FICTIONAL LOVE

MATTHEW SMITH

To Julie

from

Matthew Smith

X

ISBN 978-1-7391975-6-8

First Published 2023 United Kingdom
Copyright © 2023 Matthew Smith
Cover design by Matthew Smith

ACKNOWLEGMENTS

I would like to say thank you to my Mum and Dad, Cath and Robert Smith, and all my family for always been there for me, and have help me out through the hard time and never given up on me even when I have given then a hard time in the past.

Thank you to my Friend Sammie Miller, we have been friends now for many years and she always believed in me and encouraged me to write this book.

Thank you to all my friends who have supported me and been there for me through the good times and the bad times.

And thank you to you my Readers who have supported me

ABOUT THE AUTHER

MATTHEWSMITH

I am Matthew. I was born in the town of Halifax in West Yorkshire, UK. I grew up just outside of Halifax in a Town called Elland, where I lived for most of my life.

Life was a challenging time for me, as I was born with some medical complications. I was not able to talk until I was 7 years old, and I could not read and write until the age of 15, and then I was diagnosed with Dyslexia.

Due to my medical complications, School was very difficult, and I was at the bottom of every class and failed all my exams. I left with no qualifications and no hopes for life.

I went from job to job as I could not hold a job down and was also bullied in the Work-Place. With no friends, no relationship and no Career prospects, I fell into a depression. It was at that point where I started on a Spiritual Path to fix myself.

I got into a few relationships that were very toxic and failed, but it didn't stop me. The more times I fell, the more I got up, stronger each time. After years of really reflecting and doing daily Spiritual Practises, I started to get ideas to write a Story.

I had never written before, as I did not have the time, due to working. I started to feel ill at work, and I didn't have time for anything outside of work. My Manager would expect me to work over even if I did have plans. It got to the stage where my Soul was screaming out at me to quit, but I didn't, I just carried on until the day came when I couldn't carry on, and I had an emotional break-down and had to go on the sick.

After 2 weeks of rest at home and self-care, I would sit at night and meditate, and that's when this Story was born. I started to write not knowing where it would go or even how the Story would go, but as I sat writing, more and more seemed to flow out, like I was being guided.

I never returned to my job in the call-centre, and I am now living my dream, doing the things I love, writing and making people happy.

I now live in a small town on the Coast just North of Liverpool, and I write. I believe that everything happens for a reason, and life guides us to where we need to be.

You can contact me and reach out to me if you have any questions about the Book, or if you just want a chat, I'm always happy for a nice, friendly conversation.

Facebook: Matthew Smith
Instagram: @heavenearthconnection
Email: smithmatthew.1983.2020@gmail.com

FORWARDS

This Fictional Love Story is a perfect example of how we should view our Lives as our Time on Earth is only short and it is also of uncertain length, so we need to make the most of it whilst we still can, accepting that 'EVERYTHING HAPPENS FOR A REASON'.

The Story is told as it unfolds from many different angles, using the Characters and utilizing the Props to re-tell the Events in the Story, consistently throughout the Whole Book. The Story-Line is gripping, intuitive, intriguing and informative, giving the Reader a suggestive, Spiritual Perspective on how to view Life and Living, being grateful of what you have got and being accepting and respectful of your Life's Journey and the importance of enjoying Life.

Ultimately, being mindful of your Purpose in Life, acknowledging that it can change significantly in the blink of an eye, in a split second, altering your Path considerably with its many twists and turns. It just goes to show that no-one is certain of what's to come in our Life, making it important to take each Day as it comes and to Live out our Lives with Hope and Love in our Hearts.

A truly remarkable read, constructed Beautifully with a Spiritual Insight, keeping us in suspense as the Story is told, being revealed gradually when the Mind is ready and in gradual Steps.

This Book will have you sitting on the edge of your seat, wanting to find out the Eventual Outcome, giving you a Spiritual Dimension in understanding Life, which you may never have considered before.

It is cleverly written in a Fictional Form, interweaving Themes in Reality and Every-Day Life Encounters to present to you a Story of Recovery, Discovery and Spiritual-Relief and Belief. A Must-Read for those Ghost-Story, Suspense and Drama-Love

PROLOGUE

Have you ever read a Book that you got lost in? You picked it up and started reading. The next thing you look at is the clock and hours have passed, but yet, you have been so unaware.

You get to know the Characters in the Book and build a Relationship with them. It feels like you know them on such a personal level, then you finish reading. There is a sense of sadness, almost like you are grieving the Characters in the Story.

I am not really into reading myself. I always struggled to get into Books. They were just words on pages, but then I guess you have to have a good Imagination to get lost in the Story, and I did not have that good of an Imagination. I prefer Films and Box-Sets, because I can see what is going on. I remember this one Box-Set I watched years back.

I don't remember what it was called as my Memory isn't so good since my Accident, but it was about 5 Seasons long and each Season had about 10 Episodes. There was one Character that I sort of had a crush on, there was just something about her, and I felt like I got to know her on a Personal Level. I got to know her likes and dislikes.

I was sad when I finished watching the Box-Set as I would not see her again, and that was it. It was over like a Relationship that had come to an end. I did start watching another Box-Set with the same Actress, but it was not the same. She was different like she was a completely different Person, but I guess she was.

Anyway, you are probably wondering why I am telling you about me having crushes and falling for Characters in Stories and Films? Well, it will all make sense very soon as I tell you my Story.

***

My name is Danny. I am 33 years old. I am just a regular Guy, 5' 8" tall, average-build, light-brown hair, short back and sides and blue-eyes. I am nothing special, just a plain-looking regular Guy. I live in a little Seaside Town on the West Coast, called Palm Bay. It's tucked away in the Hills and Cliffs, it has a Beach and a few Shops, but its main feature is 'The Old Harbour' that they revamped a few years ago. It looks so nice at Night when it's all lit up with the string-lights that run from One end to the other.

'The Old Harbour' is the Life and Soul of Palm Bay with the Bars, Pubs and Restaurants that run alongside the Water, even there is an old Fishing Boat that got turned into a Coffee Shop.

In the Centre of Town, there are little Independent Shops that have their own products and one Supermarket on the Main-Road as you come into the Town. There is not much around Palm Bay as it's surrounded by Hills and Trees. The biggest Place is the City about 40 miles East. That is where I am from.

***

I live with my Girlfriend, Becky. We have been together now for about 6 months. We live in a little Apartment in Town about a 5-minutes stroll from the Beach and Harbour, so it is the perfect Location. We are looking for a new Place within Palm Bay as our Apartment is pretty small.

 Becky is a little younger than me. She is 31. She works in a little Crystal and Healing Shop down on the Beach with her Friend Willow who owns the Shop. She used to be a Nurse working at the local Hospital, and that's where we met. She was my Nurse helping me recover from the Accident, but it got a bit too much for her working there, as we didn't spend a lot of time together, as she seemed to work long-hours just to put a roof over her head. Now we were living together, she didn't need to Work as much, so she quit and got a Job at the Shop.

***

Before moving to Palm Bay, I lived in the City and worked for an IT Company. I would work about 50 to 60 hours a Week. I enjoyed that Job and had just got a Promotion to Head of my Department. It was more money and fewer hours, so I could

3

spend Time with my Girlfriend, Sian who sadly is no longer here. We were going to move to Palm Bay and I would commute to Work every Day. Sian didn't want me to do that as it would make my Days longer, and the Idea was to take the Promotion so cut down my Hours.

I wanted to leave the City for a long time. I did Love it there, but it was too busy and chaotic for me, everyone living Life in the fast-lane. Sian had Family there, but I didn't. My Mum and Dad died when I was 9 years old.

They were in a Plane Crash. They never went on Holidays. They would have long Weekends away as my Mum never really liked to Travel, but my Dad had convinced her to go to Portugal for 2 weeks. She said no at first, but after some persuasion, she finally said yes. I was so excited for them.

Me and my older Sister, Alisha were going to stay with our Gran and Gran-dad, and they were going to take us away to their Caravan. My Mum and Dad never made it Home - The Flight out never made it to Portugal. The Plane's Engines failed, and it went down over the Water.

I felt a lot of anger after that toward my Dad for making my Mum go. It took me a long-time to come to terms with it.

The only Family I have now is my older Sister, Alisha who is 36 and her Partner Tom who is 39. They both live in Palm Bay in a Villa-Type House just about a mile from the Town, up on the Cliffs. Alisha worked in an Office part-time but did most of her 'Work from Home' as she never really liked being in the Office with all the gossip, and her Manager was always going on about Targets and trying to make her work past her finishing-time, just because he had no Life. He thought that everyone should have no Life, so 'Working from Home' made life a lot easier for her. Tom managed a small Team of People in a small Family-Run, Events Marketing Company.

Tom's Grand-parents had left him quite a lot of Money when they passed, so they both were able to get a nice Villa in Palm Bay.

***

So, that's a little about me and my Family. I have a nice Life here in Palm Bay. I don't work in IT anymore or the City. My Life is very different now from what it used to be, as you will find out later. Now I write. I was guided to do this, and it helped me get my Memories back. I had never read a Book in my Life and never written one, so this was a complete change in my Life. After the Accident, a lot happened. I have always been a Man of Science, but things were about to change.

Science can explain a lot, but there are other things out there, other Forces, other beings and other Worlds that go beyond Science. I am not Religious, but now I do believe that there are Higher Powers out in the Universe that we just cannot comprehend. My Gran always used to say to me that everything happens for a reason, and even when things don't seem to be going your way, it is for a good reason. When I got turned down for the first I.T Job I went to, I was really upset, and my Gran said it was because something better was coming and that Job was not for me. Then a year later, the Company had got closed down for Money Laundering.

I now believe that Life is for Living and doing the things you enjoy, and yes, we have to Work, but don't make that your 'Main Focus'. My Gran-dad had worked hard all his life saving up for his Retirement. He worked 6 days a week, some days 14-hour shifts. His Dream was to retire to Spain, but that Dream fell apart as when he did come to Retire, his body was that exhausted from all the years Work he had done that he could barely walk and he got all sorts of illnesses, which made him a 'Grumpy Old Man' in his final years.

Anyway, I could go on all day, but here is my Story of how I got to where I am Today.

***

I will warn you now, you may need to keep a box of tissues close-by, as the recent, past events have been an 'Emotional Roller-Coaster', but it all made sense as to why it all happened and has brought me to this moment now.

This is my Story...

CHAPTER 1

Wake Up, Wake Up".

A voice shouted in my ear, I turned with half-open eyes. It was Sian, my Girlfriend.

"Come on, wake up Sleepy-Head, it's a Beautiful Day, and I thought we could head to the Coast to see your Sister and then head down to the Beach".

I felt like the luckiest Guy in the World to wake up next to Sian every Morning. I still wonder how it happened, how I came to be with her. We met last year at a Bar in the City; I had gone out for a Drink after Work with my Friend, Sean. I looked over to the far side of the Bar and I saw her. She was standing on her own, looking anxious. After half an Hour, she was still standing there on her own, now looking worried and sad. I could see the look of disappointment in her face like her World had fallen apart, and now she was lost, wondering what to do.

I smiled at her with half a smile, letting her know I had noticed her; she smiled at me, the smile that told me she had noticed me too but was trying to figure me out to check if I was 'Normal' and not a 'Weirdo'. I'm not sure why, but I plucked up the courage and walked over to her. I have never done that before as she was way out of my League. I don't know what pulled me to her and as I approached her, my heart was pounding, and I started to sweat. I wanted to turn around and walk away, but my heart would not let me. I guess it was my Intuition. I mean, what's the worst that could happen? She rejects me and I feel hurt for a Moment then I go back to my Friend and we enjoy the rest of the Night. I didn't have anything to lose.

She was wearing this black dress that just hugged her and fitted her body perfectly. The top-half was low-cut, not that I was looking purposefully, but it wasn't that hard to miss. I had never seen anyone look so Beautiful in all of my Life. She just stood out in the Room. Those big, green-eyes, that long, blonde-hair, her slim-figure with all the curves in the right places, plus she was smaller than me. I would say about 5'4": Something like that. She would fit in my arms perfectly. I imagined what it would be like to be with her, holding her close to me - Even the way she drank her Wine - Everything about her was Amazing.

Hang on a Minute - My Mind was going crazy. I had not even spoken to her yet, and I was planning our Life together. When I got closer to her, she just looked at me. Her eyes not moving away as she took a Drink. As I got closer to her, I smiled again, letting her know that I was a Friendly Guy. I asked her how her Evening was going, and she turned and smiled and told me that her Date had not turned up. I was sad and disappointed for her, as I know that feeling well. Getting ready for a Date, even going to wait for them to turn up, but I was also relieved and kind of Happy too that he had not turned up, as I would not have got to talk to this Angel as I could only describe her as this. That she was. She picked up her glass and took a big sip of the last of her Wine.

"I am going to go now. I'm feeling kind of tired, but it was nice chatting with you", she said in a soft, friendly manner.

Her voice was so calm and soft. We talked a bit more then she got up to go. I thought to myself... I'm not going to just let her go and not see her again, so I asked her for her Number. I have never asked a Girl for her Number, but I could not hold back, like there was something that had taken over me. She smiled and took my Phone out of my hands and typed her Number in.

"Ring it if you like, so you know it's me, and then I will have your Number", she said. "I'm Sian by the way. It's nice to meet you... Umm, what's your Name? I don't think you told me".

"I'm Danny, I hope to see you again".

She smiled and walked off. When I got Home that Night, I looked at my Phone but nothing. I couldn't think about anything else but her. I felt so restless, hoping she would Message me. About an Hour or so had passed, then my Phone flashed, my heart jumped into my throat. Could this be her? I hoped so and hoped it was not just some Marketing Company trying to sell me something. I picked up my Phone, shaking with excitement but nervous at the same time. It was her, and I started to sweat as I went to look at the Message The Message read...

'Danny, it's Sian from the Bar. It was nice meeting you - Hope to see you again xx'.

I was so excited, I was shaking. I text her back, trying to be cool, but inside, I felt like a Child on Christmas Morning going into the Living Room and seeing all those Presents. I replied, asking her if she wanted to go out for Dinner.

***

On the following Friday, we met up and went on our first Date. She looked a little shocked to see me, like she was expecting me not to show up, and when I walked through the Door, her smile lit up the Room, her Beautiful, white teeth, shining. I'm sure she was an Angel sent from Heaven. We sat down and talked. She told me all about her Life, how she had just moved here from a very small Town, and she didn't know Anyone.

The Guy she was meeting the other Night, she had met on-line, and they had been chatting for a few Weeks, and they had arranged a Date for her 30th Birthday, but he never showed up. How Anyone could have stood her up. She was stunning and such a Beautiful Person.

"Oh, was it your Birthday? What - he stood you up on your Birthday?", I said, feeling a little upset and angry.

"Yes, but I believe that 'Everything Happens for a Reason'. You see Danny, if he would have shown up, would we have gone on this Date? Would you have come up to me? Would we have met...? No, we wouldn't, so by him not showing up, you came over to me, and now we are on this Date, and who knows what could happen?", Sian said, with a smile on her face.

***

After that Date, we started to see each other. First, it was once a Week, then she would stay at my Place on a Weekend, then once in the Week. Each Time she stayed, she would leave Something of hers at mine to remind me of her and then she slowly moved in. She even claimed her drawer and space in my wardrobe. She knew what she was doing, but I didn't mind at all as I loved her being here.

We had been seeing each other for about 3 months when I asked her to move in. I knew she was the one I wanted to be with. My Friend Sean thought it was far too soon and that I should get to know her more, but Love doesn't do Time. It was very easy for her to move in as she didn't have a lot to bring with her as half of her things were already in my Place. Everything was perfect in my Life. I was so happy. I was with this Amazingly Beautiful Woman, and my Manager had put me in for Promotion at Work. This meant that I would be getting a lot more Money, and me and Sian could move to the Coast near Alisha and Tom: My Sister and her Partner. We had seen this little Beach House we liked, over-looking the Water. It was only small but perfect for both of us.

It was only about a 5 minutes' drive from my Sisters. The City was such a Great Place if you were younger and loved that fast-paced Life, but it wasn't for me now, and I wanted to move to the Coast. It had been my Dream for a long-time.

***

Today was the Day Sian picked up her new Car. She was so excited.

She had been saving up a while for it, but I had offered to help her out as I was being Promoted, so Money was not going to be much of an Issue anymore. She wasn't really into Cars. To her, they just got you from A to B, and the one she had was falling to bits. She had bought it when she had passed her test, it was second-hand, so she wasn't sure how old it was but knew it was ready for the scrap. This Car however, just stood out to her. I think it was the colour she liked. It was a bright-yellow Convertible. We had arranged to pick it up at 11am and then go for a drive over to Palm Bay where my Sister lived.

"Come on, get up! We have a Car to pick up", said Sian, shaking the bed.

I almost fell out of bed; I loved seeing her happy and excited. It made me feel really happy. She had cooked me a nice Breakfast with everything on there you could think of. It was only 9am, but the Sun was already shining, and there was hardly a Cloud in the Sky. It was going to be a hot Day. Sian had already packed her Bikini and the Beach Bag before I had even woken up. Once we had had Breakfast and finished our Morning Coffee, we set off to the Car-Place to pick up the Car.

***

When we entered the Show-Room, we were greeted by a tall, well-built Man with dark-tanned skin, glasses and a shaved-head. He looked at us and smiled.

"Hi - You must be Danny and Sian. My name is Peter, and you must be here to pick up the Car. I'm sorry for the delay. It was ready in the Week, but we like to give them a check-over, and it's a good Job we did as we just had to check something over on it".

"Oh... What? Danny said. Is it Ok?".

"Yes... It's nothing to worry about - Just had to check the Brakes over as there was a warning light that flashed up, but I can assure you, it's nothing to worry about. If you both would like to follow me into my Office, and we can get the Paperwork Signed over".

The Office was cold. Peter must have had the Air Conditioning on full, as I started to shiver a little. He asked Sian for her Details, and he typed them all in on his Computer, on her File then pulled some Papers from the Printer.

"Please could you Sign these Papers Miss, then you can be on your way. So, have you got any Plans on this nice, hot Day?".

I looked out at the Car in the Showroom from the Office window. It was a nice Car, not the cheapest to run as it was a two and a Half-Litre Engine. The Car Sian had was only a One-Litre, but she deserved a nice Car, and she had worked hard for it.

"We are going to head over to Palm Bay to my Sisters and then to the Beach", I said to Peter.

Sian had finally finished Signing all the Papers. It seemed never-ending. I'm sure they just like to chop down Trees for the sake of it.

You would think after all this Modern Technology that it all could be done On-line. Once Sian had handed the Papers over to Peter, he checked through them, smiled then handed over the Keys.

"It's all yours now, Miss... Have a good Day, and if you have any problems, Here are our Contact Details. Please let me show you to your new Car".

Peter led us through a side-door out the back where the Car was waiting for us. It looked Amazing, it was shining in the Sun, the top was down, and it had that new smell to it.

Sian looked at me and kissed me.

"Thank you, Babe. I Love You", she whispered in my ear.

Little did I know that I would never hear her speak these words to me again. We set off, out of the Car Show-Room Forecourt, onto the Road and headed West for the Coast. The Wind blew through Sian's long-hair; I looked at her in her sun-glasses and thought how lucky I was. She was just loving Life, driving with the top down. This was Heaven. The Sun was shining on this hot Day and that I am going to spend on the Beach with the Love of my Life... What more could I ask for?

In the distance, we could see the Ocean and smell that fresh-clean, Ocean-Air.

"Babe... Shall we stay on the Main-Road or go down the Scenic-Route?", Sian said in her happy, cheerful voice.

I got a feeling that we should stick to the Main-Road as with it being a new Car and faster, then it would be safer driving on the Main-Road, and we would get there quicker, but Sian had other Ideas.

"Well... I think we should just stick to the Main-Road with it being a new Car. We don't want to spoil it with bumps in the Road", I said, trying to make up excuses. There was just something not right. I felt a little uneasy going the Coastal-Road even though it was such an Amazing View.

"Oh... It will be fine. I know the Road well. My Dad used to take us down here all the time", Sian shouted over the Wind.

So, we pulled off the Main-Road and started to see more and more of the Coast now. I've got to admit; this way was a lot more Scenic. We could hear the Birds singing in the Trees and feel the warm Sun on our faces. Sian had only been driving a few years, but she was a safe, good Driver. She seemed quite confident behind the wheel. It was nice to be a Passenger for a change too and just enjoy the ride and just relax. I felt the Car start to speed up as Sian slowly put more pressure on the Accelerator but nothing too much to bother me.

"Hey Sweet-Heart... Just be careful. We are not on the Main-Road now. This Road can be dangerous".

"I got this Babe. Oh, I know this spot just a mile away. We can park up - It's like a Viewing-Point".

We pulled up at the spot that Sian had told me about. It was a little lay-by built into the Cliff... Only space for two Cars. We got out, crossed the Road and went down some over-grown Steps. I could see the Ocean through a clearing in the Trees and an over-grown Path that cut down a small Hillside, to an opening. There was a Park-Bench facing the Water, surrounded by Plants, Flowers and Trees. I had never been here before.

We both sat down. Sian looked into my eyes and kissed me. I put my arms around her and held her tight. I never wanted the moment to end, the sweet- Smell of her Perfume and the warmth of her Body close to mine. Sian could go from being Child-like to being a super-soft Romantic Woman. She was just so perfect. We took some Photos and chatted for a little while.

After about half an hour of being at the Look-Out point, we headed back up the Path, onto the Road, crossed over to the Car and set off to Palm Bay. We could see it in the near distance. This small Town nestled in the Hills on the Coast. What a view it was. I was so excited at the thought that we were going to be moving there. As we were driving, the Engine check-light came on then the Brakes warning-light.

"Should we call Peter, Babe?".

"No, I'm sure it will be fine. Just drive carefully on these Roads... It's gone off now - It's all good - Must just come on when you start the Car".

Sian drove a little slower, just to be on the safe-side. We were not far from Palm Bay now. I could see it in the near-distance. Sian and I were so excited about getting a Place there. Her Dream was to write a Book.

She just loved writing and wanted to be somewhere where she could get the Inspiration. We had seen a few Places that we had liked but the one we really liked was a little two-bedroom Modern House, overlooking the Beach and not far from 'The

Old Fishing Harbour' that they have now turned into a Marina with Bars and Restaurants. The Car was now starting to speed up again. I could feel something was not quite right and a feeling of dread washed over me. I tried to ignore the feeling, hoping it would pass.

"Hey Sweet-Heart... Just go steady", I said nervously.

"I am... I am", said Sian, sounding a little worried.

"What's wrong?".

"The Brake is sticking, and I can't slow down".

"Ok Sweet-Heart... Don't panic... Just take your foot off the Accelerator and the Car will start to slow down'.

As Sian took her foot off, the Car started to slow down but wasn't slowing down as quickly as they wanted it to.

"What the fuck is wrong...? Why aren't the Brakes working?".

Sian was now in a panic as the Car didn't seem to be slowing down much at all. She turned the Wheel hoping that that could slow the Car down. She turned the Wheel left and then right, the Tyres screeched, but nothing seemed to be working to slow the Car down. Then out of nowhere, a Car appeared, coming in the opposite direction.

It blasted its Horn and then again, and Sian jumped and turned the Wheel so hard that the Car skidded across the road, making another screeching sound. Sian waved for the other Car to move in sheer-panic. That sound will always haunt me. Sian screamed in fear as the Car went over the edge of the Cliff.

We were falling, the Water and Rocks getting closer and closer to us. It was almost like slow-motion like time had slowed right down, and in front of us, faced our fate. I looked at her and she looked at me with fear in her eyes. She grabbed my hand as if to say our last Goodbye to each other.

The Car hit the Rocks and Water with such Force like a Bullet was fired from a Gun. I managed to break-free from my seatbelt and pull myself out of the Car. I'm not sure how as my leg was caught between the seat and the door, but with a little pull, I was able to break-free. The Car hit a large Rock, and I felt an agonizing pain in the back of my Head.

I turned to see the Car disappear below me, deeper into the murky Water, and all went blank.

CHAPTER 2

I saw Light above the Water. I knew it wasn't the Sun as I was been pulled to it, and I could look at it, and it didn't hurt my eyes. The more I looked at it, the more I was drawn to it. I felt like it was pulling me in. I did not feel any pain but a great sense of Peace. I could hear Music. It was so Beautiful like Harps and Violins, but I could not make out where the Music was coming from, and as I got closer to the Light, I started to wonder where Sian was. I felt a little panicky as I wanted to go back and get her, but the Light wouldn't allow me to.

The Light started to reach out to me, wrapping itself around my Body, pulling me in, further to it. I saw a Figure come towards me. I realized it was Sian She grabbed hold of me and pulled me into her embrace. She looked into my eyes, and there was a bright flash. I didn't care for anything at that Moment. I didn't care what had happened as long as I was still with Sian. That's all that mattered to me, and we were together, wherever it was that we were going. It sure felt Peaceful here.

We both appeared in the Bar that we had met in. It was like watching a Home-Movie and seeing us both standing at the Bar together, chatting. I stood there with Sian, watching this Life-Clip of how we met.

I turned to her, and as I was confused as to what was happening, she just looked at me and smiled then nodded and pointed to a Doorway with a Bright- Light, shining out from it. We walked through. I looked, and we were now on our first Date together, sat at the Table, laughing and drinking Wine. Tears started to fill my eyes. I wasn't sure if I was happy or sad but felt a mixture of emotions. I tried to think, but I couldn't. The more I tried, the more I couldn't.

I looked at me and Sian, chatting and laughing at the Table in the Restaurant. I started to realize what was happening. I was dead, and Sian was showing me all the happy times in my Life. We both then walked through another Door, and I found myself at my Place. It was the Day that Sian was moving in, that special Day when we were bringing all of her boxes into the Place. She was so happy on that Day, as this was going to be the start of our Life together. She then took us to the Car-Place where I watched her sign the Papers and drove out in her new Car, to head for the Coast.

She looked at me again, kissed me and smiled at me. I felt this Love that I had never felt before. I knew she was very special, but she was different. Now, she gives off this Love that I cannot put into words. I knew I was dead, but it was ok, because I was with Sian. She looked at me again, and then we appeared on this Beautiful Beach with white, golden-sand that looked like it had never been stepped on. It was so smooth and soft. I had not recognized the Beach. It was not familiar to me. The Sky was a deep-blue colour with big, white, fluffy Clouds that had a golden-edge where the Sun was lighting them up. There was a gentle, warm-breeze coming from the Ocean. The water was so clear and you could see all the little fishes and Sea-Life, happily swimming.

The only Sound was the Waves crashing on the Shore. Set back from the Water, the Beach was full of Trees that crept up the Hills. In the distance, there was a House amongst all the Trees and a Waterfall behind the small Building. We approached the House. I heard someone singing, her voice was something I had never heard before... Almost Angelic. Me and Sian got closer to the House, the Door was open, the singing was coming from inside the Kitchen. I was confused about whose House we were in. I had thought this was our House - The House we would spend Eternity together.

Inside the Kitchen, there was this young Woman. I would say she looked like she was in her late 20s. She was to be a few inches smaller than I, slim-build, shoulder-length, brown, silky-hair. Her skin was slightly-tanned and she had big, hazel-coloured eyes. She looked over at Sian and I but didn't say anything. It was like she could not see us. She was just in her own World, preparing food, singing in the most 'Angelic Voice'.

I gazed at her for a few moments, trying to figure out who she was and what she was doing in mine and Sian's Beach House. She seemed to look at me but yet not see me. I saw a Uniform that looked like a Nurse Tabard hung over a Chair. There was a Name-Badge pinned on the Tabard. It read 'Becky' on it. I was not sure who this Becky was and why she was in our House. I wanted to Question it, but yet, I was unable to. Sian looked at me once again, not saying anything, and we walked out of the House and back to the Beach. She looked into my eyes and said in her soft voice.

"It's time, my sweet Danny".

"What do you mean, it's time - Where are we going next?".

Sian just smiled at me and then said, "It's time to live your Life. I Love You so much".

She pulled me closer to her. I felt her Loving-Energy wrapping itself around me. I didn't want to let go. I wanted to stay in her arms Forever. I had died, and I thought this was it, and we would now be together in this 'Beautiful Place'.

"Please don't leave me, Sian. I Love You. We have so much to do together... So many Places to go".

I started to get teary as she pulled away from me and stepped back. A ray of golden-light shone down on her from the Sun, her Body started to fade away and turn into white-light. The light spread outwards, in every direction, filling the whole Beach with a warm-glow of Energy. After a few seconds, the light started to fade away, turning into 100s of white Butterflies that ascended upwards, towards the Sun into the Sky and disappeared. I looked down and saw only one white Butterfly left, the rest had gone into the Sky above.

The Butterfly flew up, onto my hand and just rested there for a moment. I watched it, it looked at me for a moment then turned into a white-ball of Light that floated up to my face and shot into my mouth and down my throat. I felt its warmth going deeper and deeper into my Body.

The feeling seemed to reside in my chest; I took off my shirt and looked down at my bare-chest where there was a warm-feeling and saw a white-glow in my heart, and I knew then, that that part of Sian's Spirit was in me. She would live on in me.

***

I started to feel pain and sadness, but yet at the same time, so much Love in my heart. I had so many Questions. Where was I? What was this Place I was in? Where is my Sian? Who was that Woman with the 'Beautiful Voice' in the House? I dropped into the soft-sand and looked out into the Ocean. In the distance, I could see a Boat coming up to the Beach and could see someone in the Boat but couldn't make them out as they were blurry from the tears in my eyes. As they came closer, I could make out a figure of a young Guy. I had never seen him before but yet felt like I had known him. The Boat came up to the Shore and the young Man got out and walked over. He hugged me.

"Hello Danny, come on... Hop on, my Son", he said in a soft, Irish Accent.

"Who are you?".

"I'm Patrick... I'm here to take you Home".

"Home?".

"Yes... Home - You know that Place where you come from".

"But I don't want to go Home. I want to stay here with Sian".

"Sian is not here, Danny - Son. She has gone", he said in a very soft, quiet tone.

"Gone where?".

"Gone Home, back with the Big-Man".

"Big Man?", I said puzzled.

"God... She has gone back to the Big-Man, God".

The Man paused then said, "Well, God is not a Big-Man in the Sky, but it is the easiest way to explain to you something that can't be explained by the Mind. Now, come... Let us go. You have many People waiting for you".

"I just want to stay here so I can be close to Sian. I don't want to go back, nothing to go back to".

"I remember talking to you here before you were born on Earth. We were sat up there". Patrick pointed to a Rock on the Beach. "We were talking about your life on Earth and we talked about this moment when you had to say goodbye to Sian, and you said that it is fine, because it's not Forever. You and she sat with me and made the Agreement".

"I didn't know it was going to be so painful at that time".

"No, you would not have done, because there is no pain up here... Just Love, but you agreed that you wanted to experience this".

"How can I go back now, knowing all of this?".

"You won't remember any of this, you won't even remember me".

"Why?".

"It wouldn't be fun if you remembered, would it? Imagine coming to Earth, knowing everything, how your Life was going to be, what will happen. That is not fun is it? Takes the Mystery out of Life. It's so much fun, watching things unfold in Life".

"Will I remember you, Patrick?".

"You might do, Son. I will show up, now and then, in your Life, just to check up on you, but you won't see me as I am now. I can come in many different Forms, and I will give you little Signs, now and then. I might give you some Life-Lessons to help you along".

"What I will say, Danny is that you have a lot of People that Love You, and you are going to be very happy in Life. It's going to be an Amazing Journey, so different from how it has been".

Patrick and I started to walk to the little Rowing Boat that now was moored up on the Sand.

"Jump in Danny, Son. I will pull us out to Sea".

"Where are we going?".

"We are going Home... Well... You are. It is time, Danny. Oh, you are going to have such an Amazing Life', Patrick said in a very excited 'Tone of Voice'.

Patrick jumped in the Boat and started to row out to Sea. As we went further out, I could see the Water getting deeper and could no longer see the Ocean- Floor. I looked back at the Beach and it started to fade away into the distance as we went further and further out to Sea. A thin, white-mist started to appear around the Boat. Within a few moments, I could not see the Shore anymore or even the Water that surrounded the Boat. It looked like the little Rowing-Boat was just floating in a Cloud of this thick, white-Mist.

"Nearly home now, Danny - Son", said Patrick.

I looked at Patrick as the Mist got thicker and thicker, surrounding him until I could just make out his out-line. I started to hear a beeping sound but could not make out where it was coming from as I was in a Rowing-Boat in the Ocean, so there was nowhere it could be coming from. The beep was getting louder and louder.

I could not see any part of Patrick now, as the Mist was so thick. I looked down at my feet and they had vanished into the Mist. The white-Mist now surrounded my Body, entering my nose, ears and mouth. The beeps started to become very loud now, and I could hear familiar voices. My eyes hurt. Like someone had put a Bright-Light on in a Room, but this Light was not like the warm, comforting one I saw. This one was painful and felt cold and artificial.

CHAPTER 3

Blackness, Nothingness and no Memories of anything, that's all I saw. My eyes wanted to open, but yet, my Mind wanted them to stay closed. What would I see when I opened them? I was scared. My Mind had so many Questions, but yet, I could not provide the Answers. My Body felt so weak and cold, it hurt all over like I had been run over by a Bus. The pain in my legs was something I had not felt before at all. It felt like hot-needles were being poked all over me from top to bottom. My face was cold as there was a chill in the Air. I was in a Void. I was neither dead nor alive, just in a Space of Nothingness.

I heard voices that sounded very familiar to me, a Male and Female voice, their voice soft and quiet, so I could not make out what they were saying, just the Sounds. The beeps seemed to be getting even louder. Maybe that was because I was fully coming back now, back into this World. I opened my eyes slowly and turned slightly, using up the little strength I had to see where the beep was coming from. There was a large machine with a screen full of graphs and numbers, tubes running through it, into my arm. I scanned the room with my eyes, but it all seemed a little blurry.

The Sun was shining in through the window to my left; I could feel its warmth on one side of my face, and I tried to turn to face the window to warm the other side of my face up. To my right, some more windows that looked out into the Nurse Station and a Door that looked to lead out onto a Hospital Ward. I closed my eyes again. "Is this a Dream...? Maybe if I go to sleep, I will wake up", I thought, but when I re-opened my eyes, I was still in the same Place. More of the Room had become clear now as my eyes were adjusting. Two people walked into the Room with cups of Coffee. They both looked at me and froze for what seemed like a Life-Time. The young Woman looked at me and dropped her Coffee. She came running up to the bed I was in with tears in her eyes. Her long, black-hair tickled my face, and I coughed as the strong-scent of her Perfume hit the back of my throat.

"Oh my God... Oh my God", the young Woman cried. "You are awake". "Tom... He is awake... Come over here".

The young Man came running over. He too had tears in his eyes.

"Welcome back, my Friend", he said in a low, soft voice.

"Danny, I thought you were never going to wake up. I thought I had lost you". She pulled back and looked at me. "I thought we had lost you", she started to sob. "Do you know who I am...

It's me Alisha, your Sister and Tom, my Partner. You remember Us don't you?".

I recognized them, but my Memory was fuzzy. I closed my eyes again, trying to remember, then the smell of Perfume hit me again. I recognized it. Alisha had always liked her Perfume. When she was a Teenager, I would walk past her Room and be hit with the smell of it.

"Alisha, Tom... Is that you, or am I Dreaming?", I said quietly.

"Yes... It is Us. We are here now and you're not Dreaming. Let me get the Doctor and tell him you're Awake", Alisha said in an excited voice.

She rushed out the door, crying, racing to the Nurses Station to get them to call the Doctor. Tom waited in the room with me. He didn't say much, but the look on his face said everything. He was so happy to see me awake. A moment later, the door flew back open and Alisha had come bounding back in.

"The Doctor is on his way", she cried.

A minute later, the door opened again and a tall Man walked in. He was slim and had short, grey-hair with glasses and wore a long white-coat with a Stethoscope around his neck. He looked at me and smiled - Very pleased to see that I was now Awake.

"Hello Danny, I'm Dr. Walker. How are you feeling?".

I didn't know how to respond to that Question as I had so many Questions. Before I could even think of an Answer, Dr. Walker had pulled up a Chair and was looking at a File he had in his hand, skimming through the bits of Paper. He kept looking up at me and then back down at the File. After a few moments, he places the File down on the Table.

"Danny, what is the last thing you remember?".

I tried to think hard but nothing. Before I even could talk, Dr. Walker must have seen the confused look in me as he started to tell me what had happened.

"Danny... 8 weeks ago, you were in a Car Accident. The Car's Brakes failed, and it lost control, and it went over the Cliff. The Police, Ambulance and Rescue Team were there in minutes. They managed to get you out, but not the Driver". Dr. Walker looked down, his eyes were sad. "The Driver didn't make it. They found her a few days later".

I looked at Alisha who had tears rolling down her face and was sniffing up.

"Driver?", I asked. "Was I not driving?".

"Danny... You were not driving, you were going out for the Day, coming to see me and Tom. You and... There was a pause as Alisha sniffed up again. "You and Sian. Oh Danny... I'm so sorry", Alisha said, as she started to cry.

"Sian?".

"What - You don't remember?", Alisha looked at Dr. Walker, "But, how can he not remember?".

Dr. Walker began to speak again. "Danny has been in a coma for the last 8 weeks. It is common for People to lose their short-term Memory".

"But why and how?", Alisha asked.

"Well, some people say that the Memory-Loss is to block out the Trauma from the Incident".

"Will he ever get his Memory back?".

"Bits may come back in time of what has happened".

"What if he remembers everything... How is he going to cope? He has been through enough suffering when we lost our Parents".

"He will be fine... We have Support Groups and Therapy. You and Danny will not have to deal with this on your own".

Tom looked at Alisha and held her hand. He looked into her eyes. "It will be Ok... I promise".

They were all talking like I wasn't even in the Room, but I didn't have the energy or strength to speak. I just tried to listen, even though it was a Challenge, as I still felt like I was not fully here and present.

I wasn't even sure who I was, and this Driver Sian - Who was she? But yet, when I heard the Name, it sounded familiar, but yet, I wasn't sure who she was. I just had to listen and try and piece together what had happened to me. Maybe if I closed my eyes and opened them again, I would walk up out of this strange Dream. I closed my eyes once more and counted down from 10. When I opened my eyes again, I was still in the Hospital bed. Dr. Walker was still talking to the three of us. Maybe this was not a Dream but real. I didn't remember anything about any Accident though. Could this be a Game Show like one of those reality TV Shows?

"Dr... Can Danny come Home, now he is Awake?".

"Oh no... Not yet. We are going to keep him for another 2 weeks. He needs to build his strength back up. Don't worry... We will look after him and you can come to visit any time. What I would say though is that when we have discharged him, for him not to be on his own for a while. When he starts getting his Memory back, he will need all the support he can get, and it's not advisable for him to be on his own".

"Oh... Don't worry about that. Me and Tom have already sorted out the Spare-Room. He is going to live with us for as long as it takes, and he will Love our little new Puppy, Charlie". Alisha started to cheer up, now thinking about all the nice times they would have ahead of them.

"Tom... Is it Ok to stay with you both? I mean, I don't want to be a burden on you both".

"Don't be so silly Mate. You are staying with us for as long as you need to. Charlie will Love You". "It will give him someone to play with as he seems to like to play on the Evening when I sit down to relax for the Night after Work", said Tom, smiling.

***

My stomach started to growl at me. I was so hungry, it felt like I had not eaten in a long-time, but then it had been 8 weeks since I was in a coma. 8 Weeks without eating, yet to me, it felt like I had just been asleep for a few minutes, and to my stomach, it felt like I had not eaten in a Life-Time.

"Dr... Please can I have something to eat? I'm so hungry".

The Dr. smiled, "I will get the Nurse to bring you some Toast. I will check on you again in a few days, but you will have Bella looking after you as of Tomorrow. You will like her, and I'm sure you will get along great. She is about your age. She will make sure that you are looked after and comfortable. She will be helping you with a few light exercises as well. Don't worry though, Danny. We will not have you weight-lifting or running a marathon... Just a few little exercises to get your muscles back working again. It will properly feel like you have done a session at the Gym. Anyway, I have babbled on enough now. I will get the Nurse to make you that Toast. It's good to have you back with us my Friend", Dr. Walker said, smiling and leaving the room.

Ten minutes after Dr. Walker had left, the Nurse came into the Room; there was this nice smell that made my stomach growl. She wheeled in the trolley with two slices of thick, hot Toast with a cup of Tea. I am not a Toast Person but this was different as I'd not eaten for 8 weeks. I just wanted to fill my stomach. I could see the steam rising from the Tea as the Nurse placed it down next to me on the table. The smell took me back to when I was a Child, and when I was ill, my Mum would always make me some Toast and bring me a nice cup of Tea. For a moment, a wave of sadness washed over me as Mum and Dad were no longer here.

I didn't often think about it, but now and then, I would have these moments where I did miss them. I know that I didn't die in that Car Crash for a reason. My Mum and Dad stopped me. I needed to be here for Alisha. Alisha always seemed much stronger than me. She seemed to be able to deal with things better, but I knew that this was just a front with her. She had to be strong for me.

When Tom came into her Life, it was a big Blessing as she had him for support, and she could then take the pressure off herself and stop being the 'Emotional Crutch' for me. I liked Tom. He was a nice Guy, a genuine caring, authentic Guy who would do anything for her.

It had not been easy for them as when they first met, Tom's ex, Melissa would call him up and cry on the Phone saying she wanted him back and that she was pregnant with his baby. This is a lie as Melissa had cheated on Tom several times when they were together.

One night, she threw him out when he came home from Work and he found her in bed with his Best-Friend Paul. One Friday Night, he was bored and feeling a little lonely, so he decided to pluck up the courage to go 'Speed-Dating'. He was very shy and had never done anything like this before. He stood at the Bar, waiting to be served before the Event and saw a Woman staring at him. She was with a few others. It looked like a Works Night Out. He noticed she had kept looking over at him and when he turned, she would turn away.

The 'Speed-Dating' didn't go to plan. Some of the Women were nice, but Tom just didn't connect with any of them. After the Event, he went to the Bar and got another Drink. Alisha and her Friends were still there; she went to the Bar to get a Drink and introduced herself to Tom. A few moments later, they were laughing and talking together. They have been together ever since. She can be a bit bossy with him sometimes, but they Love each other so much.

***

As I bit into the first piece of Toast, it was like Heaven. The hot-butter had started to melt into the Bread.

"Just go easy on that Danny. Take it slow. You have not eaten in a while, and your stomach won't be used to eating", said Alisha.

I just wanted to eat it so quickly and enjoy it, but I knew I did have to eat slowly as I would probably throw it back up. The smell and taste of it seemed a lot stronger and more intense as I swallowed my first piece and then washed it down with a sip of Tea. The Nurse had made it perfect for me.

"Right Danny, my little Man, me and Tom are going to get off now, but we will be back Tomorrow Afternoon". When they had left, the Nurse came in and told me that they had come over every Day and just sat by my bed, hoping and praying that I would wake up. There were times when hope seemed like it had gone as my Body was Life- less and it had got to a point where the Doctor had talked about giving it another few weeks and then thinking about turning my Life-Support Machine off. Alisha had kicked off at that idea as she knew that I would wake up soon, some Day. She never gave up hope completely and it was why I had woken up Today. I was still very confused with no Memory of what happened, but I was happy to see Alisha walk out of the Room, smiling and knowing that I was Ok and getting better.

***

The next Morning, I woke up to this Beautiful Humming Sound. The Sound was very familiar. I recognized it but yet could not place it. I opened my eyes to this Beautiful Young

Woman in my Room, opening the curtains and letting in the Morning Sunshine. I could barely see her, as the Sun was so bright - Just the Silhouette with long-hair.

She stepped over to the bed and smiled at me. I got a full view of her now, the Sun shining behind her, creating a golden-glow around her. She had long, dark-brown, straight-hair and tanned-skin that looked so soft and smooth. I had noticed her big, hazel-eyes and her smile, and I felt like I had seen her before Somewhere, but I couldn't remember where.

"Good Morning Beautiful - Nice to see you. Are you Awake? Dr. Walker told me that you had woken up, and I just couldn't wait to meet you. How are you feeling? Well... That's a bit of a silly Question... You have been through a lot. You have probably got so many Questions. Oh, by the way, let me introduce myself. I'm Rebecca, but you can call me Becky, everyone else does. I'm going to be looking after you for the next two weeks, and then I will be coming to check up on you once you are back Home every 2 weeks, so I

I guess we will be seeing a lot of each other. Aren't you the lucky one, Danny... Danny, you look confused Babe".

"You are called Becky?", I said, sounding confused.

"Well... On my Birth Certificate, it's down as Rebecca but everyone calls me Becky, and last time I checked, I was called Becky", she smiled and giggled. "Dr. Walker said someone called Bella would be looking after me".

Becky laughed again and shook her head, smiling. "Oh... I wish he wouldn't do that... We are supposed to be Professionals here". Becky paused for a Moment. "So, Dr. Walker has a Daughter called Bella and he started calling me it as he said I remind him of an older version of his Daughter. He shouldn't be calling me that Name to the Patients but hey, you seem a cool Guy, so I will let him off".

She was well-fit, I thought in my head. That long, brown, silky-hair, her hazel-eyes and her tanned-skin...

That Perfect Body. I hate Hospitals, but seeing Becky every day was going to make my stay here pleasant, and she seemed so nice and friendly.

"So, Becky... If we are going to be spending a lot of time together, I would Love to know more about you".

"Oh... You would, would you? Becky looked at her Watch, "Well... I have plenty of Time anyway before I start my Shift. So, I'm Becky. I am 28 years old - Single. I live alone with my Cat in Palm Bay in a little Apartment. I work here in the Hospital, and I also help my Friend out, Willow. She runs a Crystal-Shop down by the Beach sometimes", Becky laughed.

"What are you laughing at?", I said, chuckling to myself.

"Just sounds like some cheesy Dating Show doesn't it? Anyway, I will continue... So, I moved here from a little Town about 60 miles from here. I hated the Place; it was one of these Places where nothing changed there, only the age of the People. The People who were born there, lived there, went to School there, worked there, had their Kids there, and it was just a repeat of that Cycle. I am sure that the People of that Town were in-bred as no-one new ever seemed to move there and no-one left".

"I did meet a Guy there. He moved there but only because his Family was there. Things were great with us. I met him on the Bus going to Work one day. We got chatting, exchanged Numbers, went on a Date and ended up living together, but that's when it all changed. He lost his Job and wouldn't even bother looking for another Job. He said that he was going to Work for himself, which I was fine with at first, because I know that getting a Job is hard these days, so we made a Deal that I would work and he would stay at Home like a modern House-Husband until he set up his Business. He loved that Idea, but it didn't work. I would come home from Work, and there would be beer cans all over the House, no Food on the Table or Meal made - Piles of washing and ironing, and it was always the same excuse".

"Oh... I didn't know what time you would be Home and I was going to do it". I got fed up with it, Danny and needed to get out of this backward in-bred Town. I wanted to be a Nurse and care for People. My Friend was going to meet this Guy she had met On-line from Palm Bay. I had never been, but just the name of the Place sounded nice, so we went. I took her, and it's a good

Job I did as he never showed up. We decided to stay and check out the Place, go down to the Harbour and get some Food. I liked it here - It felt like Home. I loved the Beach and the Sea. I could just sit there for hours, sat on the Beach, looking out to Sea, wondering what is out there. I started to go over to Palm Bay every Weekend with my Friend Jess, and I met a Girl called Willow who had the Crystal Shop. We became Friends, and I ended up moving here, helping her out in the Shop until I managed to get this Nurse Job and my own little Pad".

"Oh Wow... That is Amazing. I'm so happy for you, Becky. Sounds like it's all worked out for you and your Friend Jess. Do you still see her?".

"Yes, I guess it has all worked out, and No, I don't see Jess. When I moved here, she stopped speaking to me, along with my Family". Becky's Tone of Voice had changed, and it wasn't as cheerful and as happy as it was.

"They fell out with me... They couldn't understand why I wanted to move. My Mum said I hated her and wanted to get away, but the truth is Danny, I didn't hate her. She was very Toxic, and I felt drawn to live by the Sea since I was a Child. I wanted to live on the Coast. There is a little Village just up the Coast called West-Point. I had seen Photos of it looking so cute, and I wanted a little Cottage there, but I moved here, and I like it here, Danny. Maybe one day, I will move there, but for now, I'm here".

"Dr. Walker is like my new Dad, and then there is Willow. She is like my Mum even though she is only 10 years older than me, but she is an old Soul. The only thing that I guess I'm missing in Life now is a Boyfriend - That 'Special Someone'. I believe though, that everything happens for a reason, and Life will connect us with the right People through Events and Circumstances. The Events and Circumstances might seem challenging, even cruel at times, but the Bigger Picture is that Life brings us to this point now. The Universe guides us all the way, and we just have to Trust".

"Well, you have me now, Becky. I'm sure we can be Friends when I'm out of here. Maybe, you could show me this Crystal Shop".

Becky smiled and laughed. I felt a little embarrassed saying that 'you have me now' - Where the hell did that come from? Nothing like making a Moment awkward. I had just met her. She was my Nurse, and there I was, forcing a Friendship onto my Nurse, hoping maybe, it could be something more, one Day.

"You don't look like a Guy that is into Crystals and Spiritual things", Becky said, frowning and looking confused. Was that her way of saying that she wasn't interested in me, but then to be honest, I had just come out of a coma and probably looked like I had just been dug up. "Well, I have always been more Science, but I am just not sure anymore. Since I woke up out of the coma, I feel different. Not the Danny I was, something happened, but yet, I don't have any Memory of it".

"When you get out of here and I'm not your Nurse anymore, I will take you to my Friend Willow. You will like her. She may even help you if you wanted it".

***

That night, I lay there in the Hospital bed. It was silent. It almost felt like I was alone in the Whole World. I couldn't stop thinking about Becky. Not only was she Beautiful, but I felt a Real Connection to her. Had I seen her before? She looked so familiar to me, but how?

Maybe I had seen her passing by and not noticed her before. What if she was right? - Everything and every Event is Connected, bringing People together?

If I wouldn't have been in that Car Crash then I wouldn't be here in this Hospital and have met Becky. Who was driving the Car? I thought. What if that Person driving the Car was supposed to drive that Day and lose control of it to Crash it so I could be with Becky?

"Danny, you are being stupid now. You only just met her Today, and she is your Nurse. She is nice to Everyone, not just you. You're nothing special to her - Just another Patient. She probably tells the same Story to Everyone to make them feel better".

My Mind was so cruel at times, always doubting. I put my head on the pillow and closed my eyes, feeling sad and happy that I had met Becky even if she didn't like me in that way. It was going to make my stay more pleasant to see her every Day.

***

Every Day that passed, I was getting better and better, feeling stronger and stronger. I could walk a little better now, but still, I had a long way to go. Becky would come every Day, and we would do Exercise together. She would come to see me on her Break-Times, and we would chat and laugh. We had started to get to know each other well.

I wanted to ask her out on a Date, but part of me was scared. We had built up this strong Friendship, and I didn't want to ruin it, and there was the fact that she was my Nurse. Not only that, there was Something that told me, I can't move forward just yet. It is too soon for me to move forward. I needed to remember so I could then let go and move on with my Life. I knew that there was Something that I had to face up to. Every day, I tried to remember by closing my eyes but nothing. It was just blank like that part of my Life had been erased.

***

It was my last Day here at the Hospital. I was happy to leave but scared and sad too, as this was the Place I was born in - Well... I'd come out of the coma, but it was like being born again, as I didn't remember anything. What World would I walk into...? What would my Life be like now once I left the Hospital? Alisha had turned up to pick me up as Tom was working; She bounced through the door, all happy that I was finally coming Home.

We were chatting about my new Home and how I would like it there, and I would Love their new Puppy Charlie who would be so happy to meet me and have a new Friend to play with. After about 20 minutes, Becky came into my Room with the Discharge Papers for me to Sign. She pulled up a seat next to the bed; I was now sitting on the bed. Not like 2 weeks ago when I was in the bed with tubes coming out of me. I felt quite sad, leaving and saying Goodbye to Becky. I would see her for a few more weeks, but not like here, where I would see her every Day.

"Well, Beautiful - It's time for you to go".

"I will miss you, Becky".

Becky laughed and threw her arms around me and kissed me on the cheek. I felt myself blush a little as I knew Alisha was standing there, watching me. "You're going to miss me... Why Danny Babe... You have not seen the last of me. I am still going to come over every two Weeks to check on you and we shall hang out when you are better when I'm not your Nurse anymore, if you like?". Becky winked at me.

I could see Alisha looking over at me and Becky smiling, but she didn't say anything. I was happy to be going Home. Well...

Back to Tom and Alisha's. I wasn't sure what would happen now and where my Life would take me, but my Main Focus now was recovering, and I guess, then starting over again with Life.

CHAPTER 4

Alisha's House was about a 30 minutes' drive from the Hospital. This was a new-start for me to leave the old behind and start again. I was excited about staying by the Beach. As a Child, I always loved the Water and the Beach. There was just something about looking out into that endless Ocean and contemplating Life. Waking up every morning to the sound of Sea-Birds, there was just a Magic about it.

I felt happy and excited about my Life and the Amazing things to come, but at the same time, I felt this deep-pain in my heart like something was missing, a piece of my heart, gone like the feeling where you are hungry and eat but you're not filled up and still hungry for Something. I was still hungry, trying to find Something to fill the void I felt in me, then the thought came rushing to me to what happened and who I was. Had I died and was I just Dreaming all of this up? What if my Life wasn't Real at all and that's why I could not remember anything?

I felt a tear roll down my face, but yet, why was I even crying when I don't remember anything? There must have been some Thoughts or Memories there for me to cry. I closed my eyes for a Moment and took a deep breath in, and I saw a flash of yellow and what looked like a young blonde-haired Woman, smiling at me.

I did not see her face, but I knew she was smiling at me. Before I could make out who she was, she disappeared. I snapped my eyes back open and jerked back in my seat. Alisha pulled to the side of the Road; She was looking at me puzzled as to what had happened.

"Danny, I'm here for you, Ok. Me and Tom are here for you. Don't think you have to do this on your own. I know you don't remember what happened, and maybe this is good for now, but when you do remember, we are here for you and you can stay with us as long as you need, until you are fully Healed".

Knowing that, made me feel better as I never like to be a burden on anyone or bother them. My Gran-dad was the same. He was a proud Man and didn't like to bother People. He always said a Man is there to look after and protect and should not put his pain and woes on anyone. I did not agree to that as everyone needs help and support sometimes, but I guess I carried that guilt from him with me.

"What happened to me, Sis?, I said with another tear rolling down my cheek. ''I remember a Car and that is it".

"Danny - Take one day at a time, Lovely. You will remember when you need to remember. Life will show you when you are ready to remember". Alisha smiled and pulled out onto the Road again.

"You will Love Palm Bay Danny, it's perfect. They did all 'The Old Harbour' up last year and made lots of little Bars and Restaurants, even put a little Nightclub there. There is the Train Station that they refurbished and modernized as well, so you can get to the City, but I don't think you will be going there anytime soon, if at all. Oh, and me and Tom are going to take you to our favourite Restaurant on Friday. It's called 'Little Paradise'. We got to know the Manager quite well there, and he always gives us the best-seat, over-looking the Beach. We have told him that you are staying with us, and he is excited to meet you".

I felt my energy pick up again and a little bit of excitement came in. Maybe I might stay here in Palm Bay. It sounds so friendly, and I might make Friends here and even Date Becky. There was something about her. I felt like I had known her before, and I had seen her before. I was getting more and more happier and excited about Life now. I did need reassurance a lot.

"Becky likes you Danny. You never know in time, what will happen", Alisha said grinning at me.

"How do you know that?", I said, trying to hold back a big grin.

"Oh, I know... I'm a Woman. Remember... We know everything, especially when it comes to stuff like that".

"But, how she is my Nurse, it has to stay Professional".

"She won't always be your Nurse though will she?... And come on Danny -Did you see the way she was with you - Not very Professional. I bet she doesn't hug and kiss all her Patients Goodbye and spend all that time with them when she is on her Breaks".

I could feel my cheeks turning red and my face getting hot, as I started to blush a bit. I could not hold the grin back, and it turned into a big smile, and a chuckle came out of my mouth.

We had left the Town now and were driving on the Main-Road that led out of Palm Bay. The Road cut through a dense patch of Trees with a steep Hill-Side on our right. It felt like we were in the Jungle with all the different types of Trees. Alisha turned left onto this Narrow-Road that gently ascended up a Hill; I could see the Ocean down below, the Waves crashing on the Cliffs. There were a few big Houses scattered on one side of the Road, but I couldn't see much of them as they were hidden by big Gates, Walls and Trees.

It looked like something you see in Films, where all the Big Stars lived. The Car slowed down and stopped, and Alisha pressed a Button on her Key Chain, and two big Gates opened.

She turned in, and we seemed to go up another Small-Road. In front of me was a big, white House. There were a few Trees and lots of Flowers around the edge. In the middle of the Front Patio, there was an Island of grass with two Palm Trees and lots of Plants with two little Spot-Lights that would shine a Light up the Trees when Dark. This Place looked Perfect and would be my Home for a while now.

There were two Lamps mounted on the wall at both sides of a Dark, wooden-arched Door with a door mat that said, 'Welcome'. Alisha had always wanted a nice House and when Mum and Dad passed, they had left us quite a lot of money so that we would never be short of anything again, but my Dad once said that when the time comes, we would still have to Work to appreciate the value of Money.

Alisha only worked 3 days a week though in an Office. She was quite the 'Lady of Leisure', Old-Fashioned as well as she loved to stay at Home and look after the House when Tom was working and have his Dinner there for when he got Home from Work. They seemed to have a nice little cosy, Life together.

***

I entered the front door and stepped into a big Room with little passages going off into different sections of the House. I hadn't been to this House as they had not long been here, about 2 years but they always came to the city to see me.

"Down there", she pointed, "This the Wash and Utility Room. That Door there is the downstairs Bathroom and the Door into the Garage. Here we have the Lounge".

I took off my Trainers and walked into this cozy, yet modern Space. It was Amazing. One of the walls was taken up by a big Open Fire-Place with a huge mirror above it and a few photos of Alisha and Tom. To the side of that, there was a big TV mounted on the wall and two massive Couches that if you sat on them, they would eat you up as you would just sink right into them.

The Room was very well-lit by the Bay Window that looked out onto the Front-Garden and Patio. In the corner of the Room was a huge, Indoor Plant that pretty much touched the Ceiling. At the back of the Room was an open Staircase with old wooden beams. Alisha then showed me the Kitchen. She pushed back some big sliding doors that opened up the Kitchen Area. Everything looked so clean and untouched.

On the far wall were some big, glass doors that went out onto the Decking Area and then onto the Lawn. At the bottom of the Garden was a Gate.

"Where does that go?", I asked.

"Come with me and I will show you".

We walked past lots of Flower Beds and Plants. It was a little Tropical Paradise. They had even fitted a Water Feature in there.

Alisha opened the Gate, and there were some Steps going down the Cliff and onto the Beach, a little Private Cove that you could only access from the House. By this point, I started to believe I was dead and in Heaven. The whole Place was out of this World. They had lived in a small House when they first moved to Palm Bay, but this was their Dream Home. It was my Dream Home.

"Now, come on... Let me show you the rest of the House and your Room".

We went back inside and up some Steps, to the 1st floor. She opened the door to her Room.

"This is mine and Tom's Room. We love it in here, especially on a Night when we will sit out on the Balcony and have a glass of Wine".

We went out onto the Balcony, and it was more like a big, Sun-Terrace, you could see the Ocean, and it was so Peaceful. Just - The sound of the Waves. The room had a King-Size bed and a Walk-In wardrobe. Above the bed, hung a huge canvas of Palm Bay Beach with the Sun-setting.

We then walked back out onto the Landing and she pointed out another Room. "Now, that Room there is the Bathroom, and you are really lucky because you have your own En-suite Bathroom in your Room".

I was expecting the Guest-Room to be a tiny Box-Room, full of junk that no-one wanted but yet could not be thrown away. I was so wrong... There was a big King-Size bed in there, a Desk with a Lamp on and a window just to the side with a sofa built into it that over-looked the front Garden and Patio.

Alisha had decorated this Room in nice, soft, neutral colours. It felt warm and cozy in there. Half of the Ceiling sloped down as the Room had been built into the Roof. On the far wall, there was the Door to the Bathroom and then another Door next to it. I looked in, and it was a Walk-In wardrobe with all my things already in it. Alisha had gone to my old Place in the City and got my things and brought them back here.

***

Once I was settled in my new Room, I felt at Peace and calm as the Week before, when I was in the Hospital. I thought that I might be a burden on Alisha and Tom, but now I realized that they did want me to stay with them. She had made up my Room and got all my things here. She wanted me to feel at Home here. I felt a little overwhelmed by it all. I had gone into a coma and then woken up to a whole new Life, like I had been re-born into another Life-Time.

Later that Evening, I was in my new Room, on the bed, getting settled in, and the smell of Something really good hit my nose.

Alisha had cooked Dinner. She had made Spaghetti Bolognese, which was my favourite Meal. I followed the smell down into the Kitchen, the Table was already set, and Alisha had started dishing it out. I was still very hungry, but I guess that was because I had not eaten for 2 months in a coma, and it would probably take some Time for my stomach to adjust to solid Food again. I did wonder what would happen to my old Place in the City. This was going to be something I would have to face. After Dinner, I helped Tom clear up and do the dishes, then we sat outside as Alisha watched TV. She loved her Reality TV shows, but Tom hated them, so he would sit out on the Decking until she had finished.

"Tom, Thank You so much for this, for having me stay here".

"Oh, you are so welcome, Mate. How could we even let you just go back to the City on your own".

"What will happen to my Place as I have not been there for 2 months. Do I still have it?".

I looked at Tom and he paused for a moment, trying to think of what he could say. "Danny, you do still have the Place, but your Sister is going to talk about that with you as we don't feel that you should go back, not unless you wanted to, but I think your Sister is going to take you there this Week to pick up some more Stuff. We would rather have you here in Palm Bay, and maybe, once you are better, you might make Friends here and meet a Girl. There are so many Beach Chicks here". Tom said, laughing. "Alisha said Becky had a thing for you, so you never know Mate - What's around the corner".

"Oh, we will see", I said smiling. Maybe I won't go back, maybe this is my Home now. I wanted to leave the City anyway, it was getting too much for me. At one time, I liked the City Life but not anymore. I had fallen in Love with Palm Bay, it was just like the Place I had Dreamed of as a Child. I couldn't go back. I didn't have anything to go back to, all my Work Friends had probably forgotten about me. What I had learned in Life is that you have Friends and Work Colleagues. Sometimes, you would make a few good Friends at Work but most of them... You would be Friends at Work and even go out to a Bar, but if you left that Job, they would not keep in touch, they would forget about you. I guess that's Life - People come and go, and some will stay who are meant to stay. We have to move on, and the time that we spend with them People, created good and bad Memories.

I headed off to bed but wasn't feeling tired. I just felt I needed to be alone. I looked over at the Desk with the Lamp on it. It was an old Oak-Desk that looked like it had come out of a Time-Machine from 100s of years ago. Alisha liked collecting old Antique Stuff. She said they told a Story, they had a Past. I wonder what the Story was behind that? Even the Lamp on it, looked old. As I turned to turn off the bed-side Light, there was a very strong smell of Perfume. It was not Alisha's as it had a different scent to it. It was very sweet and reminded me of a Summers Day. I had smelt that smell before but couldn't place it. As I shut my eyes, I felt a slight breeze on my face and a whisper in my ear.

"I Will Love You Forever".

I jumped up and looked into the Dark, but nothing was there just the Darkness of the Room. I heard Tom and Alisha downstairs talking, could it have been them, but no it can't have been as it was close to my ear. Maybe I was just Imagining it as it had been a long and emotional Day. I closed my eyes again and slowly drifted off to sleep.

CHAPTER 5

I woke up the next Morning, feeling a little strange; I had this deep sadness in me that I could not put my finger on. It was the same feeling that you feel through a break-up, that heart-ache and deep pain and a sense of loss. What did I have to be sad about? I was now living in an Amazing Place with Alisha and Tom, this was the start of my new Life. I looked over at the old Oak Writing-Desk, wondering how old it was and where it had come from. I jumped in the shower and got ready and went down for Breakfast. Alisha was already up. She had Breakfast waiting for me, Eggs on Toast. Yum.

"I thought we could go into Town today, Danny and you can get familiar with the Area - That is if you are up for it?", Alisha said, taking a drink of her Coffee. "Danny, are you Ok? You look a little sad".

Alisha came over and put her arms around me and hugged me. This made me feel even worse. I looked at her and I could feel a tear roll down my cheek.

"I'm Ok, I just feel a little sad, and I'm not sure why. Why would I feel sad if I don't remember anything, I don't understand?".

"You have been through a lot, Danny - Memories might start to come back up, but the feelings are still there - They never go".

"This is why you are a little confused as you have these feelings but no Memories to put them with. We don't have to go into Town if you don't want to, we can save it for another Day and just hang out here".

"No, let's go. I need to get out. It will do me good". I wanted to go out. It would be nice to see the Town and go for Lunch with my Sister. Over the years, we had become more like Best Friends than Brother and Sister. It was a nice Relationship we had with each other, and her and Tom were my only Friends now - They were all I had.

***

Just as we were about to leave, Alisha's Phone rang. She answered and left the Room. I went and sat down, waiting for her, then my Phone beeped. I had not checked my Phone in a while. There was no need to as I had no Friends and the only People who would contact me now, I lived with. I looked at my Phone and I had one Voicemail and a Text Message that I had not read. I opened the Message and it said...

'Danny Babe - Hope you are having a nice Day at Work. I am not going to cook Tonight as I thought we could go out for Dinner and then, when we pick up the new Car Tomorrow, we can go visit Alisha and Tom at their new House. See you Tonight. I Love You. xxx'.

There was just a Number with no Name. I wondered who it was. It hurt my Mind to think about it, so I rang the Number but there was no answer, it just rang and rang. Then I called the Voicemail that had been left for me. It sounded like Waves and Wind in the background, the Sound got louder and then faded. A second later, a soft voice said.

"Danny, I am so sorry for leaving you Sweet-Heart. I will always be with you. Remember me... So, you can move on".

The line started to crackle and then cut-off. Her voice was Beautiful, so soft and gentle, like Music in my ears; It seemed familiar, like I had heard her voice before. I tried to call the Number, but yet, there was no Number to call back on. I listened to the Message again, trying to figure out who it was. I heard Alisha still talking on the Phone. She sounded as though she was getting frustrated with the Person on the other end. I turned to look out of the front-window onto the Patio and saw a Figure standing by the Trees. It looked like a Person but I couldn't quite make it out. It seemed to just stay there, looking right at me. I closed my eyes and rubbed them as I had not long been up. My eyes still might have been adjusting to the Day-Light, but when I opened them, a few seconds later, the Figure was still there, looking at me.

I went outside, onto the front Patio to see who it was. Maybe, they were lost?

As I approached the Trees where the Figure stood, it seemed to fade away as I got closer to it. I looked all around and it was nowhere to be seen. There was a gentle breeze that blew past me; it carried a sweet-scent with it, like Summer Flowers. It was really strong that I nearly started to choke on it. I felt a little blow in my ear, and something soft touches my cheek like a kiss. I looked to my side and jumped back, nearly falling over, but there was nothing there or no-one there. The only sound was that of the Wind and Waves crashing onto the Beach in the distance. What was that? What had just happened? I heard a voice call me.

"Danny, Danny", Alisha called out.

"Danny, I'm so sorry about that. That was Helen at Work. She wanted to know what I had done with some Files. I told them not to bother me when I'm not at Work. Like they think I have nothing better to do, I even left her a Note telling her where the Files were. Oh, I bet Patrick has moved them... Sorry Danny, listen at me complaining about Work. Why were you out here?".

"I thought I had seen someone over there, and I went to check it out as they were looking in here".

"What... Over there? Are you sure... No-one can come in that way as behind those Trees is the Cliff and it's all walled off. Are you sure it was over there, who was it?".

"I don't know... When I went out, they disappeared. I couldn't see their face, but there was something strange. I could smell this Perfume in the Air, it came close and then just disappeared".

Alisha didn't know what to say at this, she just smiled as she always did when she did not know how to Answer. I felt a little silly telling her as she probably thinks I'm Nuts.

***

We got in the Car and pulled out of the Driveway, the Electric-Gates closing behind us. The drive into Town was nice as the Sun was shining, and just at the back of the Trees, you could see the Ocean on the right of us. On the left side were Rocks climbing up the Hillside with Trees and the odd House in-between. Alisha pulled into the Main Car-Park next to the Main-Beach and Harbour. Palm Bay wasn't that big of a Place. It had a few Shops that were set back; the Shops looked mostly like little Independent Craft Shops.

There was a big, new Supermarket just on the edge of Town; They probably didn't want to build it in Town as it would spoil the surrounding Area. There was a Train Station at the front of the Town where People would have to cross the Tracks to get to the Harbour and Beach. The Trains terminated there from the

City. The Town itself was mostly made up of little Villas and Apartments that were dotted in amongst the Trees. The main feature of the Town seemed to be 'The Old Harbour' that they had done up with all the nice Bars and Restaurants and an 'Old Fishing Boat' that had been turned into a Coffee Shop.

I looked around and wondered where Becky lived as it wasn't a big Town so she would be close by. I was looking forward to seeing her again; She seemed to just cheer me up with her presence and we had built up a good Friendship in the Hospital.

She would be coming to see me in a few days to check up on me and I was quite looking forward to seeing her. When I had recovered and was fully better, we could be good Friends and hang out together and maybe more.

That's what my Hope was anyway.

CHAPTER 6

The Town was busy to say the least. It was a Week-Day and People should have been at Work. It was now Lunch-Time. As Alisha was on the Phone, we did not set off till late Morning, and we were now both quite hungry and the smell of fresh doughnuts was making my stomach growl. Alisa pointed to this little Cafe on one of the Side-Streets with a few Chairs and Tables outside on the Pavement. It was one of these Family-Run Cafes, small and friendly that if you were new in Town, you would feel welcome in there, and it would then become a Local Place to go and eat. Alisha was a Local there. She would go every Week for Lunch so she knew the People who worked in there very well.

"Let's go in here. You will like it", Alisha said.

When we walked in, we were both greeted by an older Lady with white-hair and quite a big-built Person. She reminded me of a big cuddly Grand-ma who you could go to if you had a problem in Life, and she would just know the Answers to your

Questions and make you feel better. She has that warm-glow to her, that could have been the sweat from the heat of the pans in the back, but still, she looked friendly.

There was a younger Girl, I would say she looked about 20, but it was hard to tell - Quite small, a good few inches smaller than me, and she seemed very energetic, running up and down with Food and Drinks. I watched her as she cleared a whole Table just with one hand, balancing all the plates and a cloth in the other arm. She looked over and smiled at me as if she was trying to impress me. I smiled at her back and then sat down at a Table just in front of the Main Counter. The smell of cooking was making me very hungry as it wafted from the back of the Kitchen through the Cafe. I looked to where the smell was coming from and saw a large-built, tall Man, standing over a big frying-pan, frying Bacon; He had a Native-American look about him.

The Woman smiled at Alisha and me and came over with a Pad and Pen to take our Order. "You must be Danny", said the Woman. "It's lovely to meet you. Alisha said you were coming to stay with her. My name is Margaret and this is our little Lucy. She is a Waitress here. Just ask her if you need anything... Oh, and the Man in the back is my Husband Alo. He is Native-American".

"Oh... That's an interesting Name", I said. I had come across many unusual Names before but never that one. I suppose I had never met a Native-American before.

"Yes, it means Spirit-Guide. Come over Dear, this is Danny - Alisha's Brother. He is staying with her".

He walked over with half a smile on his face. He put his hand out for me to shake it. His face looked very stern and aged but not old-looking... More like Wise.

I could see the Wisdom in his eyes, this Guy could tell you the Story of Time and how everything came to be.

"Hello Daniel".

His handshake was firm; he looked into my eyes and took a small step back.

"Daniel, you are sad but yet you do not know where your sadness comes from as you have no Memories", the Man said, in a quiet voice. "The Memories shall return and you shall then be able to let go and move on. The blackness of Night shall end, and the Sun shall rise to bring a new Day".

He then opened a Door and went up some Stairs; Alisha and Margaret were too busy talking, to hear anything that Alo had said. They seemed to be chatting about Work and just the usual chatter Women have.

"Danny, have you been down the Beach yet and met our other Daughter, Willow. She has a Shop there, she sells Crystals, she gets all that Stuff from her Dad", laughed Margaret. '

'Willow... Does she have a Friend called Becky that is a Nurse?", I said.

"Yes, she does".

"Oh Wow, Becky is my Nurse. She said that she would take me to the Shop and meet Willow". "Oh, what a small World it is".

Alo walked back into the Cafe from upstairs and he handed me something. There was a smell that I had smelt in Alisha's House. It was some kind of Incense, quite sweet and natural. I looked at the Object Alo had handed me. It was a wooden Pen that had been hand-made with a calving on it. I had never seen a Pen like it. There was a 'White Feather' on the end of it and one side was carved out with an Inscription on. 'Remember me'.

"This is a Gift for you, Daniel. This Gift shall change your Life".

"Thank you, Sir", I said nervously as I took the Pen from him.

"I shall get back to my Duties now or I shall be meeting the Great Spirits in the Sky sooner than I expect to". Alo laughed as Margaret pushed him back into the Kitchen.

"Yes, you will Dear as it will be me that will send you up there if you don't get this Food made".

It was nice to see a Family working together and still laughing and joking around. I looked down at the Pen in my hand and rubbed my finger over the engraving that read 'Remember Me' and placed it in my pocket, making sure it was safe. I didn't know what it meant, but it was a nice Pen and was Hand- Made, which made it special and unique. A few moments later, our Food came out. I had ordered a full Breakfast with everything on it. Alisha had ordered Egg, Beans and Toast. She wasn't as hungry as me. It didn't take me long to finish as I was still hungry. My stomach had a lot of catching up to do.

***

Once we had both finished our Lunch and Alisha had paid, we said Goodbye to Margaret and Alo and left the Cafe, crossed over the Street and walked down the other-side until we reached another little Side-Street. This was another little Street filled with small Craft and Independent Shops that sold little Hand-Made Things and other Knick-Knacky bits.

We entered a small Shop with lots of old Furniture on display in the window, there was a Bell above the Door so when you opened to enter, it rang. The Shop had an old, dusty-smell to it as it had just been left to age in Time. The first thing I noticed was a tall, old Grand-Father's Clock. The Time said 3.00, it had stopped as the Second-Hand was still, and the Pendulum had stopped. As we walked down through the Shop to the Counter, the smell of old wood and old Furniture became stronger, I started to cough a little.

It just reminded me of when I used to visit my Gran. The Shop was very dark, just a few dimly-lit Lamps around. At the far-end was a big, dark, wooden Counter with a Door that went into the back. A Man appeared out of the Door, he was small and chubby with long, grey-hair and a beard, and he had large, round glasses on that made his eyes look big, and a big white-beard, not much of his face was on show. He looked at me with a smile and then looked at Alisha. He was definitely born to Work in a Shop like this.

"Ah Hello, Alisha and how are we Today?", he said in a gentle, soft voice.

"Hey Bill, I am very good Thank-You. We were just in Town and I thought I would call in to check if you had managed to fix that old Watch I brought in the other Week".

"Ah yes, let me get it for you".

The old Man disappeared into the back. He did not suit that Name, Bill. He should have been called Father-Time. On the side of the Counter was a pile of very old Books. I picked one up and opened it, it was dated 1874. I had never really been a big Reader, and Books didn't seem to interest me at all. I much preferred TV, but seeing this old Book did fascinate me as it was like holding a piece of History.

I Imagined what it was like back then, a Person sat at a Desk with a Feather and some Paper. The only Light they had was a Candle. Would it of been better back in them Times? I mean People had very little but they made do with what they had and there weren't any distractions, so their Imagination would have been pure and their Writings would have been very Wise and even Inspirational. After about 5 minutes, Bill returned from the back with the Watch, and he placed it down on the Counter.

"Oh, by the way, this is my Brother, Danny. He is staying with me for a while".

"Ah, Hello young Man. I see you like that Book". Bill took the Book from me and held it close to him. "Books are very special, they have a Magic to them, they can bring the Past back to Life and create Worlds. Every Reader will see the Story in his or her own way. Just one Story can create endless Worlds as each Person that reads will use their Imagination to create their own World. I used to be a Writer and I remembered writing my first Novel back then. It was all Hand-Written - none of these Computers. I did get a Type-Writer and that made my writing a lot easier and saved time. Do you like to read, Danny or maybe you're a Writer?". Bill smiled at me.

"Well, to be honest Sir, I never really thought about reading a Book or writing. I don't think I could. I mean I wouldn't even know what to write about. I don't have a very good Imagination". "Well, not many Authors do. They will just sit down then the next thing they know is that they have written a Book or they will get an idea for a Story, and as they start to Write, more will unfold, then they will have a Best-Selling Book".

I thought about what Bill had said to me, but yet, my Mind was still very blank, so there was no way I could even come up with any Ideas about writing a Book at this Moment in Time. An Author needs to think of a good Story and once they have written it, they then need to find a Publisher or to Self-Publish and I didn't have a clue about any of that Stuff.

"Have you found a Home for that Desk, Alisha?"

"Oh yes, Bill I have, it's in the Spire Room that is now Danny's Room. It was a Beautiful Desk - Where did it come from? It does look very old, but it's Beautiful and that's why I bought it".

"Well, I'm not too sure where it is from, a middle-aged Couple brought it in when they were clearing out their Dad's House when he passed away, but they said it was given to him, so I'm not sure how old it is. Lovely Couple though they were. They said that her Dad told them a Story about it when they were younger".

"Oh, what Story? I love a good Story behind an old Antique". Alisha's eyes lit up with excitement.

"I'm not sure if it's true or just a Story they told me, to get me to take it off their hands. Bill paused for a second before continuing. Well, its original Owner made it by hand. He carved it all out himself, he worked on the Boats and he was going to Sea for months of course, back in them days, there were no Phones, you couldn't call each other - The only way was to write when in the Ports, so he decided to craft his Wife a Desk so she could sit and write to him. He placed the Desk next to the Window under the Moon-Light, he even engraved her Name into the Desk and a Message that read", 'Nancy - We Will Never Be Apart - For Our Words Will Eternally Bind Our Love'.

He had told his Wife what Ports he would be stopping at so she could send the Letters there. They would write to each other every Month. At each Port the Man stopped at, there was a Letter waiting there for him. After Months of being away, the Man stopped receiving Letters, his Ship would pull up at the Port and he would go to the Local Inn where the Letter was sent, but there was no Letter. After a few more Months with no Letters from his Wife, he returned Home.

He found Nancy at the Desk with the Ink and Paper, her Body was Lifeless, and she had passed away. He picked up the half-written Letter and it read...

'Dear Thomas, my Beloved. This is my final Letter to you. I wanted to tell you, but could never find the right moment, and

if I told you before your trip, you would never have gone. I am very ill. I have little time left.

Every day, my Body gets weaker and weaker, by the time you return I shall be gone, for the Angels will have taken my Soul to rest. I want you to get on with your Life. You are still very young and you shall find Love again. Know that our Love shall never die for Love is Eternal. Goodbye, my Love…'

"She passed away before she finished the Letter".

Bill had a little tear in his eyes and he quickly wiped it away before anyone could see. Thomas was devastated he had lost the only thing in Life that was worth living for, and now she had gone. A few Nights later, he sat at the Desk and started to write his final Goodbye to Nancy. He sat in the window, under the Moon-Light, at the Desk and wrote his final Letter to her. A tear fell from his eyes onto the Paper. He woke up the next Morning and looked at the Letter, and underneath where he had written, there were some words but it was not his writing and not the same Ink. It read - 'Thomas, We Will Never Be Apart - For Our Words Will Eternally Bind Our Love'.

"Thomas would write to Nancy often and he would wake up in the Morning with a Letter back from his deceased Wife, Nancy. A few years after, Thomas passed away and the Desk was sold and passed on", Bill concluded.

I felt a sense of real sadness for some reason, it hit me right in the heart how he lost his Wife, the Love of his Life and he never got to say Goodbye. I looked at Alisha who was now sniffing up, her eyes all red and filled with tears.

"I'm not sure how true the Story is", said Bill.

"I would like to think it's partly true as when I lost my Wife, Norma, a few years ago, I would like to think she is looking down on me and is in a better Place, and we will be re-united again One Day". Bill sighed and looked up. "Oh, look at the Time. I will be getting ready to shut soon".

Bill had quickly changed the Subject. I could see in his eyes that he missed his Wife. How does Life go on when you lose Someone you Love? I mean... Can it go on, waking up every Day and looking at their side of the bed where they once slept? I felt I tear roll down my cheek. Bill looked at me and smiled.

"Danny, Son - Life does go on, and we move on. We can't give up on Life. People will come into our Lives and they will leave. It's all part of the big Cycle". Bill handed the Watch back to Alisha.

"There you go, it's all fixed up, just needed some tweaking, that should run for a while now".

***

As we were heading back Home in the Car, the Sun had started to set. Where had the Time gone? The day had just passed.

I was thinking about the old Books and the Desk, everything Bill had said. I wanted to start reading, but I just didn't know what to read. I did once try to read a Book, but there were just words on pages. Maybe that wasn't the right Book for me. When we arrived Home, Tom was already Home. He greeted us and was cooking Dinner. I went upstairs to get a Shower. I looked over at the Desk and there were some blank pieces of Paper. I never remembered putting Paper on there. In fact, I didn't have any Paper. I lifted the Paper and stacked it neatly to one side. There were not just a few bits of Paper now, but as I was stacking it more and more - Sheets seemed to appear out of nowhere. Under the Paper where the words are inscribed in the Wood, 'Danny, We Will Never Be Apart - For Our Words Will Eternally Bind Our Love'. I jumped back in shock, nearly tripping up over some Trainers I had left on the floor. I walked back over to the Desk and the words had disappeared. Maybe I was just seeing things, the Mind playing tricks on me. I reached into my pocket and got the Pen out that Alo had given me and closely inspected the Message that was on the side. 'Remember me'. My finger slid over the Pen, feeling the engraving on it. I placed the Pen next to the Paper that now looked like it was twice as high as before. Maybe, I was starting to lose my Mind from the Trauma I had been through. After all, I had been in a coma and lost my Memories. I knew I had so much to deal with but without any Memories - How could I even begin to Heal and move forward? Would I just end up in a Home for People who had gone Mad?

I had tried so hard to be strong in front of Alisha and Tom, but part of me was so sad, and I felt this Void in my heart like something was missing, and when Bill was telling the Story about Thomas and Nancy, it really seemed to hurt me more than it would have done before, and yet, I just could not understand why. Yes, it was a sad Story, but it shouldn't have made me feel that way. It felt like I was Thomas and I had lost the Love of my Life, the way it made me feel.

I got in the Shower and went down for Dinner. Tom had cooked Steak and Chips with Mushrooms. We all sat around the Table and ate. I looked out towards the Back Garden and the Ocean, the Sun had gone down now and the Sky was a pinkish, red-colour that merged into a purple then a blue. I noticed a Figure looking at me. I could not make out who it was but the shape of the Body looked very slender like a Woman. She just stood there watching me. Alisha and Tom didn't seem to notice her. They were just interested in eating their Food. I jumped up to run over to the Door and slid it open, but by the time I got to the bottom of the Garden, she had gone. I opened the Gate and looked down. There were steps that led to the Beach, but there was no- one there. All I could hear was the Waves crashing on the Shore. Alisha and Tom came running out, startled and surprised to see what I was doing. "What is it Danny?", Alisha said in a startled voice.

"I thought I saw someone in the Garden".

"There is no-one there, Mate", Tom said.

"But I saw her, she was there, looking at me".

"Saw who?", said Alisha.

"I don't know, she was looking at me, and it felt like she was calling me to go out, but when I got there, she had gone. I saw her earlier Today too before we left for the Town. She was standing among the Trees, and I went out but she had gone".

"How can she have been in the Trees Mate as there is nothing there just the Cliff and the Ocean. Come on - Let's go back in and finish Dinner", said Tom.

After Dinner, I went up to my Room as it had been a long Day, I could hear Alisha and Tom talking downstairs but couldn't make out what they were saying. I was starting to feel worried now.

'What if I am going Mad?'... I thought to myself.

***

"I'm going to call Becky Tomorrow to find out if she has sorted the Therapy. We should get it sorted out now as the poor Guy has got a lot to deal with and he will need all the support he can get as his Memory returns. Oh Tom, how is he going to deal with it when he finds out that he lost his Girlfriend, Sian. I just can't Imagine what he is going through. He is feeling so much sadness, pain and grief, but yet, he has no Memory of it. He must be so confused". Alisha started to cry into Tom's arms. Tom pulled her in close to him and held her. "It's going to be fine Sweet-Heart, he has all of us here with him, and Becky will be there for him too. I know she has a soft-spot for him and they may even become more than Friends when she has finished being his Nurse".

"Oh, that would be nice. She is lovely and he can stay around here then instead of going back to the City".

"Oh, he won't be going back there, we will sort it out so he can stay around here. I will even look at him getting a Job at my Place but only when he is ready".

"I Love You Tom", Alisha said, looking into his eyes.

CHAPTER 7

I lay on my bed just looking out of the slightly open window; there was a gentle breeze in the Air Tonight. The Moon was so bright, shining in through my window, lighting up the Room. All the Paper was piled up, still there on the Desk with the Pen next to it. Maybe Alisha had put it there so if I got bored, I could maybe draw. She was like a Mum to me sometimes. We had our moments when we were younger, fighting like Brother and Sister do, but I always looked up to her and loved her. When our Parents died, all we had was each other, but when she met Tom, she got more Motherly over me. I guess she didn't want me feeling alone as I had no-one else apart from a few Work-Friends in my Job, but really, these were just Work-Colleagues and didn't care much for me.

I turned over and shut my eyes, it was getting late now and Alisha wanted to take me back to the City Tomorrow so we could pick up some more of my Stuff.

I guess I wasn't sure how I felt going back there, and if I would ever return to live there, that was my old Life - How could I return to that? - It would be like going backward and I didn't even know if I would still have my Job -They all probably thought I was dead as not one of them had tried to contact me, even my Supervisor who was my Friend, so I thought had not made contact with me or at least tried to. I guess Life goes on for them. It made me think about how nothing is permanent in Life and People come and go throughout Life, and we just have to accept that and not hold on to Anything.

***

There was a sudden drop in Temperature, the Room seemed to go ice-cold, and I could see my breath. I lay there thinking, should I get up and close the window, but I was too cold to move. After a few Moments of thinking about being cold. I climbed out of bed, my whole body feeling numb; I was cold down to the bones now. I made my way over to the window and pulled it closed.

Something drew my attention to look over at the Trees across the Front Patio. The Moon was so bright - Shining down on the Trees, lighting them all up, then I saw her. She looked right at me, she stood there amongst the Trees, the Moon lighting her up. She had this golden-glow around her. I rubbed my eyes, thinking I was seeing things, but she was still there, looking right at me. I could not make out her face but her glow filled me up with warmth and comfort. I felt like I knew her. She felt so familiar to me that my heart was pounding and I could not take my eyes off her.

I stood there for a long moment then grabbed my slippers and raced downstairs and out the front door, but she had gone. I went over to the Trees where she had stood and scanned the whole Area, but there was no-one there. All I could hear was the sound of the Waves, breaking the silence of the peace. I started to make my way to the back of the House to see if she had walked there. I did not hear the Gate open. I undid the Latch and pushed the Gate open slowly, trying to not make a Sound. The Gate creaked open, and I walked through into the Back Garden and scanned the Area but nothing. There was no-one there. She could not have gone far for there was nowhere to go apart from the Bottom Gate, down to the Beach, but there were no signs that anyone had been about in the Garden.

I started to walk slowly down to the bottom of the Garden, still looking around to see if she had hidden anywhere. I leaned over the Gate and looked down at the Beach at the bottom of the Cliff-Face, but the Tide was fully in, so it would have been impossible for her to go down there. I turned quickly and was startled as the light flicked on in the Kitchen, lighting up the entire Garden. The Patio door slid open, and Alisha walked out.

"Danny, are you Ok? I heard you get up".

I looked at her and told her about the Figure I had seen and how she just looked at me like she knew me.

"Do you know who she is? Does she live around here?".

"I have seen her a few times", I said to her.

Alisha looked at me with a puzzled look.

"No, I'm sorry Danny, I can't think of anyone who lives round here who fits that description. How often have you seen her? And what would a young Woman be doing, hanging around on her own this time of Night?".

Alisha looked even more puzzled, trying to work out who it could be as she had never seen Anyone like that before around there. She stepped closer to me and put her arm around me to comfort me and warm me up as I was now shivering.

"Come in now, Danny. Let's go inside and get some sleep. We have a big Day Tomorrow". I went back up to my Room and turned the Lamp off that was on the old Desk. The strange thing was that I didn't remember even turning it on, but there it was, shining down on the Paper that now looked to have doubled in size. I climbed back into bed and snuggled into the covers as the Room was still chilly, but not as ice-cold as it was before. I closed my eyes once more and got settled.

"I Love You Danny Babe, Remember Me".

Just as those words were whispered in my ear, there was a Beautiful smell that wafted under my nose. It smelt like Flowers in Summer. The smell got that strong that I started to cough. I felt a cold-breeze on my left cheek then a soft-touch like a kiss, very soft and gentle.

Was I being haunted by a Ghost or was it just my Imagination as I had been through so much, and I didn't believe in Ghosts. I never had seen one so why should I, but then the thought would have been nice as I like to think that my Mum and Dad are watching over me and looking out for me.

**

I got up the next Morning, feeling good. I had not felt as good in a long-time, but today seemed different, the Sun was shining and I just felt happy and positive like I knew everything was going to be Ok. Maybe it was because Becky was going to come over, then I was going to go over to the City with Alisha so it was going to be a nice Day. I went down into the Kitchen to the smell of Eggs on Toast. Tom had already left for Work and Alisha was washing the dishes, humming a nice tune and looking out at the Birds, flying over the Sea, trying to catch their Breakfast.

"Good Morning, how are you feeling Today?", said Alisha in a happy, smiley voice as she plated up my Eggs, Toast and Coffee. "Are you ready for the Day?".

"I feel good this Morning", I replied. "I still can't work out who that Girl was though. I have seen her a few times now around here. I hope she is not lost and wants help".

"Well, I will keep my eye out for her and if I see her, I will have a chat". Alisha paused for a moment... "Maybe, she is a Secret Admirer who has seen you around and wants to get close to you".

"Well, if she was, I would be a bit spooked out by her hanging around at that time of Night in the Trees looking in at me through the window".

"Yes, good-point Danny. Would you even want to be with a Person like that?".

We both laughed about it, and I headed back upstairs to take a Shower and get ready for the Day ahead. I felt good Today, but had mixed emotions about going back to the City. Would it trigger any Memories for me, and what if it did and it was something I didn't like...? How would I deal with it? Becky would make me feel better though. I was looking forward to seeing her. The last time I saw her was when I was in the Hospital, so it would be nice to see her out of that Place, even though she was still working. Just as I had got dressed and was combing my hair, there was a knock at the door. It was Becky. When I saw her, I felt this big smile wash over my face. She was also really happy to see me as she flung her arms around me and kissed me on the cheek. I'm sure that's not very

Professional, but then again, Becky wasn't Professional, and I didn't care.

"Right Guys, I'm going to leave you to it. I've got to go into Town and run some errands. I will see you later on Danny, and we will go to your old Place to pick up the rest of your Things. See you later Becky", Alisha said, winking at me.

She closed the door and left to drive into Town.

"Would you like a Drink?", I said to Becky as I walked into the Kitchen and started making Coffee. Becky took off her jacket and sat down in the Lounge, making herself at Home. I smiled to myself, visioning us both sitting together, her cuddling up to me, one Day.

"Hey, Day-Dreamer - What you thinking about?" Becky called.

She had made me jump and I soon snapped out of the Day-Dream. "Ummm... Nothing... I was just urrmm... Do you take sugar in your Coffee?".

"Just one please, with milk".

I brought the two mugs of steaming Coffee out of the Kitchen and placed them on the Coffee Table. Becky was there, smiling and looking at me with her big, hazel-eyes. Oh, she was so Beautiful. I could see into her Soul. It was at that Moment, I knew that we had a Connection. I wasn't sure what it was, but I just knew. I sat down next to her, and she moved slightly closer to me and picked up her Coffee and took a sip then placed the mug down in her lap, holding tightly onto it.

"So, what's your plans Today then Danny, Babe?"

"I'm going back to the City to pick up some more of my Things this Afternoon".

"Oh, you're going back to your 'Old Place'. How do you feel about that as it's been a long-time, are you still renting it?", Becky said in her cheerful, happy voice.

"Well, I'm going to pick up the rest of my Things there I think. I still have some more Stuff there and the Land-Lord was kind when Alisha explained to him what had happened. He said that he would not rent it out until all my Stuff was out and to take my Time".

"Oh, so you won't be going back to stay there then after you're better".

"No, I'm getting to like it here in Palm Bay and think I could have a Life here once I am recovered. I will get a Job and my 'Own Place' here".

"Oh, that is wonderful that you're wanting to stay here, it's only a small Town, but I love it here. I couldn't imagine being anywhere else now".

I looked at Becky and could see her smile and a sparkle in her eyes when I told her I was staying here, did she like me more than a Friend or just a Patient? The way she was and behaved around me was a bit strange, did I like her like that. I mean... She was so pretty and her long, dark-hair and tanned-skin were so attractive to me. She was a bit smaller than me; She would fit perfectly in my arms.

"Oh, get a grip, Danny, it's Becky, it's her Job to be nice", said a voice in my head. I quickly snapped out of that moment of falling in Love with her. We chatted for what seemed like Hours. I told her about the Girl I had seen several times. She looked interested when I was telling her and moved closer to me even more. She took another sip of her Coffee and kept her eyes fixed on me for a few Moments then got up and went into the Kitchen to take her Coffee-Cup back and placed it in the sink. As she washed her Cup up, she was humming this Beautiful Tune. It sounded very familiar to me, but yet, I couldn't place it.

I had heard it somewhere before, even the Kitchen and the whole Room were familiar like I had seen this moment in a Dream. I walked into the Kitchen, drank the last sip of Coffee and stood next to her by the sink. We both looked into each other's eyes, it felt like an Eternity. There was such a strong urge to pull her into me and kiss her, but I couldn't. She was my Nurse, and I had to keep it Professional just like she did. I was falling for her but then what about this other Girl that kept coming to me, 'The Tree Girl' - That's what I had decided to call her as I always seemed to see her in the Trees. Maybe she lived there...

"Right, Darling... It's time for me to go, but I will be back in the next couple of weeks to see you", Becky said in her soft, gentle voice, turning away from me before she did something Unprofessional.

"Ok, Becky. I will look forward to that, urm maybe when I am better, we could hang out sometime? That's if you like, I mean. I don't have any Friends around here, so it would be nice. That's if you want to". I felt my cheeks going red and started to sweat. Becky grabbed me in a big-hug and kissed me on the cheek again.

"Of course, we can. I would love that, Danny. We can go for Food, have nice walks on the Beach and have lots of fun. Right. Well, I had better go, Danny but don't miss me too much will ya!". Becky turned around and left. I looked and waved as she drove down the Drive and out of the Gates.

***

Not long after she had left, Alisha pulled up with lots of shopping bags. I helped her unload the Car and put the shopping away.

"How was your time with Becky?".

''It was nice", I replied, smiling.

"You two like each other don't you? I can tell by the way she is with you, and when you see her, the smile on your face. I think that's cute. You deserve it, after what you have been through".

"I do like her, but she might not like me like that, and I don't know if I like her in that way".

"Oh, come on now my little Brother... Even a Blind Man could see you both like each other. It's so obvious".

I just chuckled and smiled. "Well, who knows what Life will bring eh? I do like it here in Palm Bay, and when I'm ready, I can start looking for a Job and my 'Own Place' ".

"Yes, but there is no rush what so ever Danny, you know me and Tom are happy to have you stay with us for however long it takes you to feel better, and don't be worrying about getting a Job. You have been through so much and still recovering, so just take each Day as it comes".

That was the difference between my Mom and Sister. My Mom would have had me looking for a Job the Day after I had come out of the Hospital, but Alisha was cool and wanted me to just feel happy and fully recover. It made me feel better as there was no pressure.

It got me wondering if that's why so many People take their own Life. I had a Friend, years ago that took his own Life. The poor Guy just felt that he had no-one, he had me but his Family wasn't very supportive of him. They were all about Work and

Success. They pushed him and pushed so hard to be Successful that he ended up getting Sectioned then taking his own Life. I often think of him, it just makes me feel angry the way the World is, there is no Love and Compassion anymore. It's like we are told what to do and how to behave. We Work for a Company who pay us very little Money for our Time. We work so many Hours, then at the Weekend, when we do get Time off, we are so tired to do Anything with that Time.

I just had got that Promotion in my Job, it was a lot more Money but also would have taken a lot more of my Time even though they had told me it was fewer Hours but Bosses tell you that to sell it to you. Sometimes, we have to think about what is more important in Life: Money or Time and happiness. Money might be able to buy you nice things, but you can't take it with you when you die. Living here in Palm Bay made me realize that I don't want to go back to the Corporate World or the Slave World as I call it; I would be quite happy selling Ice-Creams and Doughnuts down at the Beach.

CHAPTER 8

After Alisha and I had had Lunch, we got ready to go back to the City to my 'Old House'. It was about an Hours drive to my 'Old Place' as I just lived on the outskirts of the City. I felt a little anxious, my heart started to beat faster as we left for the City. I wasn't sure why I was feeling this way, it wasn't like I was moving back but then I don't know what to expect. The Drive seemed to take a long time and was quite boring as it was just one Main Road with not much Scenery.

I felt the Energy change, the further away from Palm Bay we got. The Weather started to change too, more Clouds started to appear in the Sky, turning from big, white, fluffy Clouds to dark, grey ones that seem to take over the blue Sky. We drove through one of the worst Areas in the City as we had been diverted due to a burst Water-Pipe in the Road.

I felt sick going through the Area. It was a part of the City that People had forgotten about and had just been left to rot and decline. Palm Bay seemed like a different Planet compared to this Place. Some of the Houses were boarded up with gangs of Kids throwing bricks through the windows of abandoned Buildings.

The walls were covered in Graffiti, and 'Homeless People' were begging on the Streets. If Hell existed, this was it. I could see Alisha was getting uncomfortable driving through this part of the City. She checked to see if all the doors were locked and windows were fully up. After another 10 minutes of being in Hell, we finally came to the Place I used to live, we drove into this little Avenue and I saw my old House. It looked the same as it did before, nothing had changed. I felt dread in the pit of my stomach and started to get a little Nervous. I was greeted by my old Neighbour, Mrs. Warrington. She was a lovely Woman in her 70s, she had lost her husband 10 years ago and liked to know Everyone's Business, but I guess that was down to her being lonely. She saw me and raced towards the Car as I was getting out and hugged me so tightly that I lost my breath. She was a larger Woman, so her grip was tight. She was like my Grand-ma - That sort of loving, warm, Energy but quite full-on too. Sometimes. I would be out in my Garden chilling out, and then I would hear this voice call to me over the fence, and she would start gossiping about the other Neighbours and her Friends.

"Danny, is that you my Dear?" she said in disbelief. "Oh Danny, it's good to see you, Love... Hey, listen to this. Have you heard about Jim? He has split up with his Wife after 30 years and he has come out of the Closet and is Gay".

Alisha stepped in and Mrs. Warrington let go of me. "We are not here to talk about who is and who isn't Gay now, are we? Danny has been through a lot. We have just come to get some Things and then we will be off again", Alisha said in a firm but friendly voice.

"Oh, I am sorry my Dear. It's just that I have not seen our Danny for ages and so much to tell him. I can come round after you have done what you have come here to do, Dears".

Mrs. Warrington smiled. She was so happy to see us, I felt sorry for her. She didn't have Anyone, and with me moved out, it must have been lonely for her. A moment later, she then burst out in floods of tears and pulled me into her again. "I'm so sorry for your loss. I hope you are ok, I'm sure you will be fine, you are strong".

What loss I thought to myself. I have not lost Anybody. "Mrs. Warrington -What loss - I have not lost Anybody", I said to her, very confused. She too looked confused as if I was a different Person, maybe she was getting confused with Someone Else as People do start to get confused at that age.

"Danny, your Girlfriend, Sian. Do you not remember? Oh, I'm so sorry Dear, always here if you need to talk about it. I remember when I lost my Derrick. I cried and cried until there were no more tears to cry".

I looked at Mrs. Warrington again, confused. Who was Sian? Was she mistaking me for Someone Else? Alisha's face was angry. She stomped over to Mrs. Warrington.

"Danny, please could you just get my Phone out of the Car. I think I have left it in there", Alisha now sounding angry.

She pulled Mrs. Warrington to one side.

"I don't want you to mention Sian to Danny. He lost his Memory of her in the Accident and the last thing he needs right now is to deal with that on top of everything else. We have sorted out Therapy for him when he is ready. I know you mean well Mrs. Warrington, but please, don't bring it up again to him".

"Oh, I am so sorry. I had no idea he didn't remember. I won't talk about it".

She felt upset that she did not know about Danny. Alisha felt a little bad and hugged Mrs. Warrington, "It's Ok, you weren't to know".

I found Alisha's Phone in the Car and walked back to where they were standing. I looked at the front-door of the House, wondering if anything had changed behind it, since I lived there.

Alisha handed me the Key, and I walked up to the big, grey front-door, put the Key in and struggled to turn it. After a few moments, I realized I was turning the Key the wrong way and laughed to myself as I finally opened the door and stepped in. I scanned the empty Room, it looked and felt Life-Less, no Love there, no People, no Energy - Just a void of Nothing. It wasn't a Home, it was just a Brick-Shelter and this made me realize that I never wanted to return here. I went upstairs and looked around. It was just like I had remembered it. I did like the House, but now it felt like it was missing Something or Someone, but I got the feeling I wasn't the only one that had lived here. It was very strange as I felt like there was another Person here with me. I could feel a Presence as I walked into my old Room.

There was a card on the bedside table with a picture of a Teddy Bear. I opened the card out and it read.

'Danny, Babe. I am so proud of you for your Promotion at Work. You deserve it. I Love You with all my heart'.

I could not read the name on the bottom as the Ink had smudged. It looked like it started with an S but I couldn't make out the rest. I opened up the wardrobe to find lots of Women's clothes and nice Summer dresses. Wow, Whoever wore these, I bet they were really Pretty. I raised my arm to the top- shelf in the wardrobe and felt around, not knowing what I was looking to find. A Photo fell from the top-shelf, I quickly picked it up and turned it around and took a look at the Picture. When I saw the Photo and who was on it, it fell from my hands as I fell back onto the bed. I couldn't move, I wanted to but could not as my legs were frozen. I bent down and picked up the Photo and looked at it again, it was of a young Woman. She was Beautiful with long, blonde, flowing-hair, green-eyes, slim-build with rosy-cheeks. I was confused. Who was she? What were her clothes here for? And the Photo, did she live here after me? But the Land-Lord had told Alisha that no-one had moved in after me.

I looked again at the Photo, trying to figure out who she was. I realized that she looked to have the same-shaped Figure as the Girl who I had seen the other Night, looking in at me through the window but how and what was she doing here? Alisha walked into the Room and saw me looking at the Photo, her eyes filled with tears. She tried to cover it up, but she just made her eyes all red. She came and sat with me on the bed and put her arm around me to comfort me.

"Alisha, I don't understand who she is? What is her Stuff doing here in my House? This was the Girl I have seen in the Trees. I am sure of it. I have not seen her face, but the outline and her whole Figure are the same, and that card on the Table, none of it makes sense to me, I am so confused".

"Danny, it's Ok... Come here". Alisha pulled me into her. She took a big sigh.

"Danny, I Love You, and maybe it was not a good idea for us to come here Today, as I feel it's still too soon. You have been through so much and feel you just need to take things slow. You don't remember much about the Accident, do you?".

I pulled back a little from her and looked at her. Was there something she was not telling me, hiding from me, why would she do this to me?

"What is it Sis, what is wrong, what are you hiding from me? I feel there is something you are holding back from me". I felt scared that it was Something that had happened from the Accident, and I didn't remember Anything at all. "Danny, the Doctor said you lost your short-term Memory, but it will start to return in Time and when it does, we have sorted out Therapy for you, as there are things that happened that you do not remember, yet things that are quite painful".

I spoke to the Therapist, and she said that it was better I don't tell you until you start to remember, and we can all talk about it together. I'm so sorry, Danny, but I don't feel you are ready yet, it is still too soon and you are physically still recovering".

"It's Ok, Sis. I know you Love me and only want what is best for me, so I Trust You, but I'm confused as that Photo of the Girl is the one I've been seeing. It certainly looks like her, even though I have not seen her face, but it just feels like it's her".

Alisha looked at the Photo. "Are you sure that is the Person you saw in the Trees?".

"Yes, she was looking at me and smiling, and I didn't tell you this, but last Night, when that happened, I went back to bed and there was this smell of Perfume. It smelled like Summer Flowers. I'm sure I have smelt it before, but I can't remember where. Anyway, I felt this kiss on my cheek and someone whisper in my ear, saying I Love You. It just looked like this Girl. Do you think it was here - Maybe she had lived here after me and had died, and she is trying to tell me something but why?".

Alisha had another tear rolling down her cheek, she quickly wiped it away before I could see, but I could not miss it as she wasn't very good at hiding her feelings and emotions. A smile appeared on her face as she looked at the Photo and held it to her heart. I looked at the Photo one last time and looked into the Girl's eyes and it felt like she was looking at me and smiling. She was so Beautiful.

***

On the way Home, we went through Hell Town again. It seemed to be scarier now as more Gangs were hanging around, looking at us with such angry faces.

As we left the City, a big Rainbow appeared in front of us, like it was the Gateway home back to Palm Bay. I couldn't stop wondering about the Girl in the Photo. Who was she? And why did I see her at the House in the Tree. Was that her who kissed me? I had so many Questions.

Alisha turned the Radio on as she seemed quiet and not said much, we are both not big fans of the Radio but Palm Bay had just produced a Local Radio Station that had only been airing for a few Days. Maybe the Background Sounds and Music might take my Mind off Things.

"Good Afternoon Guys, so Today's Topic of the Day is Messages. Have you ever received a Message from someone that you did not know, but yet spoke to you like they were trying to tell you Something".

"What do you mean - From the Other-Side like the Spirit-World?".

"Yes, that's right Bob, do you believe in all that Stuff?"

"Well, I'm not sure. I'm not going to say I do or don't but my Aunty used to go to this Church and she said they were People there who could talk to our Loved Ones that had passed over and get Messages from them".

"Anyways, talking of Messages, we received one when we got in Today. I'm not sure where it is from but I saw it on my Desk, it's like it just appeared out of nowhere, it has no Return Address on it, it just says - Read me out".

"Well, I guess we shall read it out. This will be for Someone out there".

'My love, I am still here. I am with you in your Dreams. I kiss you Good-Night. I watch you from afar. Your Memories of me have temporarily gone, but they shall return to you, my Darling through your written word. Know that your Life is going to be Amazing and I'm here to see it all. Looking down on you. I'm

so proud of you. I am the Butterfly you see in the Garden, I am the gentle breeze in the Air, I am the Sun lighting up your way in the Day, I am the Moon at Night providing that soft glow. It is me that shall take you to your next Chapter in Life and we shall meet again, my Love, in another Life-Time, but for now, I shall remain, to watch you from afar and see your wonderful Life grow'.

There was a silence on the Radio for what seemed like Forever.

"Oh Wow, my Goodness. I don't know what to say", said one of the DJ's, sniffing up, trying not to cry on Air.

"Well, it's not like me to be lost for words, that's why I got this Job on the Radio as I like to talk but this has got me lost". There was a little embarrassed chuckle from the radio DJ. "Well, I hope Whoever that was for, was listening. I just wish we knew who it was from and for".

I looked at Alisha and she looked at me, but no words were exchanged. We both then burst out crying, the tears could not be held in any longer. What a Beautiful Message that was to Someone. It was almost like it had been sent from Heaven. I cried and cried like it was the Letter that was written for me. Alisha pulled over the Car and hugged me. She whispered to me... "That Message was for you".

I could not understand, but yet I felt in my heart, it was for me. The part that said you shall remember me in your written word, what did that mean, but yet, somehow a part of me knew.

CHAPTER 9

That Night, I lay on the bed thinking about what had happened in the Day. Alisha had changed my bed sheets so my bed was all nice and fresh. I Loved a nice, clean, fresh bed, the sheets were nice and cool. I wasn't too keen on the pattern though on the duvet, it was very floral like something my Nan and Grandad would have, but I couldn't complain as I had my own Room and Alisha and Tom had made me feel so welcome here. They had made it my Home.

I felt a little guilty though as Thoughts would come up in my head like do they want me here, am I intruding on their Space? I mean it was their Home and they had both worked for it, and I just come here and stayed for free. My Sister Loved me, and I'm sure she wouldn't have taken me in if she didn't want me there. I must not try to think like this. I have always been a little insecure. I remember when I was in my Teen years, I must have only been about 13 or 14 so, not very old but I went to call for my Friend to hang out and his Mum answered the Door and said that he wasn't in, saying that he had gone to the Cinema with his Friends. I came back Home feeling very sad as he had not asked me, so this made me not feel welcome at Places. I felt welcome here, but it was still not my 'Own Place', and Alisha and Tom had their 'Own Life' to get on with, how could they do that with me here?

***

I rolled over on the bed and eased myself up and sat on the edge of the bed for a moment. The Moon was bright again Tonight, but it wasn't shining directly in my window, but still lit up my room like a pale-silver Light. I walked over to the window that looked out over the Front-Garden, hoping to see her Tonight. The Air was still and calm. I couldn't even hear the Sound of the Ocean Tonight, I looked over at the Trees where she stood last Night, but there was Nothing, just the tall shadows of the Trees in front of the Dark Sky back-drop. Maybe she wasn't Real and it was just my Imagination. I pulled the window shut and locked it.

I had been tired on the drive Home, but I seemed to have woken up now. I walked over to the Door, opening it slowly, trying not to make a Sound so that I didn't disturb Anyone. I slowly made my way downstairs, trying not to bang into anything as my eyes adjusted to the Dark, and trying not to disturb Alisha and Tom as they had gone to bed quite early that Night. I went into the Kitchen to get myself a glass of Water, the Air was cool, and Everything was still. Now I was downstairs, it was safe to turn the Light on.

As I took a sip of Water and headed back into the Lounge, a sound emerged out of the 'Silence of the Night', a little rustling Sound coming from the Back-Garden, my heart started to beat faster, and I didn't want to turn around, but curiosity got the best of me. As I turned, Something caught my eye from outside. I took the final gulp of Water, placed the glass down on the Breakfast Bar and slid opened the Patio door slowly, trying not to make a Sound and stepped outside.

The Grass was cool and soft on my bare-feet like a cool carpet. The Air was still and warm, it seemed warmer out here than inside. I took little slow-steps down the Path, scanning both sides of the Garden to see where that Sound had come from. I quickly looked to my left as I heard the Sound, thinking it was Alisha, had she heard me and got up, but there was No-one there. The Swing at the bottom of the Garden started to move slowly, swinging back and forth but how as there was no Wind and it would take a big gust of Wind to even move it slightly as it was one of them Swings that looked like a big Sofa.

I didn't think too much about it and carried on down the Path to the Gate that led down the Rocks to the Beach. I stood there looking out to the Ocean. It was so calm and still, I had not known it to be this calm like Time had just stopped and everything was at a standstill. I looked up at Alisha's and Tom's Room to check if they were out on the Balcony, and wondered if it was them making the Noise, but their curtains were drawn.

The Temperature in the Air had dropped slightly and I felt a cold spot of Air next to me, it could have been the Sea-Air, but it was a warm Night and there was no explanation for the sudden drop in Temperature. I shivered as I could see my breath and tucked my arms in closer to me to try and keep warm. The scent of Summer Flowers wafted under my nose. I closed my eyes and took a deep breath in taking in more of the sweet-smell. An Image started to unfold before me.

I was sitting at the Table with lots of Book-Shelves around me, and there were people on seats in front of me, asking Questions. They looked very excited and were smiling and happy to be there. On the Table, there was a Pen, it looked like the one that Alo had given me that had the Inscription 'Remember Me' on it. To the right of the Table, there was a big pile of Books all the same. I picked up one of the Books and the Title read 'Together Again' by Daniel Carpenter. On the back, there was a Photo of me and a description of the Story. A Woman put her hand up who was sitting in the front-row, she smiled at me and was just about to ask me a Question then the Vision started to fade away and her voice also faded out. All went Dark again as all I could see now was the inside of my eyelids. I opened my eyes and found myself in the Garden, standing there, looking up at the Moon as it had now come into full-view. A Moment later, that smell of Summer Flower Perfume had come back, but this time stronger. I began to cough as the smell hit the back of my throat, the scent was so familiar to me, if only I could remember where the smell was from. I heard the rustling sound again, this time from behind me then footsteps.

I could feel them getting closer and closer to me until they stopped right behind me, a shiver ran right down my spine as I felt an arm touch my left shoulder. I quickly spun my head around, nearly falling over and made myself dizzy to find that there was No-one there, then I felt the Presence at the other side of me. I turned back around, facing the Ocean, and she was there, in front of me, but I could not see her face, just the slender outline of her. "Who are you?", I called. "Please show me your face - Are you the Girl in the Trees and the Photo and why are you not showing me your face?".

She stepped closer to me and pulled me into her. I had never felt anything like this before. The Love I felt was nothing that I could ever put into words. Was I dead, was she an Angel coming to take me to Heaven? "Please show me your face". She pulled me in closer to her and whispered,

"When you are ready, you shall see me Darling, when you remember me, you shall see me".

I could not see her face, but I knew she was Beautiful. Her outline looked like the Girl I had seen in the Photo, but it might not have been just the same slender-type Figure. She leaned forwards and kissed me on the lips. I kissed her back as I was so lost in that moment, it felt like the World had stopped and there was just me and her - Whoever she was, I should have been scared, but yet, I felt no fear at that moment, just a Love so strong. I could not even put it into words, an Energy that just wrapped itself around me and in me. She then pulled back and faded away into the Night. Maybe it wasn't the Girl from the Photo as when I saw her in the Tree, I couldn't make out her face, just the shape of her Body, and now she had no face. I took a Moment to try and work it out, but my brain was getting tired now, so I headed back inside to bed.

***

The next Day, I woke up to a loud Sound. I looked out of my window and there was a Man with a big hammer, banging on a wall, trying to knock it down. I had not seen him before. I wondered if he it was a Neighbor as I had not seen any People around here. He looked up and waved when he saw me. He looked like a Friendly Guy, the sort of Man that you would bump into and have a long conversation in the street with. He looked like he was hot and could seriously injure himself if he was not careful. He was well out of his youth years, wearing weathered, dark-skin, like he had spent the last 30 years in the

Sun. I would guess his age to be in his late 60s but could have been younger - Just been out in the Sun too long.

I went down for Breakfast and wanted to tell Alisha about the experience last Night but also felt that she would not understand and might think I was crazy too. The House was quiet. I went into the Kitchen, Alisha had left me a note on the Breakfast Bar.

'Danny, I have had to go to the Office for a Meeting - Breakfast is on the side. I will see you later this Afternoon. Call me if you need Anything. Love your Big Sis xxxxx'

I poured the milk over my Cornflakes and turned the Coffee Machine on. After a few minutes, I took my Coffee from the Machine, pulled up a seat and ate Breakfast. I started to think about last Night's Events as I took a sip of my Coffee, washing the Cornflakes down. When I had finished Breakfast, I could still hear the banging, so I went out to see who that Man was, as I had nothing better to do Today, as Tom was at Work and Alisha was at Work, and I had no Friends here or didn't know the Area well enough to explore yet, and I couldn't walk that far anyway, as I was still recovering and building my Body back up from the Accident.

As I approached the old Man, he looked up at me and smiled, wiping the sweat from his fore-head with his arm, and panting. He looked like he could collapse at any minute. A Man of that age should not be knocking down walls, he should be sitting out in the Sun, relaxing.

'It's going to be a hot Day Today, young Man... You must be Danny, it's very nice to meet you".

The old Man wiped his fore-head again and put his hand out; we both shook hands and exchanged a smile.

"Yes, that's right sir. I am Danny. Who are you?".

"I'm Jim. I live in that House there".

He pointed to a House next to Alisha and Tom's House. "Tom had asked me if I could get rid of this bit of old wall and well... As I'm Retired now and got nothing much to do nowadays, so I said I would help him out, keep me out of trouble", the old Man laughed.

"Would you like a drink, Jim? You do look a little hot".

"Oh, Thank You Son - That would be nice".

I went off to get Jim a Drink, what a nice Friendly Man I thought to myself as I walked back into the House to get the old Man a Drink. When I came back out with his Drink, he was sitting on the Bench in the Garden looking up at the Sky, just staring into Space. I handed him the ice- cold Drink and he gulped it down and then wiped the sweat off his head once more. "I wish I could help you. I don't want you to get hurt".

"Oh, don't be so silly Son, you have been through enough. Anyways, it keeps me busy - Nothing else to do".

"How are you settling in here Danny? Tom told me all about you and what happened. Do you remember anything that happened?".

"Not really, I woke up in the Hospital and the Doctor told me, but I don't remember anything, and I'm finding that quite hard as it feels like I'm missing Something or Someone".

"Yes, I know that feeling well". Jim had a sad look in his eyes; he looked up at the Sky then looked back down, reached into his Wallet and pulled out a Photo. "This is Sandra, my wife. Beautiful, isn't she? She passed away 2 years ago. She went to visit her Friend a few days up the Coast. When she was there, she had a heart-attack. I felt so lonely, we had just got this Dream- House we had wanted for years, in Palm Bay. We would drive past and I would say, one day Sweet-Heart, we will live there. When we moved here, it was like a Dream-Come-True. We were both Retired, and it was now time to enjoy Life. When she passed, I found it hard to stay here, this was our House that we had bought together, how could I live in it on my own? - The Memories of her are here. I was going to sell up and move, maybe rent a little Place. One Night, I was sitting watching TV, and I was visited by Sandra. I thought I was seeing things as I was over-tired, but no it was her, she told me to keep the House as it was our House and she watched over me all the Time, making sure I was Ok and staying out of mischief". "Even though she can't be with me here, she is with me in my heart. She said that Life goes on and Life's about making new

115

Memories. One day, I might meet Someone Else and it will then be their House as well as mine, to create new happy Memories in. She told me, just because she is not here anymore with me that I should never give up my Dreams and create new happy Memories".

Jim's Voice started to shake and his eyes were tearing up. I could feel his sadness. "When you lose Someone you Love, it is so easy just to give up on Life, stop doing the things you enjoy, stop going out to the Places you loved going together. We used to go to this nice little Fish and Chip Restaurant down the Town, you might have seen it, that one over-looking the Beach. Well, I loved it there, we would go every Sunday. When Sandra passed, I stopped going. How could I go there now without her? Then one day, I decided to go there. It was hard, but I walk in and the Staff were so happy to see me again".

"I sat on our Table that we would sit at every Time we went, and I ordered the same Food as what we did. I kept going back and eating there each Time. Once I had gone a few times, it wasn't as hard, although I did cry a few times. Bob, the owner was so Friendly and told me that I was so brave for doing that. Now, when I go in, I'm fine, I have even met a Lady-Friend who comes in. She lost her Husband and we started chatting. So, Danny - I'm making new Memories there now. Anyway, Danny, I don't want to keep you all day, you probably have things to do, but I'm always here if you need me. Well... Until you make

Friends here rather than just talking to an old Man". Jim chuckled.

"I like talking to you, Jim".

"Well, Danny - When you are fully recovered, you get yourself down the Town, there are lots of People down there about your age". "It is a Friendly Place, and Everyone makes you feel welcome here, and you never know you might see that nice pretty young-Lady, down-town, buy her a Drink".

"Who?"

"That one that came over yesterday, really pretty. She was small, dark-hair, tanned-skin".

"Oh, Becky - That's my Nurse, she comes and checks on me to see how I'm getting on".

"Oh, I bet she does Danny". Jim said, winking "Well remember, Danny. Life's all about making new Memories and being happy, don't forget about me though, I want a Wedding Invite". Jim laughed again and smiled then walked away, back to his House.

I smiled to myself as I walked back into the House. I liked Jim. He was a nice Man and funny, he had a naughty sense of Humour, it was always nice to meet new People - Maybe I could hang out with him, he was older, well a lot older than me, but I didn't have any Friends my age and what is age anyway?

***

That Afternoon, I just chilled out in the Back-Garden thinking about my Life, I felt so much gratitude for being here. I had been in a coma and been through a nasty Accident, but I was Ok. I was alive and recovering in a Paradise Place with People I Loved around me and I was grateful for that. There are lots of People who just want more all the Time. They Work long Hours to save up for that new Car, thinking it would make them happy then they get it and they are so happy, but a few years later, they bring out a new Model and they want that... It's all wanting the best of Everything all the Time, and deep down, they are never really happy. Then comes the Day they die and they have to leave all that Stuff behind and regret their Life.

I heard a voice shout my Name. I got up on the Sun-Lounger and turned to see Alisha, she had gotten back earlier than she thought she would.

"Hey, my little Bro - How are you? - How have you been Today? - Hope you didn't get too lonely".

I told her about my Morning with Jim and she looked puzzled, trying to work out who Jim was. I could see the cogs going around in her head.

"Where does Jim live?".

118

"Oh, he lives in that House next to ours. That one hidden away in the Trees, he said. Tom had asked him to help him knock down a wall".

"What wall?", Alisha looked even more puzzled now.

I started to feel anxious - Was I making this up or were these just some strange Dreams I was having like the ones where you think you are awake and doing normal Day to Day Stuff but you're asleep. I ran to the front Door and told Alisha to follow me, I took her to the wall where Jim was Working, and I looked around but there was no wall. I then looked at the House Jim said he lived in, it was overgrown and boarded up. I started to feel dizzy, and I collapsed.

I woke up with Alisha and Tom knelt next to me by the Sofa. I slowly pulled myself up.

"What did Jim look like Buddy?", Tom asked.

I described Jim and told them all about his Wife and when they moved and what happened to his Wife, the heart attack, and how Jim would go to the Fish and Chip Restaurant. Alisha and Tom looked at each other and then looked at me surprised at how I knew all this.

"Danny - How do you know this Buddy?", Tom said in his soft voice.

"I was woken up this Morning by a banging Sound. I looked out of my window and saw a Man knocking a wall down, so I went out to him as he looked like he was going to pass out with the heat, so I got him a Drink and sat with him for a while, talking to him. He was telling me about his Life and how his Wife passed".

"Danny, Jim died a year ago. We met him when we moved in. He had lost his Wife, Sandra and asked me if there is anything we needed to do as he had lots of Time on his hands and so he was helping me with that wall but he passed away from Natural Causes. Are you sure it was him Buddy?".

"Well, it must have been him coz how would Danny know of his Wife Sandra and what he looked like", Alisha said. She paused for a moment "Do you think that if Someone has been in a coma that they can somehow unlock the Door to the Other-Side? I mean you do hear these stories of these unexplained things happening to People when they have been in a coma".

It was at that point that the opportunity came in to tell them about my experience last Night with the Vision and the Ghost-Girl. I started to tell them both, Tom rolled his eyes as he wanted to believe, but his logical Mind wouldn't let him. Alisha was very interested.

"Tom, why roll your eyes? - What if when Danny was in a coma - What if he somehow opened a door and is able to see and talk to People that have passed - There is no other explanation". Alisha was getting frustrated with Tom now. "We just don't know do we? - There is so much out there that Science can't explain, we think we know so much and understand Everything but we don't do we? Science can come up with all these Theories but does it know, has it been there? Just look at the Sun in the Sky and the Stars - Yes Science tells us what they are and we believe that, but has anyone ever traveled to the Sun or traveled into the Stars, Moon, and other Planets so how do we know what they are if no-one has been there? - We just get told Something and believe it".

Tom put his arms around Alisha and kissed her, feeling a little guilty for mocking her.

"I'm sorry, Sweet-Heart - When you put it like that, you are right, how do we know what's out there? Like you say, we have not been Anywhere, we have just been to the Moon, and did that even happen? I'm starting to think not and why haven't we gone back?".

"Danny, I have got no plans Tomorrow. I want us to go into Town, there is a Crystal-Shop, but the Woman in there - Willow is very Psychic. She may be able to explain things to you and make sense of Things".

"Is that the Daughter of the People that owned the Cafe we went to and Becky's Friend?',' I asked. I was still in a bit of shock after Today's and last Night's Events. Could I see dead People? Did the coma do something to me? Is this why I saw Jim and the Ghost-Girl. I was now calling her, not Tree-Girl anymore but Ghost-Girl.

***

I decided to have an early Night as I was really tired from the Night before and the Events that went on Today. I made my way over to the window and looked out to see if Anyone was there Tonight but No-one, just the Darkness of Night. The Moon wasn't in view Tonight, so my Room was nice and Dark for me to have a good sleep.

I looked over at Jim's House and was still in a little bit of shock. How had I been talking to a dead Man like I had gone back in time as his House was not overgrown and boarded up when I saw it this Morning. I looked over at Jim's House now thinking it might have been there again, but it was all overgrown and boarded up and crumbling away. Nature had claimed it. I closed the window and locked it. I'm not sure why I locked it as No-one was going to get in, but I guess it was just habit. I pulled my covers back and slid into bed, closed my eyes and I was gone.

CHAPTER 10

The alarm went off. I woke up and looked at her. She was so Beautiful. I was so lucky to have her in my Life. Her smile in the Morning, her gentle kiss. What more could a Guy ask for?

"Good morning, Sweet-Heart".

"Good Morning Babe. You excited to pick up the new Car Today? Come on... We better get up and make a move. I thought we could go see Alisha and Tom today up in Palm Bay and give our new little Car a test spin".

"Oh yes, Babe... That would be wonderful. We can drive up the Coastal Road"...

"Here are the Keys. Enjoy you two. What have you got planned for the rest of the Day?". "We are going to see my Sister and Boyfriend up in Palm Bay, take the Car out for a test spin".

"Oh, how wonderful. Well, if you have any problems with the Car, you just give me a call. Here is my Business Card...

"Danny, the Brakes are stuck - I can't slow down".

***

I screamed out and woke myself up, sweating. Alisha came diving into my room.

"Danny... Danny... Are you Ok? What's wrong?".

"I had this Dream, I was in my 'Old Place', and we went to pick up a new Car. I was with this Girl. I Loved her but I'm not sure who she was. We were driving to yours, here in the new Car. She was driving but the Brakes failed, and she lost control. The next thing I saw was Water all around me and then I woke up. I wish I knew who she was. I couldn't see her face, but I loved her so much". I felt myself starting to cry as I was so confused as to who this was and the Car Crash. Did I have a Girlfriend that was in the Crash with me.

Where was she now?

"Danny, just slow down... What happened?", Alisha said, putting her arm around me.

"I woke up next to this Beautiful Girl. I'm not sure who she was but we were getting a new Car. She was so happy and excited. We picked it up and were coming to see you and Tom. We drove on the Coastal Road, the Brakes failed, and then I

124

woke up". My voice was shaking. Could this be the next part of my Healing? The Flashbacks...

"Danny, I'm going to make a call Tomorrow to your Therapist. I think your Memories are starting to return. We are here for you all the way".

"Thank you, Alisha - Good Night". She kissed me and left my Room, closing the door behind her, leaving my Room in Darkness again. I turned over and went back to sleep. My Body felt light, another Image started to appear before my eyes. I saw myself in a Room surrounded by Book-Shelves and lots of People. I was sitting at the Table, the same Table I saw in my Vision. There were a pile of Books and a Pen. Everyone was so excited. A Woman and her Teenage Daughter approached me. They were so excited to see me.

"Hi Dan... I am urm LL-Lisa. This is my MM-Mum Cat. Hi, just want to say I Love your Book, and I'm a big Fan. Please, if it is Ok with you, cc-can we have a ph-photo with you, and cc-can you please Sign my BB-Book, if you don't mm-mind?".

"Of course, you can. Please don't be nervous. It's Ok. I don't bite".

"Oh, when she saw you, you were doing a Book-Signing. She wanted to come so much, she couldn't sleep".

"Well, I will tell you a little secret, Lisa. I was nervous coming here as I didn't think People would turn up or that there would be too many People and I would get shy", Lisa smiled at me. She handed me the Book, but it was all torn.

"What has happened here?".

''Well, some Girls took it off me in School Today and threw it in a puddle and told me that I should be hanging around with Guys, not reading Books".

"Well, we can't have that can we? Here, take this - a brand new copy, and I will Sign it for you, and don't let anyone ever tell you what you should and should not do".

She was so happy that I had given her the Book. I had made her and her Mum's Day and that's what made me happy, seeing other People happy and enjoying my Book. They both walked off smiling and talking. The Room went silent and everything seemed to freeze. I looked at the Clock and it had stopped. The door opened into the Book-Shop and a young Woman walked in. She smiled at me as she came closer. I could see her face this Time. She had this golden-glow around her.

Her long, blonde-hair had sparkles running through it. I looked into her big, green-eyes, and she was perfect in every way. She walked around to the other side of the Table where I was and wrapped her arms around me and kissed me. She was a few inches smaller than me and very petite. She fitted into my arms perfectly like we just went together like two pieces of a puzzle. She Looked directly into my eyes, I could feel her Soul, and it felt like I was Home.

"I'm so proud of you my Darling". She picked up the Book and whispered in my ear.

"You must write Darling. It will help you remember, and you can make new happy Memories. Never give up on your Dreams".

She stepped back and faded away. There was a rumbling Sound, and Everything around me started to shake, and Books started to fall off the Shelves. I looked up and the high-ceiling, It started to crumble and fall. I felt a hard-blow to my head and fell, hitting my knees, hard on the old floor. I could see the door ahead of me, so I started to crawl toward it, but the door seemed to get further and further away from me. I looked up and saw a big wooden beam, falling toward me. All went black.

I jumped up out of bed, sweat pouring off me, but no sooner had I woken up, the Dream quickly started to fade until I could only remember small bits of it.

I woke up the next Morning feeling very disorientated, not remembering anything from my Dream, just small snippets like the Mum and her Daughter and the Book-Shop falling apart around me. The sun was shining through the window, and it took me a few moments to come around and get my bearings. I heard the sound of pots banging around and then the smell of Coffee, seeping under my door, which fully woke me up. I got dressed and went down to see Alisha who had just finished cooking Breakfast. I sat there and

ate in silence, contemplating Everything that had happened to me.

I knew that my Memories were trying to come back and that my Mind was still trying to make sense of Everything. Everything felt like a Dream like nothing was real anymore. What if I had died and this was all just a Dream that my Soul was having and I could wake up any-time?

I took a sip of Coffee and that seemed to bring me fully back into this Reality. I watched Alisha as she hung the washing out in the Garden, in her own little World

CHAPTER 11

Willow was bored. She had no Customers in all Day. I guess it was just one of these Days where there were not many People about. She loved her little Crystal Shop, it was her Dream to have her own little Shop that sold Crystals and other Magical Things. It seemed to be so quiet every day until 10 minutes before 'Closing Time', then Customers would all come in at once like they all knew she was closing. She has had this Shop for 10 years now, and it was her Life. Her Parents owned a Cafe in Town. They had moved here when Willow was young. Her Dad Alo was Native-American and had bought the Shop for Willow as she was very gifted, and he said that no Gift should be wasted as God has given you it for a reason. She carried out her Work at her Shop, but from time to time, she would go to Client's Houses if they could not come to her, but she always preferred to do her Work in the Shop as that was her 'Magical, Healing Space'. She was a Healer and a Psychic, and she looked the part too - What you would expect a Spiritual-Psychic to look like.

She had long, light-brown hair that was all braided.

A little nose-ring, big ear-rings with feathers in and lots of Crystals around her neck. She was only small and thin, and her skin was slightly tanned and so smooth, not a wrinkle on it so it was hard to tell her age as she looked younger than she was. It was a good thing but also not so good at times as she attracted younger Guys and they would just come in the Shop to check her out, not to buy anything, just hang out there. She did think maybe they like the Energy of the Shop, but from what some of the Guys said to her, it was more like that they liked her Energy rather the Shop.

She always caught on to what they were and why they were hanging around. One time, there was this Guy who would come in and flirt with her, it wasn't much flirting as he had no idea. At first, it was a bit of fun, but he never bought anything, and this was a Shop, not some hang out. He looked like he was in his early 20s, and when she told him that she was 38, he never came back. This made Willow think about her age and Time was passing by fast. Sometimes, she would get a little sad that she was Single but she was fine for the Time-Being. She had a little Shop down by the Beach with her Family and Best Friend Becky who worked with her sometimes on her Days off from Nursing, so her life was good.

***

She opened up the Shop as usual and got set up for the Day. She had no Clients booked in Today as Saturdays was a Walk-In Day where people could just turn up and require her Services without having to book. Her Phone rang. She picked it up from the Counter to see who it was.

She didn't get many calls, so when her Phone did ring, it always alarmed her. As she was talking on the Phone, she felt the Temperature drop and walked over to the door that had blown open with the Wind. She looked out at the Sky, it had started to turn dark, big black Clouds that started to roll in from the Sea, covering the Sun, turning Day into Night. The Lights around the Harbour flicked on as if they were on a Light Sensor. It felt like there was a Storm on its way but it's what it needed as it had been hot over the last few Days and the Air had needed to be cleared. She looked out of the door, but there was not a Person in sight. It was unusually quiet for a Saturday. If it didn't pick up within the next Hour, she would be closing early. Maybe, it was the Weather keeping People away. Most of her Customers would come in the Shop from the Beach to check out the little Spiritual Crystal Shop. Willow was constantly cleaning the floor of Sand that was the only problem with being next to the Beach. She did make a sign telling People to wipe their feet before they came in, but it didn't make a difference, but it kept her busy. She had a Back Room in the Shop where she did her Readings and Healings that Customers were not

131

allowed to go into, only if they had booked in with her, as this was a very 'Special, Sacred Space' where her Dad had blessed and protected so not Everyone could go in.

There was only ever one Time when she had trouble in the Shop. A Customer had come in demanding Healing from her and saying that if Willow did not Heal her, then she and her Shop would be cursed. Willow was shocked at the Woman's behavior but being the nice Person that she was, she led her into the back, and as she opened the door to the Healing Room, the Woman had just stopped dead. She could not enter the Room. Willow had never experienced this before and was a little worried. She reached out for the Woman and had to practically drag her into the Room, but as she reached out, the Woman looked and hissed and jumped back.

Willow tried again to reach for the Woman, but she hissed again and jumped back. It felt like there was this invisible barrier stopping Willow, taking her in her Healing Room. She called Alo, her Dad for advice as she had never seen anything like this. Within minutes, her Dad was down in the Shop. He took one look at the Woman and insisted that she leave and never return. The Woman left, muttering to herself, and as she left, Alo spoke some words that Willow did not understand. It was a strange Language, and her Dad told her it was called Light-Language and was for Protection.

"Willow, my Dear Daughter. She was not any normal Woman".

"Her Soul had been taken by Darkness, the Light had stopped you from taking her into your Room. If she would have entered and you started to Heal her, the Darkness would have transferred to you".

"But what if she needs my help? She knew she had Darkness in her and needed it clearing".

"Oh, she knew she had the Darkness, but she liked it being there. She just wanted to take your Energy. We can't help Everyone my Dear Daughter".

That was the only time that Willow had any bother at the Shop. She did have a few regular Customers but most of them would be Tourists or just People passing by.

She looked at her Watch. It was getting on for 2pm and still no Customers. The Sky outside had become Darker, it looked like it was Dusk, and it was kind of creepy. Willow was just about to lock up and close early when she got the scent of Perfume in the Shop. It smelt of Summer Flowers, and the smell was getting stronger. It was so strong that Willow started to cough. She looked at where the smell could be coming from. Maybe, it was the Incense she had just re-stocked this Morning, but she did not recognize that smell.

She walked over, but all she could smell there was the Incense, not that same smell as was in the Room. Willow looked around, puzzled as to where the smell was coming from. She walked over to the door and closed it, thinking the smell might have been coming from outside. She was just about to lock the door when the Wind-Chimes chimed that were just hanging above the front Counter. She walked over to them, trying to figure out how that was making a Sound as there was no Wind in the room. "Hello, who is there?", she called. After a few seconds, she got the Message...

"Do not close. Danny's Coming. Tell him to write a Book... Remember me".

It had been a while since Willow had received Messages like this so she wasn't sure what it meant, but her Intuition was telling her to keep the Shop open as Someone called Danny was coming in. Willow tried to work out what the Message was about and who it was that was trying to get through to her. She sat down on her Chair behind the Counter and just took a deep breath and closed her eyes.

A Vision appeared before her eyes. A Car with two People in, a Guy and a Girl. They were smiling and laughing. The Car had pulled up at the side of the Road and the Couple got out and were taking Photos of the View. They got back in the Car and drove off. A few moments later, there was a screech and a Female voice shouted 'Danny' then all went blank. Willow opened her eyes, coughing and trying to catch her breath like she was in Water, drowning. The Vision was so clear and Real.

What had she just witnessed? She got up from her Seat and went to grab her bottle of Water. She picked up her Phone and rang Becky to tell her what had happened and that she needed someone to talk to about this. Becky was quick to Answer.

"Hey, Willow Chick. How are you?".

"I'm...".

"Everything Ok? You sound in shock, what has happened?".

"Well l... I... I'm not sure", Willow said in a shocked voice.

"I'm coming over now".

"No, it's Ok Beck. You don't have to, but Thank You anyway. I'm just in a bit of shock that's all".

"Well, are you going to tell me what's happened then Chick?".

"Yes, well it's been a quiet Day, so I was going to shut the Shop up early and get off, but as I'm closing the Shop, I smell this Perfume that I haven't smelt before. It smelt really nice like Summer Flowers. I went to look around the Shop to see where it was coming from, but I couldn't find it, then I went back to lock the Shop up, but as I'm locking up, the Wind-Chimes start to chime and I go check it out, but there is no-one there. I then get this Message saying,

"Do not close. Danny's coming in, write, Book, remember me".

"Oh, Wow, what do you think it means?", Becky said excitedly.

"I don't know, but it gets even more strange, so I sit down for a Moment, close my eyes and I have this Vision of two People in a Car, a young Guy and a Girl and she screams Danny then the car goes over this Cliff and all goes black. I open my eyes, coughing and trying to catch my breath. It felt like I was under water, drowning".

Becky went silent for a moment.

"Hey, you still there?".

"Yes, Sorry - I am still here, Chick. That sounds like the Guy I'm seeing at the Moment".

"What - You're seeing a Guy and you never told me".

"No, not like that - He is a Patient of mine. He is called Danny. He was in a Car Accident, and he went into a coma. Poor Guy lost his Girlfriend, but the worst part is that he has no Memory of her".

"Oh Wow. Do you think she is trying to come through to me to get to him?".

"She could be Willow, but I'm not sure that you should tell him, it still might be too soon. He is still recovering and getting his head around it all".

"Can I ask you a personal Question Becky if you don't mind? I'm not sure where this is coming from, but do you like Danny?".

"Yes, he is a nice Guy".

"No, I mean do you like him like him?".

Becky chuckled down the Phone. She could feel herself blushing.

"You do, don't you? Come on - You can tell me".

"Well, he is my Patient so I can't like him like that or I could lose my Job".

"He won't be your Patient Forever though will he Becky? You are such a Beautiful Person. You deserve to be happy with someone, especially after all the shit you went through".

"Thank You Willow. I can see how it goes... I think Danny does like me too, as when he sees me, his face lights up, and he sort of blushes a bit too. I think that's sweet. We were sat in his Sister's Lounge the other Day, I had gone to see him and I thought he was going to kiss me. I could feel it".

"What would you have done if he had kissed you?".

"I would have kissed him back probably", Becky chuckled down the Phone again. "It might be too soon for him as his Short-Term Memories will come back and he will remember Everything, and when he remembers losing his Girlfriend in the Crash that will devastate him".

"Yes, but he will need Someone there, and you are the perfect one for him".

"Awww, Thank You so much. Well, we can see... If it is meant to be, it will happen".

"It certainly will".

"Well, Willow... I better let you go and get on with your Day as I'm sure Danny will be coming in soon".

"Ok, well it was nice chatting with you, and I will see you Monday when you're next in, and we can have a good catch-up then".

"OK, Goodbye Chick. See you soon".

Willow felt better after her and Becky's conversation.

She sat and thought about what had happened and if that Message was for Danny. Should she tell him about his Girlfriend or was he not ready yet. This could delay his recovery if he found this out so soon but would it be better to tell him so he could deal with it. Just as she was contemplating it, a voice in her head said.

"He will soon remember me in his own time".

Willow quickly turned her head to check where the voice was coming from. She did this all the Time and the voices always startled her, even though she had had this Gift all her Life, so she should have been used to commutating Spirits Telepathically.

That did make Willow feel at ease, knowing that she did not have to tell him but could Guide him if he needed it.

***

Willow looked around the Shop, trying to find something to do. She checked her Daily Task Sheet that she had made, but Everything was ticked on it. Sometimes, she did feel quite lonely. She Loved her life but Becky was her only Friend and if Becky did end up with Danny then who would she have to hang out with? Becky had once tried setting her up on a Date with a Guy called Mike. He seemed nice and was interested in Willow's Life and would ask her Questions about Spirituality, but when he wanted to stay over at Willows one Night and she told him no, that she wanted to get to know him more first as the Energy must be right before she jumps into bed with anyone. He left and messaged her the Day after saying that he was not interested in her.

Just another Guy. Only after one Thing, but she knew not all Guys are the same and there will be one waiting for her. He might not be in this Universe yet, but he will come.

The door chimed, opened and a Voice said, "Are you open?". Willow looked up thinking it might have been Danny, but it was a Woman on her own.

"Yes, I'm open. Sorry, I was going to close early as it's been a quiet Day".

"Oh, tell me about it", the Woman said in a Friendly Tone of Voice. I'm not sure where Everyone is Today. I have just been into Town and there is no-one about. I think it must be the Weather keeping Everyone inside".

"Yes, maybe. So, how is it I can help you Today?".

"I'm looking for a Crystal that helps protect me from Negative Energies as I'm feeling I'm getting attacked. Oh, my... I hope I don't sound too strange", the Woman laughed.

Willow put her arms out and made a Friendly Gesture at the Woman. "Hey, look around this Shop and look at me, nothing is strange to me", Willow laughed. "Now... We have two Crystals that can help you". Willow walked over to the Crystals and pulled two black chunks out. "This is Tourmaline and this one is Obsidian. They both are very Powerful Amazing Crystals". Willow pulled out a Crystal from under her top. "This is Tourmaline. I wear this one all the time around my neck. I get lots of People coming in here. I'm not saying they are bad but they carry lots of different Energies".

"Ok my Love, then I will take the two".

"Would you like a Chain for them so you can wear them?".

"Oh, yes please. That would be nice".

"If you do feel you are getting attacked or you have any unwanted Energies on you, I'm a Healer so I can help remove them from you".

"Oh... That would be nice. I will book in with you. I will have to check when I'm free".

"Ok, cool. Well here is my Card with all my Details on". Willow took the payment for the Crystals and the Woman left. The first Customer of the Day she thought. I wonder if she will be the last of the Day..

CHAPTER 12

"Danny, are you ready? We have to go before the Shop shuts and this Weather is not looking too good Today", Alisha shouted up the Stairs to me".

I was excited about visiting this Shop as it was Somewhere new and I hope that maybe I might get some answers. Was I seeing Ghosts and was some Ghost-Girl trying to get through to me? On the way there, I felt a little nervous as I did not know what to expect or what this Woman did. Was she going to lock me in her Shop and put some Spell on me? It was going to be a nice thought to be able to chat with Someone about it.

***

We pulled into the 'Main Beach Car Park', and Alisha pointed at the Shop. We were the only Car parked in there. I could see the Waves crashing onto the Beach, getting further and further in, towards the Car Park. The Sky was still dark, it looked kind of cool, I did like a good Storm and it seemed cooler being down at the Beach, seeing a Storm coming in. "Danny... I have a few things to do in Town, so I will drop you off and then come pick you back up".

"What... You're not coming in with me, why not?".

This just made me feel worse. I got out and started to head over to the Shop that Alisha had pointed to, I knew exactly what Shop it was as there were only two Shops on the Beach, an Ice-Cream one and this one. I could smell Incense coming from inside and this made me feel calm, I could feel good vibes from the Place. The front of the Shop was a light-blue colour with old window-frames with those little panes of glass.

In the front windows, there were Sea-Shells dotted about with big Crystals and Candles. There was a Sign that had been hand-painted on a bit of driftwood that read, 'Come in a Stranger, leave as a Friend'. I was a bit nervous going in but I knew that I had to for she may give me Guidance or clarity on things and tell me I'm not going Mad. I opened the door and the smell of Incense hit me. I felt very calm and relaxed, there was the sound of Waves with gentle Music playing over it. All my worries and anxieties seemed to fall away.

"Hello, is anyone in?" I called.

"Just hang on, my Love. I'm coming to be with you in just a sec".

As the Woman walked out from the back, I wondered if that was her. She was nothing like I could have imagined. When she saw me, she stopped and looked at me, figuring me out, then after a few seconds, she smiled at me.

"Danny isn't it?" she said in a very friendly voice.'

"Yes, that's right. I am Danny. My Sister advised me to come here and check out the Shop".

"You Ok there, you seem a little surprised there?".

"Yes, I was just not expecting... Urmm".

'What... Expecting someone as young as me?", Willow laughed.

"Well, yes. I had an old Lady in my head".

Willow laughed again "A lot of People think that as it's not something that People expect someone my age to do around here. Anyway, let me introduce myself. I'm Willow, and welcome to my 'World' Well... 'Shop' but it's my 'World'. I was expecting you Danny and I'm glad you're here now, as I was going to close the Shop but someone told me I had to stay open for you.

"How did you know I was coming?".

"Well... Let's just say a voice in my head told me", Willow smiled and walked over to the door and closed it then locked it, turning the 'Open Sign' to 'Closed'.

"We don't want anyone interrupting us do we, during the Sacrifice?", Willow laughed. She had a dark sense of Humour.

"Oh, don't worry Danny. I'm not locking you in. I just don't want us to be disturbed.

Would you like a Drink? I will put the Kettle on then we will have a chat". Willow walked into another Side Room and returned a few moments later with two cups of Coffee. She handed me one, it was still very hot so I placed it down on the Table next to me and just watched the steam rise from it. Willow took a little sip of hers but soon put it down when she realized how hot it was.

"So, Danny... How are you settling in here, are you liking Palm Bay?".

"Yes, well I haven't seen much of it yet, but I'm sure I will stay here as it looks like a nice place".

"Oh, it is. I've been here a long-time now and I love it. You will get settled and make new Friends here I'm sure of that, and you have already met Becky, haven't you?".

"Yes, she is my Nurse. How do you know her?".

"Oh, she and I have known each other a Long-Time. She works here sometimes when she is not working at the Hospital. She is such a Beautiful-Soul".

"She certainly is, we are going to hang out together when I am feeling better and she is no longer my Nurse".

"Oh, you are, are you...? Is that what they call it now, hanging out?' ',Willow laughed.

I felt myself starting to blush. "I don't know anyone here apart from my Sister, her Boyfriend Tom, Becky and now you".

"You like her, don't you? That's cool... Well, I am no Match-Maker - That is the Universe's Job but just watch this space, Danny", Willow winked and smiled at me.

"So, tell me what's been going on with you?".

I started to talk to Willow about the Girl in the Trees then Jim and the Dream that I had. I could see that she looked very interested, nodding her head and looking into my eyes. She grabbed her cup of Coffee and took another sip. I picked up mine once I knew it had cooled down and took a big Drink, trying to clear my throat as I was talking about such an unusual subject that was way out of my Comfort Zone.

"Danny, do you remember anything about the Accident you were in or if there was anybody else there?".

"I don't, but in my Dream, there was this Girl there. I could not see her face but she was in the Car with me".

"Have you seen this Girl any other time? After the Accident, you were in a coma in the Hospital. Did you see Anything or Anyone there?".

I closed my eyes and thought for a Moment and then a Vision of a Man in a Boat with an Irish Accent appeared. I opened my eyes and told Willow.

"Wow, Danny - That is Amazing... Well Done. So, let me explain what's happened to you".

I looked at Willow as I took another sip of the Coffee, which was now warm. I edged forward on my Seat, waiting for Willow to talk.

"So, when People go into a coma, they temporally die and can go into the After-Life. If it is not their time, they will come back out of the coma, sometimes they will get given a Key, not an actual Key but they can get abilities and open the Doorway into Heaven. This can happen if they have lost Someone close to them or they need help with remembering what happened so they can move on. The Irish Man was one of your Spirit-Guides, and he was taking you back to your Physical Body as it was not your time".

Willow closed her eyes and then started to speak again. "Danny, my Love. There is Someone who is trying to get through to you, but I can't speak much of them as you have to remember them so you can move on. She was there when your Guide was taking you in the Boat back to Earth. You did not want to leave that

Place did you?, but you see Danny, that was not Heaven, that was like a Stop-Off Point like an in-between World so you could not have stayed there".

The Room filled with the smell of the Summer Flowers again and Willow and I looked at each other as we could both smell it. The whole Room filled with the Scent, overpowering all the other Smells. I told her, I kept smelling the Scent just before the Girl appears.

There was a Whisper in the Air.

"Danny, my Darling. Write the Book and you shall remember me".

I felt the kiss on my cheek. Willow looked at me and had tears in her eyes like she could see who it was. She just sat there smiling and staring to my right side as if Someone was there. She smiled and nodded her head. "Danny, there is some Paper and a Pen on your Desk at Home, you need to write. I'm getting that this Story will change your Life and shall make you remember what happened so you can move on".

"I don't read Books never mind write one. I wouldn't know where to start and why do I need to remember what happened? That might make things worse if I did remember".

"You feel sad like you have lost Someone or Something but don't know what, and you need closure until you can move on. We all need closure on things. Years ago, I was with a Guy, we were so happy then one Day, he dumped me. Just came out of the blue. One Night, we were going to go for Food, I was getting ready and he phoned me and told me he didn't want to see me again. I was devastated, I thought that I had done something wrong and for weeks and even months after, it hurt. My heart felt so bad that I could not Date Anyone. After 3 months, I found out that he was cheating on me. I still felt hurt, but I needed to find out so that I could move on. It's all about getting closure so we can Heal from situations. You're going to get so much help writing your Book There is Someone that you have to remember but I can't say who as this is your Healing Journey and you have to find out, but I'm here for you, so is Becky and your Sister and her Boyfriend.

We all Love You so much, and I know that you are going to have a wonderful Life here, and I want you to remember that Everything happens for a reason, no matter how painful it may be".

"Thank You, Willow. Thank You so much", I said with tears in my eyes, sniffing up.

Willow passed me a tissue and then reached out too and hugged me.

"You are so welcome. You have a Beautiful, Gifted-Soul, Danny, and I'm so happy to have met you".

"You too Willow. Thank You again".

Willow reached out again and we gave each other another big tight hug. I felt so calm and peaceful now, not like before when Alisha dropped me off. After a few moments, there was a knock at the front door. Willow had forgotten she had locked it. She walked over and there was Alisha. She let her in and shut the door behind her, making sure that no-one else could come in now as it was Closing Time.

"Hey Guys, hope Everything is Ok and you feel better now, Danny?".

"Oh, I do and Willow is Amazing, she has helped me with Stuff. There is still a lot I have to figure out as she is not allowed to tell me Everything as it's my own Healing Path".

"It certainly is, and Thank You so much Willow for your Time. Here, have this". Alisha took out some notes from her purse and handed it to Willow".

"Oh no, I can't take this. I'm just here to help".

"No, take it please Willow. You have taken your Time to help Danny".

"Thank You so much... Well, here... I want to give you this".

Willow walked over to the Music Stand and pulled out a CD and handed it to me.

"This is a nice Music CD, it helps me with my Work and it will help you with yours Danny".

I looked at the CD, it had a Beach on there with the Sunset and it said calming Music with Wave and Beach Sounds.

"Thank you so much, and I will see you again soon".

"You certainly will, anytime you're in Town, call in. Oh, and Becky is in on Monday too so if you're around, wink wink".

I felt myself go red again, I said Goodbye to Willow, and Alisha and I left. On the way Home, I told her all about my Time with Willow and what she had said. I was surprised at her as she was so interested in it all and the Spirit-World I had never really known her to be like that but after Mum and Dad died, she got more into it, wanting to find out if there was an After-Life?

It was more me that came from a Scientific sort of Approach, but with what had happened to me, even Science can't explain that. I like Science but I was starting to change my view on it, it can only take us so far, but what is beyond that point? Even Religion is very limited. It cannot explain Everything, it only thinks it can. Maybe I had been given this Gift and it was going to change my Life?

***

We arrived Home, and it was still very Dark. I checked my Phone to see what Time it was as it could have been the middle of the Night for all I knew. We opened the front door to the smell of Cooking.

Tom made us Dinner, it was all there ready for us to sit down and eat and then settle down for the Night. We got ready for Dinner and all sat around the table. Tom had asked me how my Day was, but I felt a little reluctant to tell him as I knew he didn't believe in any of that Stuff, so I just told him that my chat with Willow was really helpful and I feel better after it.

After Dinner, I helped Tom with the dishes. There was a 'Loud, Crashing Sound' outside that made us all jump. We all dived to the Patio doors to see what it was.

The Garden Shed next door had collapsed from the Wind that had now picked up. Tom locked the door, making sure it was secure as Palm Bay can get hit with bad Storms. We then settled in the Lounge, and Tom put a Film on.

CHAPTER 13

That evening, I lay on my bed looking at the Writer's Desk with the old Lamp standing on it and the stack of Paper that looked to have grown even more now. I did not read Books. I didn't like Books. I could never get into them. They were just words on pages to me. So, how could I even write one? I just would not know where to start. I sat and pondered over this for a short-while, exhausting my mind and trying to think about writing.

There was no Moon Tonight lighting up the Sky, so it was quite Dark outside. I opened the window and looked out to see if I could see her, but there was no sight of her. I scanned the whole Area with my eyes, but nothing and no-one, just the stillness of the Night. I chuckled to myself as I'd been doing this every Night, now trying to find the Ghost-Girl.

If Anyone knew, I would be locked up, thinking that I was Crazy. I shut the window and drew the curtains, feeling a little disappointed that she had not come Tonight.

There was a low 'Creaking Sound' that caught my ear. I turned around slowly, looking to see where the Sound was coming from. I followed the Sound over to the Desk and tucked the Chair back under it, as I turned to get into bed. The Chair flew back out from under the Desk, and the pile of Papers fell onto the floor, scattering all over my Room. I looked at the Desk and the Lamp flickered on, making an 'Electric Buzzing Sound'.

My Emotions were all mixed up at this point, part of me wanted and should have been scared, but yet another part of me was frozen in fascination and curiosity. As I started to gather up the Paper and place it in a neat pile on the Desk, the words appeared.

'Write and you shall remember me'.

I rubbed my eyes, and the writing seemed to fade away. The smell of Summer Flowers filled the Air in the Room and I smiled, she is back. This Time, I was going to try and talk to her. If I could talk with Jim, the old Man next door who had died, then why not Ghost-Girl.

"Hello, I'm Danny, what is your Name?", I called out.

The Room was Silent, but there was something different about this Silence. It felt very peaceful. The Lamp buzzed then flickered out. The Room fell into Darkness, I could not see or make out Anything, and it felt like I was in a 'Black Void of Nothingness'. My Room had never been this Dark even when the Moon wasn't shining in. I could still see as my eyes could adjust, but not this Time. I got down on my hands and knees, feeling about on the floor, trying to find the Bedroom door. I tried to let some Light in and find the Light-Switch that was next to the door, but I couldn't even see where the Bedroom door was.

For a Moment, I thought I was dead, still in the endless coma and living with Alisha and Tom, and all the other Stuff like meeting Becky in the Hospital was just a Dream, and I was still in this Eternal coma. Was this it...? Had I just been Dreaming all this up and the Dream had ended now and I was dead? I started to feel the panic kick in, and my heart was racing. I felt something in front of me and grabbed it. It was my Phone. I turned on the Torch and could see the outline of a slender Figure, sitting at the Desk. It looked back at me, but it had no face. Was this the Girl, but yet why wouldn't she show her face to me?

She slowly got out of the Chair and started to walk towards me, my heart racing, my Mind trying to convince me I was Dreaming. The Figure knelt in front of me, and all the fear and panic just seemed to disappear from me. I felt so peaceful and calm, my heart had stopped racing and it felt soft and warm like this Energy was flowing into it. I had never felt anything like it before, a tear rolled down my cheeks, but this was not a tear of sadness. I could not put it into words. Only word I could use was Love. The Beautiful Figure got back up and held out it's arm to me. I reached out, and it took my hand, both of our Energies started to merge, and I could feel this Divine Presence inside me. There was a whisper in my ear, I could not make out or recognize the voice, but it was so Angelic and gentle. It said,

"I am within you now. I shall show you and help you remember".

I felt a kiss on my cheek and a warm glow in my heart.

The Lamp buzzed and turned back on, lighting up the Room. The 'Sweet-Smell' that had filled the Room had faded until I could no longer smell it, but I still felt that deep sense of Peace within me. I noticed the Paper on the Desk had been moved, the top sheet had been placed in the centre with the Pen next to it. There was some writing on the Paper, but it was quite hard to make out as it was faded but still just about readable if you focused. I picked up the Paper, held it close to my eyes and began to read what was written.

'Danny, my Darling. You miss me, but yet you don't remember me, Babe. I want you to enjoy Life and you will live Life to the full and be very happy and successful. I wish I could show myself to you, but I am not allowed, for you have to remember me, and it is then that your new Life shall begin, my Love. I will

help you, and I am always here looking down on you, and the
Day shall come when we are re-united again.

I Love You so much from...'

Just as I had finished reading the last words, the writing had
faded away and the page was blank again.

I knew I had to write a Book, and that would help me in some
way, but I don't know how or what to write, what would my
Story even be about? I'm no JK Rowling. Maybe if I go to the
Library Tomorrow and read a Book, it might help me.

***

The next day, I got up, had Breakfast and decided that I would
go to the Library. Alisha had to go into the Office today again,
so I was on my own. I would have to walk into Town as I don't
think there were Buses, well I had not seen one, and it can't be
that far. It only took about 10 minutes of driving, so I would say
30 minutes max to walk. The exercise would do me good.
Becky did say that I had to exercise. I was feeling stronger now,
so I thought I would take up the Challenge.

I set off down the Small Road, out onto the Main Road into
Town. It was easy to find my way into Town as it was just one
Road with a few Houses dotted about, in-between the Palm
Forest. I guess that's where they got the Name Palm Bay from
as the Area looked like a Tropical Island, littered with Palm
Trees. The Weather was not as hot Today, so it made it more

159

bearable to move about and walk. The Road was quiet, just the odd Car going past, now and then. In one direction was Palm Bay and in the other, the Road cut through the Jungle and Hills, onto the next small Town on the Coast.

I arrived in town about 45 minutes later; the Weather had started to get hotter now as the Sun was rising further into the Sky. After the long walk, I was feeling pretty tired as I had not walked in a long-time, just pottered about the House and Town with Alisha. Had I made a mistake walking here, was it too much for me? I remember too, I had to walk back.

''Oh well, I'm here now. I'll worry about that later''.

I thought I had not been into Town on my own and felt excited to check out the Place, but also a little bit anxious too. It's surprising where your confidence goes when you haven't been out in a while. The first Place I wanted to check out was the Harbour as it seemed the Life and Soul of the Town.

As I headed down to 'The Old Harbour', my legs were pretty tired and I was feeling hungry as the smell of Fish and Chips hit my nose. The Seagulls were out in full Force Today, making a right racket as they were fighting each other for scraps of Food that People had left.

It looked like a very Picturesque Place with little Shops that you only ever see at the Seaside, selling all kinds of little Things. There were Ice-Cream Kiosks and Cafe's down one side of the

Harbour, and at the other side, were the Bars and Restaurants and Palm Bay's only Night Club 'Sunset'.

Alisha had told me that not many People go as People are more into the Beach round here and going to the Bars and Cafe's rather than Clubbing. I was not much of a Clubber now. I used to like going to the odd Club in my early 20s, but now, I just liked eating out and maybe the odd, nice, little Bar. I was feeling thirsty as the Weather had got even hotter now. I didn't like over-crowded Places, so it took me a little time to find Somewhere that I could sit and have a Drink. I felt a little over-stimulated with Everything going on around me and felt like I could have collapsed, A Woman saw me as I started to feel dizzy and nearly fell. Just as I was about to hit the ground, she grabbed me and took me over to her Cafe, sat me down and got me a nice, cold Drink.

The People around here seemed so Friendly, and it made me feel happy that I lived in such a nice Place. I took my Wallet out to pay her for the Drink but she insisted that it was on the House. After a few moments of getting my strength back together, I heard a voice calling me, surprising me as to who it was, as I didn't know Anyone around here. I turned around to see who it was and saw Becky running towards me. She was wearing a Summer dress and was looking even more stunning than ever. I had never seen her out of her Work Uniform. I wish I had. I felt myself blushing at that thought. She was all done up with her make-up on, and as she got closer, I could smell her Perfume. My jaw dropped open at the sight of her.

"Hey Danny, Sweet-Heart - What are you doing here?", Becky said, in a hyper and happy voice.

She threw her arms around me and kissed me on the cheek. I wasn't sure if that was allowed as I was still her Patient, but I wasn't going to complain about that. Anyway, we were just two People out and she is not working so what is wrong with that?

"Hey Becky, how are you?". I hugged her back not wanting to let her go. I could have had her in my arms for Eternity, but I had to pull back as I didn't want her getting all creeped out. Would you like to join me for a Drink? I have just had one but I can order another one as it's a hot Day".

"Well Danny, Babe. You took the words out of my mouth. I was just going to ask you what would you like to Drink? So, what brings you? Is your Sister here?".

"Alisha is working Today, so I thought I would walk into Town and check the Place out. I'm going to go to the Library later".

"What... You walked all that way? I know I said you needed exercise but only a little a Day, not like walking the County". Becky half laughed and sounded concerned at the same time.

"What are you going to the Library for? You don't look like a Guy that reads –You are more of a Netflix Guy I'd say".

I told Becky about meeting Willow and the experiences I had been having and how I need to write the Book. I did expect her to laugh, but I don't know why as she is not the kind of Person to mock People. Her eyes widened and she pulled up closer to me, looking at me with such interest.

"Wow, Babe. That is Amazing... Well... I think you should go for it. You never know, you could become a top Writer, and you never know, in years to come, they could make a Film out of your Book".

I smiled and laughed at her, as I had never even read a Book, never mind writing one and making a Film from it. I looked at her for a moment and imagined us being together, a smile spread across my face, and I quickly came back, snapping out of it, as I didn't want to make it too obvious that I fancied the pants off her. She did brighten up my Day. She was like a 'Little Ray of Sunshine', and I'm sure she liked me, but how could I ask her out. She was my Nurse, taking care of me, but then... 'Love Breaks All Boundaries'.

'Love Breaks All Boundaries...?' Where did that thought even come from...That's not something I would say. We finished our Drinks, Becky got up to pay, and I followed her inside, and took out my Wallet, but she insisted that she was paying. "Right, Danny Babe, I've got to go back to my Apartment and sort some Stuff out, but we should hang out again Sometime. Maybe you could come around to mine or we could go for Something to eat Sometime?".

She smiled, pulled me into her, and this time, kissed me on my lips then walked off smiling away. Did she just ask me out? Did this Beautiful Goddess just ask me out on a Date? I couldn't stop smiling. The Woman in the Cafe came over to me.

"Well, she could not have made it anymore clearer and obvious that she likes you". The Woman smiled. "She is very Pretty. I have seen her around Town a few times with Guys checking her out, but she just walked past them, not showing interest. I guess she has just been waiting for the right Guy". The Woman winked at me and I said Goodbye to her and made my way from the Harbour, back into Town, heading for the Library. I had never been in a Library before, so I wasn't sure what to expect.

***

The Library was quite a big old Building. It stood out from the rest of the Town;

I wasn't even sure how it got there as the Town was modern. I imagined that the Town was built around the old Building. Inside, was a different Story. It was modern and smelled like fresh-paint. There were different sections for different genres of Books, and each section had Seats and a Table. Off to the side of the front Desk was a small Room filled with Computers and Printers. I was greeted by a young Woman with glasses and long dark hair in a ponytail. She looked friendly and approachable but quite nervous as well. She introduced herself.

"Hi my name is Sally, and I am one of the Librarians that work here".

I shook her hand and introduced myself, and we walked off into the Library together. It was all new to me as I had never been to a Library before.

"So, how can I help you today, Danny?", Sally said in a quiet, shy voice.

"I'm not sure... I'm thinking of writing a Book, but I have never even read a Book so don't know where to start".

"Oh Wow, that's excellent. What gave you the Idea?".

"Let's just say I was Guided to it".

I didn't want to go into the whole Story with a Stranger, but Sally looked like she would not judge me, but still, I didn't know her to be telling her that a dead Girl had told me to write a Book. "So, what kind of a Book do you want to write? Is it a Novel, a Fictional Story or is it based on your Life?".

"Well, I'm not sure yet. I thought, maybe if I see a Book I like, I can read it and get an idea from it".

"Oh excellent. Here, take this". Sally handed me a Book and took me to sit down.

"This Book was written by a Man who was very Dyslexic. He could not read and write until he was 14 years old, but he wrote this and it was a World's Bestseller".

"How did he do that?", I said with Amazement.

"Well, you see Danny - a good Book is not how many words or how many pages it has in it or the Front Cover. It is the Story. This Man had such a Creative Imagination, and he was able to put his Life into a Fictional Novel. It's not the Book Danny, it's the Story in the Book. Once you have a Story, the Book is born and grows from there. Right, I will leave you to it as I need to get back to my Job, but if you need any more help, just come and get me, and good luck with your Book. I'm sure you will have a great Story to tell". Sally smiled and walked off.

I sat for a few moments skimming through the pages, but all I saw was writing, nothing but words on pages. Maybe if I just try and read a page to see how I get on. I looked at all the text on the page and started to read the first page and then the second and third and so on, until I finished the first Chapter.

The Book was about a Man that had fallen in Love with a Woman but Days before the Wedding, they had both found out that they were Brother and Sister that had been separated at Birth. I was very interested to read more and how the Story would unfold, so I decided to take the Book out and continue reading it. Once I had read the first few pages, the Story started to come to Life. This could be a new Hobby of mine, to read. I looked at the Time and it was turning 3.30 - Time had just seemed to have disappeared. "It was nice meeting you, Danny. Enjoy reading and all the best with your writing", she said, looking down at some Papers.

***

I set off, walking back Home, forgetting how far the walk Home was. The Sun was not as hot now as it was late Afternoon so the Temperature was pleasant. The Town had quietened down as Everyone was going Home, settling down for the late Afternoon and Evening. I was thinking about what to write in my Book. Just what could the Story be about, and then I closed my eyes just for a second, and I saw the Car-Crash and the faceless Person next to me in the Car then that scream. I blinked my eyes back open to find myself at Home on the Sofa with Alisha beside me.

"What... How did I get here?", I said, feeling shocked and disorientated.

"You fainted on the Road-Side, it's a good job Mrs. Haven was driving past and saw you, or who knows how long you would have been there for. Just what were you doing? Alisha said in quite an angry Voice.

I had never really seen her angry at me before apart from when we were Kids, but I knew it was only because she was worried about me. I put my head down and looked at the floor like a little Puppy Dog that had done something wrong.

"I wanted a walk into Town as I wanted to go to the Library. I met Becky, and we got a Drink down the Harbour. I guess I just wanted to check out the Town", I said in a low voice.

Alisha's eyes widened and her Tone of Voice calmed down.

"I know Danny, but it's hot outside, and it's a little bit too much. I know you must be bored here when me and Tom are Working, but it's not been too long since you were out of the Hospital. Tell you what - Would you like to go for something to eat Tonight? Just you and me as Tom is working late. We can have some Brother-Sister Time".

CHAPTER 14

Alisha and I were sitting at a Table, waiting for Dinner. She had ordered a Chicken Salad and I had ordered Fish and Chips. The Restaurant was very quiet this Evening, most of the Tables were empty. There was just an older Couple, sitting in the corner and a small group of Friends at the Table across from us. It was very unusual for the Restaurant to be quiet as it was down on the Harbour, which was the Life and Soul of Palm Bay, but then come to think of it, even the Harbour was strangely quiet. To say it was a nice, warm evening.

I loved it down here, though it was a nice Place to come, especially at night when it was all lit up with the Lights. They were strung from Lamp-Post to Lamp-Post. There were a few small Boats in the Harbour, but it was more used for Leisure now than Fishing purposes. It was nice to spend time with

Alisha as I had not seen much of her now she had to keep going back into the Office for Meetings. It was a nice change to spend some Brother and Sister Time together. Since Mum and Dad had died, we had got close.

She was like a Mum but also like my Best Friend to me, as I didn't have many Friends and now I had none living here. I had met Becky who was hot and hoped that we could be more then Friends one day, then Willow... She was cool, oh and Ghost-Girl... But I'm not sure if I could class her as a Friend. I hope though... Maybe in Time, I would make new Friends here as I was sure that I was staying here now. Palm Bay was a quiet Place, though it only really got busy in the height of the Summer Months when the Tourists came to surf. I was not one for having lots of Friends. I enjoyed doing my own thing, and I had Becky now, so that was good enough for me.

***

The Kitchen door swung open and the Waiter came over with two big plates of food. I looked at the plate, as he placed it down in front of me, and my mouth watered. The food looked so good. I'd never seen a plate as big, filled with a giant Fish and lots of Chips with Mushy Peas on. I wasn't sure where to start. Should I eat it or climb it? It looked so good. I picked up my Fork and stabbed the first Chip. As I was piling the Chips onto my Fork ready to take a mouthful, Alisha's Phone beeped. She took it out of her bag and looked at it with a puzzled expression on her face.

"I'm sorry, Danny. I'm just going to go Outside. I have to make a Call".

She got up and left. I saw Outside, chatting on her Phone. She looked like she was shouting at first, then she laughed and smiled, so I relaxed, then once I knew, it was nothing too serious. I carried on eating, enjoying each mouthful. I took a drink of my Coke to wash the Chips down and sat waiting for Alisha. She seemed to have been gone ages, and I started to feel a little worried. I scanned the Restaurant to see if she had come back in, but she was not there, so I decided to go find her.

She seemed to have disappeared. I went Outside and looked in both directions, but she was not there. I opened the door and walked back into the Restaurant, worried now to where she could have gone. If she had to go Somewhere, she would have told me. The Music had stopped playing and Everyone seemed to have left, but I didn't see Anyone leave, even the Staff had disappeared. I looked out of the window and not one Soul was in sight, not even the sound of the Birds. The smell of Perfume hit me and I knew she was here, Ghost-Girl. I took another look around the Room, trying to find her, then I turned back and there she was - This Beautiful Figure.

I still could not make out her face, but she was a lot clearer now. She was a little smaller than me with this long, blonde-hair that reached down to her mid- back. She was slimly-built with all the curves in the right places. She reminded me of Someone from my past, but yet, I couldn't remember who. She had a glowing, white, golden-light around her. As she walked closer, the light touched me and I felt this Love from her. It was warm and gentle, and yet so strong and powerful at the same time. I felt my heart melt, and tears started to fill my eyes - not out of sadness, but from this Love. How did I even know what this feeling was, as if I had never felt it before, but yet, I must have for me to know of this Love.

She came closer to me, and the feeling intensified, and I started to feel this energy going through me like my whole body was getting healed and rebuilt, but only, it wasn't painful, just a tingling, buzzing feeling, rushing all around my Body. She put her hand out towards me, and this small, golden-ball of Energy appeared in her palm. The ball started to expand in her hand, then she blow it at me with a gentle blow. It went straight into my heart and then up to my head.

The Restaurant started to crumble and fall before my eyes, and I appeared in a Book-Shop like the one in my Dream. I sat behind that same Table as in the Dream with a pile of Books, Signing Copies for People. I picked up one of the Books and looked at it closely. It had the Title and my Name, written on the Front-Cover. I looked up and People were smiling and queuing up, waiting for Signed-Copies of my Book. I thought for a moment... Had I died in the Restaurant? - Maybe on a Fish-

Bone and she was an Angel that had come for me to take me to Heaven and was showing me an alternative Life? But then, my logical Mind was trying so hard to make sense of it but it couldn't. I opened to the first page of the Book and started to read the first few lines. I turned a few of the pages and then turned to the back of the Book, but the pages were blank. I flicked through some more pages, but all the other pages were blank too. I was confused as to why only the first pages had been written, but yet I was in a Book-Shop, Signing it. I looked up in confusion to find I was no longer in the Book-Shop but in my Bedroom, at my Desk with pages of writing in front of me. The Ghost-Girl Angel was there next to me, smiling. I could not see her face, but yet I knew she was smiling at me. She whispered in my ear.

"Danny, my Love, this Book shall change your Life. Once you remember, all shall be clear, and you shall have the Life you Dreamed of. I want you to know that Everything happens for a reason my Darling, even the bits we don't like in Life. They happen to help us on our Journey".

***

'Danny! Danny!! Danny!!! Wake up".

I felt my Body shaking quite hard and heard Alisha's voice; I opened my eyes and was back in the Restaurant with People standing around me, looking concerned.

"What happened?", I said.

"I went out to take that Call, and I looked in the window and saw you had fallen off your Chair. I raced in and you were choking. Fortunately, this lovely Couple saw you and came over to help you. It's a good job they did or God knows what would have happened to you", Alisha said, still panicking and her heart racing.

The Waitress came and brought me a glass of Water, and I sat in the Chair, trying to work out just what had happened. Maybe, I was supposed to die in the Car Accident but I didn't, and the Ghost-Girl was my Angel, coming to take me to Heaven, but people kept saving me and interfering in Divine Will. Could that even happen? - Can people interfere in Divine Will, or when it's your Time, it's your Time. Things seemed to be clearer now though, as I knew I had to write this Book. I didn't know what for or if it would even sell, but I just knew I had to write it as it would reveal Something and help me in some way.

On the way Home, I explained to Alisha what had happened and what I saw. I couldn't keep this to myself as if I was going Mad. I would need some support. She listened but didn't say much. I could see her thinking of Something to say and I felt that she knew Something, that she was not telling me a Secret. After a few moments of Silence, she started to talk.

"Danny, I'm not sure what is going on, but I believe you should write this Book. I don't know how or why but maybe it will help you, you are being given lots of Signs".

I had never really heard Alisha talk like this, she was more open-minded than I was but not Spiritual in any way.

"Danny... When Mum and Dad died, something happened to me. I would lay and cry at Night into my pillow so no-one heard me. Mum would come to me and kiss me Good-Night. I never saw her, but I felt her. I went to see a Psychic-Medium who told me about Mum coming to see me at Night. I had never told anyone about it, but she knew. She passed a Message to me from Mum and told me to look after you and support you on your Journey as you are going to need it. I never knew what she meant, but it all makes sense now"

CHAPTER 15

Later that night, I was in my Room, trying to figure out what happened. I heard Alisha and Tom talking downstairs, they both sounded pretty worried about me. I was starting to get a little worried myself as all these strange things that were happening to me, it was like I was losing touch with Reality. Maybe it was all in my head. I had been through so much, and yet, I just seemed to get on with Life like nothing had happened. It all seemed too Real though. I looked out of the window to check if she was there Tonight. I scanned the Trees with my eyes but nothing... Just the two Cars on the Driveway. Maybe I was going crazy, and I had not seen Anyone, and it was just all in my Mind. The Mind can play tricks on you. I looked over to the Desk at the pile of Paper that now looked and had grown twice in size. Next to it was the Pen I had been given. I went over to the Desk and picked up the Pen and looked at it closely. The Inscription read.

Remember me... I rubbed over the Engraving with my finger, took a deep breath in and closed my eyes.

Maybe, I was supposed to write this Book.

Alisha used to keep a Diary. She already said it helped her after losing our Mum and Dad, to write down her feelings and thoughts. A good Book needs a good Story and what was I going to write? I had no good Story to tell. I pulled the Chair out and sat at the Desk, sat down looking at the Paper. Had Alisha left it there for me, or had it come from another World?

I picked up the Pen and started twiddling it between my fingers, the Lamp flicked on, and a second later, my window blew open, and there was a Light- Breeze in the Air. The Air had turned cool now as the warmth of my Room had now disappeared out of the window. I made my way over to the window and closed it, making sure it was closed and locked this time. I sat on my bed, looking over at the Desk, feeling more and more pulled to it. I started to think about my Story, what I would write about and the Characters in it. I was thinking of what sort of Character I would write about. What would she look like and what would she do? I thought for a moment and realized that the main Character in the Story was a young Female. How strange, I thought to Myself...

'Why a young Woman? Why not an old Male? But that was what had come into my Mind, to write a Story of a young Woman. Now, what could she be called and what would she look like? Maybe if I just get writing, that will come to me. The name Sam came into my Mind. I should call my Character, Samantha or Sam for short. I did like the Name, Sam.

***

I looked at my Phone, and it was now 11pm. I usually was tired at this Time, but I seemed to be wide-awake. My mouth felt a little dry, so I headed down to the Kitchen for a Drink of Water. Alisha and Tom had already gone to bed, so the House was Silent. I was feeling a little excited to start my new Project. I had never read a Book, but writing one was going to be fun. Tonight, seemed very different than any other Night. I had gone from refusing to write to now wanting to get started and write about Sam. I looked out of the back-door onto the Garden. I then slid the door open and stepped out onto the cold, wooden decking. The Air was a lot cooler Tonight; It was a Sign that Winter was on its way. I looked up at the Sky and thought about my Life. Where was I going? How did I even end up like this? There was still a deep sadness in me like I had lost Something Important or Someone; It felt like a piece of me had gone, a void in my heart that could not be filled but once was, with Something or Someone. I took a deep-breath, filling my lungs with the cool Night fresh-air then sighed. I headed back into the Kitchen, sliding the door behind me. The Kitchen was now a little cold as I had invited the Night-Air to come in. I washed my glass out, placing it back in the cupboard, above my head and made my way back upstairs to my Room.

The Lamp was still flickering at the Desk when I entered the Room. I walked over and the Lamp buzzed and then stopped flickering, the Pen rolled from the back of the Desk towards me and stopped with the Inscription, facing up towards me. 'Remember Me'. I pulled the Chair out and sat there for a moment at the Desk with the Pen in my hand.

I closed my eyes and started to Visualize Sam. My Character, who I was going to write about. She was Beautiful, a young Woman in her late 20s who had moved to a new Town for a fresh-start. Long, blonde, flowing shoulder- length hair, pale, smooth, soft-skin with little, rosy-red cheeks. The perfect little nose that just was in perfect proportion to her face and big, green-eyes that you could get lost in when you looked into them.

She was slim and petite-build but with curves in all the right places. I opened my eyes and felt a smile. Part of me wished she was Real. I had just imagined this Woman up out of nowhere. How did I even do that? What even is the Imagination? Where does it even come from? Was this a Real Person that I had seen and not noticed but my Subconscious Mind had? I took one more deep breath; I felt someone grab my hand like someone was holding my hand softly then guided it to the Paper. I started to write.

***

She lay there, awake. Tears filling her eyes. Another sleepless night Sam thought. The sadness was so strong over her that she felt the pain in her heart.

She wished it was a heart-attack as she didn't want to be here anymore. What was the point? He was gone. She looked over at the side of her bed where Matt had once laid next to her in her arms. Now, there was just an empty Space. It had been a year since he had passed away in the Accident, but she still missed him so much. He was her Soul-Mate, he was hers, and yet God had taken him away from her. He could have taken Murderers, Pedophiles, Rapists and Child-Killers, but no, he chose to take him away... My Matt who didn't hurt a Fly. They had a Holiday booked. It was going to be their first Holiday together to celebrate one year of being together. They were going to go to a little Tropical Caribbean Island. Matt had always wanted to go there, but he felt it was a Place that only a Couple should go.

I knew Matt was the one from the first Day we had met. He was very quiet and softly spoken. We had met on-line through Social Media, but Matt didn't give me much attention at first as he seemed quite popular with the Women. There was just something about him that stood out from other Guys. We lived so far away from each other too, and it would seem impossible to meet, let alone be together. I messaged him, thinking he would not reply to me. Later that Day, he messaged me back and we got talking. I called him up. He was so nervous when he answered the Phone, but we ended up talking for hours and hours. After about a Week of chatting over the Phone, Matt decided to come down and meet me. I was so excited. I will never forget that day he knocked on my door. That was the beginning of our Life together.

Sam was now sobbing, thinking about the Memories of her and Matt. She had been to see a Psychic that day who had told her she would meet Someone in the next 3 months, but she was just not interested. All she wanted was Matt back in her arms, and just wanted to feel his lips on hers. She turned over and tried to go back to sleep, sniffing up as her eyes closed.

***

I took my Pen from the Paper and looked at what I had written, my eyes were filled with tears. I sniffed up and rubbed the tears from them. Oh, Wow - Where did that come from? How did I even write that?

It felt like it wasn't me that was writing, it was something that had taken over me and was writing for me. I was excited to see where this Story was going to go as I had no Idea at all what would unfold for Sam. But I knew she was going to be happy in the end. A wave of sadness washed over me as I read back what I had written. She has lost her Soul-Mate, the Love of her Life and how could anyone carry on after that? I felt a deep pain for her. It was getting late now and I was feeling pretty sleepy. I turned off the Lamp and got into bed.

***

The next Day, I jumped out of bed, excited the Sun was shining, and I could hear the Birds singing outside my window. I rushed downstairs. Alisha and Tom had already left for Work, but she had left me some Breakfast with a note next to it.

'Danny, Tom and I are going to be late Home Tonight as we are meeting Friends for Dinner. If you need me... Call me. Love You Lots Bro. Alisha xx'.

I was Happy that they were going out Tonight as they had been looking after me so much, making sure I was Ok, that they had put their Life on hold and they needed a Life too. I felt guilty sometimes for staying there, even though both Alisha and Tom had told me I could stay for however long I needed to. I sat in the Back-Garden, listening to the Sound of the Ocean, eating my Breakfast and drinking my Morning Coffee. I was wondering about my Story, where it was going to go, what would happen to Sam, hoping that she would end up meeting another Guy. I believe Life is for sharing with Someone and being happy together. I still felt a deep sadness in my heart for Sam, like it was my sadness.

I laughed to myself as Sam was just a Character I had thought up, to write a Story about, so how could I possibly feel anything for her?

After Breakfast, I got ready and went to my Room. I looked over at the Desk, the Sun was shining in through the window onto the Desk. I went over, picked up the Paper I had written on and re-read what I had written, still wondering where it had come from. It seemed to just touch me; I have always been sensitive but never cried over some writing, especially my own. I went to sit back at the Desk and placed the Paper back down in front of me I closed my eyes and took a deep-breath in, the Image of Sam appeared in front of me, she looked a little like Ghost-Girl - Same Figure and hair. Maybe Sam was Ghost-Girl, even though I had not seen her face, as she did feel quite Real to me, the way I had described her and wished that she was Real. I walked over to my Computer and put the CD Willow had given me, on. I then sat back at the Desk, picked up the Pen, took a deep-breath. I felt a hand grab mine, and then, I started to write again.

**

Sam opened her eyes, still very sleepy. The Sun was shining in. She looked at her Phone - 8am. She had slept through her alarm again. The Doctors had given her Medication to help her sleep, as since Matt's Death, she suffered from PTSD and Anxiety and had trouble sleeping at Night. She had refused to take her Medication as she knew that it wouldn't cure her, just suppress her feelings in. She got dressed and flew downstairs. She knew she was already late so rather than get herself into more of a panic, she made herself a Coffee and sat in the Lounge, hugging the Mug close to her as comfort. She opened up a Letter that she had received from her Land-Lord a few Days before but had not bothered to look at it until now. She scanned the Letter and then ripped it up and cried. The Land-Lord was selling the House and he had given her a Month to find a new Place. This was hers and Matt's Place, and if being given notice to leave the House, it would be like losing Matt again.

She took one last sip of her Coffee and then set off out for the Bus to Work. It was only a short Bus-Ride, but with the Morning rush-hour Traffic, she knew she would be late.

When she arrived at Work, it was 9.15am, which wasn't too bad. Only 15 minutes late and besides, she had to stay back an hour the Week before. Her Manager Martha was not impressed at all.

"Sam - In my Office please, now;". Sam followed her into the Office.

"Take a seat, Sam. I know things are hard for you, Sam. Believe me, I understand, but you can't keep showing up late like this Sweet-Heart. I know how hard it is for you, and I've explained to Darren, the Big Boss, about your Situation, and he is willing to make you a Deal".

Sam looked up at Martha who was looking at her with a look of Compassion. She swept her hair out of her face so she could give Martha her full attention. Martha wasn't a Bad Boss, she was a very caring, understanding and supportive to Sam, but as a Manager, she did have a Duty to run a Business Department.

"We have a new Admin Position and it's working from Home, so you wouldn't have to come into the Office or you could just come in one day a Week. You would not be having to answer the Phones, having to deal with Customers, shouting at you".

Martha had seen Sam start to get teary and upset and was concerned for her well-being as Sam seemed to be in a constant state of sadness like she had given up on Life. Martha placed her hand on Sam's shoulder to comfort her. She wanted to hug her, but she had to be Professional. Sam started to sob and Martha grabbed a tissue, and all Professionalism went out the window. Martha was a Human-Being too with feelings, and she hated to see Sam like this.

She pulled Sam into her and gave her a big hug, making Sam feel a bit better, knowing that she was not just working with Robots but they were Human that worked there too.

"You have worked here a couple of years now, and you are hard-working and so kind and caring. You are a real Asset to my Team and the Company, and I'm not going to see you go, so this is why I have fought for you", said Martha softly.

"Thank You", Sam said, smiling and wiping the tears away.

***

At Lunch-Time, Sam took a walk to the Park just down the Road from the Office. It was the Park where she and Matt had their first Date in.

She sat on the same Bench they had sat on and had their first kiss. The Memories came flooding back. Maybe it is time to move on, she thought. Now, maybe look at moving Towns. She liked the Beach and she could 'Work from Home' now, she would just need to find a Place to live and how hard could that be? A new start, a new Town and Place would be good for me. Sam started to feel excited as this could be a fresh-start for her. She looked around the Park, having a flash-back of her and Matt's first Date. She knew he liked her, but this Guy was too scared to kiss her, so she had to make the first move on him and Wow, was it Magical. As soon as she pulled him into her, he put his arms around her and held her there. As they kissed, it felt like time had stopped, and there was just that moment, nothing else mattered. When it was time for Matt to leave and returned Home, she was so sad and didn't want him to leave. At the Station, he made her a Promise that he would come back and stay as he could not be apart from her now. A few Weeks later, Sam met him at the Train Station and that was the start of their Life together. He was here to stay.

After Sam's flash-back, she looked at her Phone, and it was time to head back to the Office. She entered the Office and everyone was on the Phone. She looked over at the Call-Board. There were 10 calls in the queue. She hated having to take call after call all the Time, it was tiring, but the new Admin Job that was going to start next Week and the idea that she would be moving to the Coast made her Work Afternoon, bearable.

When Sam returned home from Work that Night, she got her Laptop out to start looking at Houses and Apartments to rent over on the Coast, working out her Finances. After an hour or so of looking at Places, Sam started to feel a little tired so she ran a bath. She got undressed and looked in the mirror at herself. Sam was a very attractive, 28-year-old Woman. Her natural, long, blonde-hair, her slim-body, her nicely-shaped bum, her perfectly-shaped boobs. She could have any Man, but she didn't want anyone, she just wanted Matt.

She continued to stare into the mirror and think of Matt. She felt his arms around her, touching gently on her breasts and him kissing her neck with his soft, gentle kisses. He stood behind her, their naked bodies touching and embracing each other. When she saw him in the mirror, she quickly turned around, calling his Name, but no-one was there. After a nice, long, hot-

soak in the bath, Sam felt a little more relaxed and went back downstairs and got settled for the Night. She poured herself a glass of Red-Wine and then put the TV on, trying to find something to take her mind off Matt, but no matter what she did, Everything reminded her of him.

***

I heard a bang outside, and it seemed to bring me back out of the writing trance I was in. I looked back at what I had written and read through. I felt Sam's pain and emotion. I was so sad now, after what I had written. It felt like this was Real in some way, and Sam and Matt was a Real Couple who had been separated by Death.

I had never written anything before, but to come out and write about a Couple who were in Love and death had taken them apart from each other, made my heart hurt. I just wanted to hold Sam and tell her it would be alright and wanted to be there for her. I felt her pain, her loss and her grief. She was so familiar to me, like I knew her. Was she a Real Person or had I just made her up? I tried to think but couldn't.

It was getting later on in the Day, and so I decided to go for a walk and check out the little Private Beach Cove down by the Cliffs at the bottom of the Garden. I had wanted to check it out before but just didn't get around to it. It wasn't a Private Beach as no-one owned it, but you could only get to it from the few Houses on our Street. I made my way out of the Kitchen, down the Path, to the Gate, at the bottom of the Garden and started to walk down the steep, Rock-Steps. I stopped half-way down and took a moment to take in the View. I could see all up the Coast, the Hills and even a Waterfall in the distance. It was quite some View.

The Beach cut into a little Cove in the Cliffs so was cut off from the Main Beach in Town by the Cliffs and Rocks. You probably could get to the Main Beach and into Town, but you would have to climb over the Rocks and the Cliffs, and it would not have been very safe as the Waves crashed up on the Rocks, making them slippery. This part of the Beach was like 'Our Own Private Little Beach' though and was very quiet. On the other side of the Beach, there were bigger Rocks you could stand on and Trees, but you couldn't go that way, as it was far too dense to cut through the Trees, so the only way was back up the Steps into the Garden.

***

I walked along the untouched Golden-Sand, listening to the Waves Crash on the Shore. The Weather was nice Today, it wasn't too hot or cold and there was a nice, Sea-Breeze. The Sky was a deep-blue with big, white, fluffy Clouds. I found a large Rock, sticking up out of the Sand and sat down looking out to the Ocean. I wonder if I will ever meet Someone Special in my Life like Alisha met Tom and Sam met Matt.

There is Becky, but maybe she is just a Friend. I mean, could I even see myself with Becky? I did fancy her but with her being so Friendly and Fun to be around, would she make a nice Girlfriend or just a Friend? Did she even have that Romantic side to her? I started to ponder over it, thinking about me and Becky being together. Now Sam would be my Perfect Girl if only she was Real and not made up in my head. Where did that Image of her even come from? It had to have come from Somewhere deep within me? My head was hurting, trying to think about it. Every time I tried to think, it hurt.

After a long ponder, down at the Beach, the Sun had started to set, so I went back up into the House and ordered Food. Alisha had left me some Money to order a Take-Away, so I ordered a 12" BBQ Chicken Stuff-Crust Pizza. I loved Pizza, it was one of my Favorite Foods. The House seemed very quiet without Alisha and Tom there, but I must admit, it was nice. I Love them so much, and I am so grateful for them taking me in, but I would like to get my 'Own Place' again one Day, when I'm ready. It would be nice to live in a small Apartment here in Palm Bay, going for nice little walks on the Beach every Night, watching the Sunset and then going down to the Old Harbour for a Night Out, once a Week.

After my Pizza, I wanted to go up and write some more of my Book, but something told me not to tonight, and I will write more tomorrow. I turned the TV on and started watching a Movie called 'VR Love'. It was about a Girl who had no

191

Friends, met some People through a Virtual Reality Video Game and met a Guy on there. She goes searching for him in Real-Life to find out who is he, and they end up falling in Love in Real-Life. It was one of those Films you put on if there is nothing else to do. It wasn't like a Block-Buster Movie with amazing effects, but it was still enjoyable and was one of these Films you had to watch until the end to see what happened. There were parts I wanted to turn off, but I saw it through until the end.

**

It had turned 10pm, and I heard voices outside. The door opened... It was Alisha and Tom - They looked so happy and pleased to see me settled.

"Hey Danny, my Baby Brother".

Alisha threw her arms around me and hugged me. I could smell Alcohol on her, it was nice to see her relaxed and enjoying herself. I have only seen her drunk once, and that was a few years ago. They both sat next to me and asked me how my Day had gone. I told them about the Book I had started writing and how my Characters seemed so Real. Alisha looked at me and put her arms around me.

"Danny, they are Real, you Created them. Whatever you Create, becomes Real", she said. "Please can I have a read if you don't mind". "Ok, but I have not written a lot, and I'm not sure how the Story was going to go".

I went to go get the Paper I had written on, I felt a bit embarrassed showing my Sister what I had written. As I passed the mirror, on the landing, I turned to look into it as Something had caught my eye. I looked and I saw Sam there. She was looking and smiling at me. She has a golden-light around her. After a moment, I stepped back, rubbing my eyes to check if I was seeing things, but she had gone. I grabbed the Paper and took it down to Alisha. She started to read it, and her face changed. She went from being happy to her eyes filling up with tears; She sniffed up and put the Paper down. Tom put his arms around her and kissed her.

"Oh Wow", she said "That is very sad and heart-breaking". She wiped her eyes again. "Danny, can I ask you Something? She wiped the tears from her eyes - Your Character, Sam... Who is she, how did you think her up, as she seems very Real?", said Alisha, wiping another tear from her eye.

"I don't know", I said. "I just closed my eyes and got an Image of her in my head, but she seems very Real. This is going to sound strange, but when I write about her, I feel her pain, and I've been thinking about her like she is a Real Person".

Alisha sighed and another tear rolled down her cheek.

"Danny, I want you to know, me and Tom are here for you. This Book will help you in so many ways, and you are going to get through this".

''What do you mean?", I asked her.

I looked over at Tom for the support - he just smiled.

"You two are just acting strange. I'm going to bed now – Good-Night Guys -Love You both". I took myself upstairs and into my Room.

***

"Tom... Sam in his Book sounds just like...", Alisha paused as she could not get the words out of her mouth. She took a big gulp, trying to clear the lump in her throat.

''I know Sweet-Heart", Tom said hugging her.

"Do you think he is remembering and that's why he is writing as it will help him remember? I will Phone Becky Tomorrow. I'm not sure how we are going to approach this Tom".

CHAPTER 16

The next morning, I woke up at about 8am and had just come out of a Dream. I was with Sam and she was a Real Person. We were together and lived together. I turned over to give her a Good Morning kiss but woke up. I laid there for a moment, looking at the empty space next to me in bed where Sam should have been, but she wasn't. A wave of grief washed over me, and I felt a pain in my heart for her. I could not understand why I was feeling like this over a Fictional Character in a Story I was writing.

I looked over at the Desk and saw the Pen and the pile of Paper. It seemed to have a golden-glow around it. I wanted to get writing again Today, but I had no idea what I was going to write about Today and how this Story was going to unfold, but I just felt like I needed to write about Sam as I felt like I knew her like she was Someone close to me. I headed down for Breakfast and was met by Alisha, Tom had already left for Work and Alisha was just cleaning up.

"Morning Danny, how are you this Morning?", she said as she was wiping the work-top down.

She put the kettle on and made us a cup of Coffee; Alisha always made the best Coffee, one scoop and some honey and just the right amount of milk. We sat at the Breakfast Bar, drinking our Coffee. She took a sip of her Coffee and gently placed the mug down on the mat then looked at me and smiled. "Danny, how are you feeling? I have not had a chance to chat with you for a while as you know I have had to be in the Office".

I looked at Alisha and knew that this was going to lead to a conversation, maybe it was about my Book or maybe Something else.

"Danny, last Night when I read what you had written, it made me think that maybe it is Time that we move forward in your recovery".

"I am doing just fine, Sis. I am going to be writing again Today. I feel like I know the Character in my Book. It is strange, but I'm not sure what I am going to write about. Something is telling me to write more as I feel like I know her", I said, taking another sip of my Coffee.

"Danny, you seem to be doing just fine but that is what is worrying me and Tom. You have lost your short-term Memory and don't talk about the Accident".

"There is nothing to talk about", I said, feeling a little irritated by Alisha's comment.

I was trying to hold back, but it was really hard as I knew that there was Something I was blocking out but didn't know what it was. I took another sip of my Coffee and placed the cup back down as it was too hot to hold on to.

"Danny, I am going to Phone Becky, and we are going to get some Therapy sorted out for you, as you are recovering well physically but it is important that you Recover Mentally too".

I trusted Alisha as she was my older Sister and I loved her and knew that she wanted me to get better so maybe the Therapy was a good Idea. There was something deep inside me, Sadness like the loss of Someone. Something felt missing, but I didn't know what it was, so maybe having Therapy was a good Idea. Alisha picked up the Phone and called Becky. She explained to her about the Therapy, and Becky agreed to come over that Afternoon to sit and talk to me about sorting out the Talking Therapy.

***

That Afternoon, Becky came over. I still had the hots for her and fancied her. There was just Something about her. She was just so Amazing. She always had this Beautiful smile, and when she saw me, she flung her arms around me and kissed me on the cheek. Alisha had gone to Work so it was just me and Becky; I made her a Drink and showed her what I had written, told her about the Book I was writing. As she was reading, I could see her smiling and her eyes started watering.

"Danny, that's Beautiful Babe. "What is this Story going to be about?", said Becky, sniffing up and taking a sip of her Coffee.

"I don't know... It's really strange as I started writing, but I didn't know how the Story is going to go. I just feel like I know Sam in some way and want to write about her. Do I sound weird?". I thought for a moment and felt a little embarrassed telling Becky about me knowing a Character in a Book I had started writing. Becky looked at me still with watery eyes and she moved closer to me.

"Danny, I love reading and can't wait for this Book to be finished. I know it is going to be a Beautiful Story. I used to read a Book by this Author. She would never know what she was going to write, she never even had a Story in mind, but she would Meditate before she started writing, and then the next thing she knew, Hours had passed, and she would have pages and pages of writing. Her Books were Magical. You could feel her pain, her sadness, her excitement, her Love, her happiness in her Books".

"Do you think I'm strange that I feel like I know Sam who I am writing about in my Story?".

"Of course not, Danny. You are Creating a Character. You have given this Character Life. She could be a part of your deep unconscious Mind, hidden deep within, and when you write, you are bringing her to Life".

I told Becky how I have felt, that Something was missing and I felt Sad, but I didn't know why, like I had lost Someone close to me but had no Memory of it.

I started to feel Sad again, and this sudden wave of sadness and loss, hit me, my heart felt so empty. Becky moved closer to me and put her arm around me. We sat there in each other's arms and hugged. I could smell her Sweet-Perfume, and her embrace was warm. I wanted to kiss her so bad, but she was my Nurse, and we had such a good Friendship, and I didn't want to spoil things between us. I could feel her heart-beat and her chest pressed against mine.

I was trying not to think about anything naughty as I didn't want to make this perfect situation awkward. She looked at me, and I looked into her big-eyes. She was so Beautiful, I felt a Magical-Felt Energy between us, but a

second later, she pulled back and laughed. She wanted to kiss me too, but she knew that if she did, she could no longer be my Nurse. I pulled back too, but I could have just sat there in Silence all Afternoon, just looking into her big, Beautiful eyes.

She pulled her Phone out of her bag and looked at it, looking for a Number, breaking that perfect moment we were having together. "Danny, I'm going to call my Friend, Lucy. She is a Therapist. She is so nice, and she is based down in Palm Bay. She will help you so much. You are doing so well, Babe".

Becky walked out of the Room to make the Call. I heard her chatting but couldn't quite hear what she was saying. After 5 minutes, she walked back into the Room and sat down next to me.

"Brilliant news, Danny. She can see you next Monday. She says that you can have as many Sessions as you need. You have all the support you need now".

I felt a lot happier but a little scared as well as things could come up that I may not be able to deal with, and a little part of me didn't want to get better as I would then have to enter back into the Real World, maybe move back to the City and I wouldn't see Becky again. That thought alone, hurt me so much. I turned to Becky and looked again into her big, wide-eyes.

"Becky, what happens when I am better? I will have to move back to the City, and I won't be able to see you. I mean, I will miss you coming around". I felt myself starting to blush a little.

"Danny, I will always be here for you, it just means I will no longer be your Nurse, and we can hang out properly then, if you want that is. I can show you all the nice Places around here. We can go out to the Movies and for Food".

I felt so excited and reassured knowing this. I wanted to get better now, and I'm sure Alisha and Tom wouldn't let me move back to the City. The heaviness started to lift from my heart, it was my biggest fear of losing all this and having to move back to a Place that was so stressful. I wouldn't have anyone there. I was determined that would not happen.

That Night, I was in my Room resting, laid on top of the bed, thinking of all the happy and exciting Things Life would bring me. Something caught my eye, out of the window. I jumped up and ran to open it, thinking it could have been Ghost-Girl, feeling excited that she might visit me again Tonight. Maybe I should give her a Name, she would have had a Name when she was alive. I scanned the Front-Patio from the window, but there was nothing there, just the same as the Night before the two Cars parked up.

Something whizzed past me like a Bright-Light, it was going so fast that I could not make out what it was. I turned to look over at Trees and there she was - The Ghost-Girl. She had returned. I still could not see her face, but she stood there, looking up at me. There was Something different about her Tonight though, she was not just a Shadow, but she had a golden-glow around her. It was like she was appearing and her Form was becoming clearer, trying to show herself to me. I could now make her out, she was quite small and slim with long, flowing-hair that went just past her shoulders. She started to walk out of the Tree, towards the House.

She stopped in the middle of the Driveway, looking up and then disappeared. I had not seen her that close before, but it still frustrated me as I could not see her face - Was it the same Ghost as I'd seen in my Room or a different one? What was she hiding? Why did she not want me to see her face? I closed the window, as it was now starting to get chilly, and the Wind was picking up. I felt this Energy wash over me and felt the pull to start writing. I sat on the Chair and pulled myself closer to the Desk, grabbed the Pen and looked at the Paper. I closed my eyes, took a deep breath in and started to write.

***

Sam was feeling a little better Today, her Friend Clive was coming over to take her Shopping. She had not seen him for a while, he had broken up with his Boyfriend but had met Someone else who he had been seeing for a while now. Clive was as flamboyant as they come, but Sam liked that, as he would always cheer her up just by being himself. He would make her laugh as he was a bit of a Drama Queen.

They were off to Manchester Today. It was Clive's Idea as he thought it would cheer Sam up. The door flew open and Clive walked in. "Hiya Babe, how is my favorite Girl? Oh, don't you look Gorgeous Today, Babe", Sam laughed and off they went to Manchester. On the way there, Clive was telling Sam all about his new Partner whom he had met on a Night out and hit it off with each other. I went into detail about the Night they had met. Sam told him to shush as it was too much information.

Clive saw Sam like a little Sister as his Family had disowned him when he told them he was Gay, so Sam was like the only Person he could talk to. When they got to the Shopping Centre, Clive pulled up at a Place as close as he could get to the Main Entrance. They went inside. It had been a while since Sam had gone out Shopping. She didn't have any Money, but Clive had said that he would treat her to Lunch and Shopping.

***

Sam has seen a few things she liked and handed Clive her Bag whilst she tried on tops and dresses in the Changing Rooms. Clive stayed on the other side of the door, chatting away to her as he always did, but then he stopped...

...And there was Silence.

"Clive", Sam shouted. "Are you still there?".

There was no answer. Sam listened and noticed that the Music had gone off in the Shop and there was not even the chatter of People. She put her top back on and opened the door slowly not knowing what to expect on the other side. Everyone had gone. There were no Shop Assistants, no Customers and no Clive. Sam wandered around the empty Shop, confused as to what was going on. She checked her Phone, and there was no Signal, and the Time had stopped at 2.22pm. She started to panic, wondering what was going on. She cried out to Clive, but he did not answer. There was no sign of him. She fell to the floor and put her head into her arms and burst into tears.

She heard a familiar voice call her. She looked up, it was Matt. She rubbed her teary eyes and blinked, making sure that she was not seeing Things. He put out his hand and helped her up. She flung her arms around him. ''I miss you so much my Darling, why did you have to go?''. Matt pulled her in close to him but didn't say anything.

"Matt, I can't do this anymore - Everything I do, Everywhere I go, just reminds me of you. I need you, I Miss You so much".

Sam sobbed into his neck and Matt held her there but said nothing. After a few moments, he stepped back and smiled at Sam.

"Sam, you have to let me go. You have such a wonderful Life ahead of you, and you are going to find Love and happiness again. He is waiting for you, and when the Time is right, you both shall come together".

Sam cried, "I don't want anyone but you Matt - How can I even think about Love and meeting Someone Else. It's you I want".

''Sam, I will always be here with you, but you shall Love again. I Love You with all my heart and I always will, but Life has some Amazing Things for you". Matt started to walk back to the changing room. Sam followed him, the door closed behind them

and Matt walked through the mirror on the back-wall and looked back at Sam.

"We will be together again Sweet-Heart".

He turned back and walked into a bright, white-light. Sam tried to get through the mirror, banging the glass with her fist, cracking the big mirror. Blood started to drip down onto the floor, from her bleeding hands. She opened up both her palms, and they were covered in blood. She fell to the floor and placed her head into her bloody hands and sobbed. Clive burst into the changing room and picked her up off the floor.

"Clive, where have you been? Did you see Matt - What happened to you? Sam stopped and looked around, she could see the Shop Workers and Customers who had gathered around, looking at her, wondering if she was Ok. Sam listened and noticed the Music was playing again.

"Clive, what happened - Where did you go?".

"I was right here all the time, talking to you, but you stopped answering me, then I heard the cry and a bang so I had to break in".

An older Woman and young Girl who worked there came over and saw what had happened. Sam felt nervous and embarrassed at what she had done as she saw the two Women walking towards her, her rosy-cheeks disappeared as the colour faded from her face and she went pale, a sick-feeling washed over her and she collapsed into Clive's arms. She thought they were going to call the Police for what she had done to the mirror. "I'm so Sorry, I will pay for the damages. I just want to go", Sam cried. The older Woman looked at Sam.

''Let's get you cleaned up, Lovely. Don't worry about the mirror. Jess, can you go make this young Lady and young Man a cup of Tea".

The young Shop Assistant darted off into the back to make them Tea. Clive apologized and explained to the Manager about Sam losing her Boyfriend, Matt and how she was struggling to cope. That's why they have come Shopping to cheer her up.

"I'm so Sorry"; said Sam, her voice shaking. The older Woman put her arms around her.

"It's fine Lovely. We will get our Maintenance Man to fix it. I lost my Husband 5 years ago now. I thought I would never get over him. We were so in Love with each other then one Day, he had a heart-attack just like that, he collapsed and died instantly.

I never thought I would find Love again, especially at my age but I did, two years ago. My Friend asked me to go on a Cruise with her. Like you, I just didn't want to do Anything but I went and that was when I met him, my heart opened back up and we have been together since. So, you see Sam, we don't just Love once we can Love again, we might not think so at the time but God will send us another Angel to Love".

''How old are you, Sam?''.

Sam sniffed up, wiping the tears from her eyes. "I'm 27".

"Oh, you have so many good years ahead of you, you are Beautiful, and I know you will find Love again".

Sam got cleaned up, wiping away all the blood to reveal the smallest of scratches on her hands. Her, Clive and the older Woman sat for a few more Moments, chatting and drinking their Tea.

"Thank you so much for not getting mad at me and calling the Police", Sam said, now feeling a little better.

"Oh, don't be worrying about it, it's only a mirror and mirrors can be replaced", the Woman said in her soft, friendly voice, putting her arm around Sam again. "Right, I better get back to Work, you take good care Sam, and remember, you will find Love again. God will send you another Angel", the Woman smiled and walked off.

Sam and Clive finished their Drinks and left the Shopping Centre. On their way Home, they stopped at a Family Pub for Food as they never got Lunch. When they had finished their Late-Lunch, that was more like Dinner now, Clive dropped Sam back off at Home, making sure she was Ok. By this Time, she was feeling a little better, knowing Matt was still around. Even if he could not be physically here with her, he was there in Spirit, and she knew Someday, they would be together again.

***

I opened my eyes, it was 2am. I was confused as to what happened as I remember sitting at my Desk and then nothing. I had blanked out and woken up to find I had written more pages. I read back to what I had written. After reading it back, I just wanted to hug Sam. I wanted to hold her close to me and tell her it was Ok. I felt Something so deep for her like a Love so deep, and I wanted her to be with me Tonight, to hold her close to me whilst she slept in my arms. It was at that point, I realized I had fallen for her, fallen in Love with her. I have heard People having crushes on Pop Stars and Film Stars but never Fictional Characters in a Story, especially my own Story. How could I even fall in Love with someone I had just made up, yet I could feel it in my heart, I longed for her. How did I know I was in Love? I had never been in Love before or had I but could not remember?

CHAPTER 17

The Next Day, I could not think of Anyone but Sam. She was there in my Thoughts, I didn't want to tell Alisha about this as I might get locked up for being Crazy. I didn't write for a few Days after that. I thought maybe if I didn't write then I would not think about Sam, but I was so wrong.

It was the Day of my first Therapy Session. I was nervous as I didn't know what to expect. Alisha had dropped me off at the Place and then went to Work. I stood there in front of a big House, there was a short Path that lead up to a dark, wooden door with a Keypad outside. The House had been converted into 4 Apartments. I walked up the Path, there were Plants and Trees on each side and two hanging baskets on the wall by the door. I pressed the button that was labelled 2, and a few seconds later, a soft voice answered.

"Hello, I am Danny. I have an Appointment to see you".

"Oh, Hi Danny. Just give me a sec, and I will let you in".

The door opened and there was this small Woman with a red and white striped low-cut top on with brown-hair, cut into a bob.

She was wearing a short, black-skirt with a length, just passed her knees. She was not what I had Imagine a Therapist to look like. She looked a few years younger than me. When I saw her though, I had Imagined some old Woman with glasses telling me to lay on the Couch whilst she made Notes. She put her hand out and shook my hand.

"Hi, I am Lucy. You must be Danny. Come on, come in, nice to meet you".

She led me inside her Flat, and I followed her to the Lounge and took a seat. She smiled at me and then walked into the Kitchen. I scanned the room, taking in my Environment; It was very Modern and bright with a big Plant in the corner and some Modern-Art on the walls. Lucy came out of the Kitchen with two big glasses of Home-Made, cloudy Lemonade.

"I hope you like it Danny, I made it myself", Lucy said.

She sat down on a Chair across from me and smiled, taking a Drink of the Lemonade. She then placed the glass on a Table and crossed her

legs and smiled at me.

"Not what you were expecting is it, Danny?", she chuckled.

"When people think of Therapists, they think of some Middle-Aged Woman sitting in a Chair in a room full of Books. So, let me tell you a little about me and what I do. So, my name is Lucy and I am 30 years old. I Moved here about 10 years ago. I have a Boyfriend, Liam who is 38. I have been a Therapist for about 5 years now, and I help People by giving them space to open up and Talk. Talking is one of the biggest Healing Tools, but yet, we don't get to Talk.

We might Talk to our Friends but do they listen? No, they don't, coz when we Talk, they are Thinking about what they can say to us back. They are thinking of a response and we do the same back, and sometimes we don't like to burden our Friends with our problems so that is what I'm here for".

Lucy pulled out a File and started looking through it.

"Right Danny, start by telling me a bit about yourself. This Session is mainly for me to get to know you".

I started to tell Lucy about the Accident. She had it all in the File, but she wanted to hear it from me. I told her about me moving in with my Sister and her Boyfriend. She started to make notes, nodding her head. I then told her about the Book I was writing and then about Sam. She stopped writing and put the Pad down then gave me a strange look.

"Ok Danny, tell me about this Character in your Book".

I started to tell her all about Sam and that I felt this Love for her but it was silly as she was a made-up Character in a Story. I felt myself starting to go red and felt embarrassed for telling her that I loved a made-up Character in a Story.

"Danny, why do you feel silly falling in Love with Sam?".

"She is not real Lucy, I made her up".

"Danny, the Imagination is Something we do not fully understand like where does it even come from, how can we just make these People up in our head, where do we even get the Ideas and Images from? It has to come from Somewhere.

Sam could be Someone you are close to but you don't know, she could have been Someone from your past or even your Future who you have not even met yet".

"What - Can that happen?" I said surprised.

"Yes, it can - The Mind can Create anything and bring it to Life. When we write, we bring all our Unconscious Thoughts to the Surface and then it is Created so Sam who you are writing about could be Someone you knew in the past or she could be a Future Girlfriend, and that's why you feel the way you do for her".

"So, you don't think I'm Crazy then?".

"Oh, not at all - It sounds like you have been Guided to write this Book for a reason and it's part of your Healing. You see also what can happen, Danny is that we block out Trauma, so after the Car Accident, you lost your Short-Term Memory, you blocked out Something so Traumatic you were not ready to face. However, for you to move forward, we have to face this and deal with it and this is why you have all the support you need. We will face this together, Danny".

Lucy smiled at me.

"Also, this Book - your writing sounds similar to your Life like the Car Accident. Danny. You could be writing this Book to remember what happened to you. What I would like to do in our next Session is to try and take you back to the Accident if you are ready for that, and we can try to help you piece

it all together". '

'Does that work?" I said surprisingly.

"Yes, it can do and is very Powerful. There was once this Man that came to see me, his Girlfriend wanted to get married in a Church but he freaked out when he saw the Church and could not go in. He was very upset at this and didn't want to let his Wife down but he just could not step foot in a Church, so he and his Wife came to see me and I regressed him back anyway. It turned out that when he was a young Boy, his Parents would take him to Church and he would get taken in the Back-Room and abused by the Priest. He was that Traumatized by it, he had blocked it out and had no Memory of it, but then when he and his Girlfriend walked into the Church, he couldn't be there and he didn't know any way I worked with him and a year later, he got married at a Church.

"Oh, Wow - That's Amazing".

"This work is not going to be easy Danny, but I want you to keep writing your Book and see what unfolds, and I will book you another Session for next Week".

I had started to feel better just after the first Session Today. I had got to know Lucy and felt comfortable with her. She had told me to write everything down that happened in the Week, and we could talk about it each Week in our Sessions, so, if I was to see the Ghost-Girl again, I had to tell her. I phoned Alisha to come and pick me up, feeling happy that I had made progress and that I wasn't Crazy, falling in Love with Sam, but she was still on my Mind, and I could think of no-one else but her. Even Becky had started to go out of my Mind, and I felt a little sad as I liked Becky.

***

I was pretty tired that Night and didn't bother writing, but I could not stop Thinking about Sam still and how much I cared for her. Maybe she was a Future Girlfriend that I was going to meet but then what about Becky after our hug last Week? I felt so much closer to her, and she knew I wanted to kiss her and she wanted to kiss me but we couldn't. So, now I had two Girls that I liked. There was Becky my Nurse and Sam my Character from my Story, but Sam was different. I felt a deep Love for her like I had not felt before. I tried to get to sleep, but even though I was tired, I found it hard to settle. I almost felt guilty for being in Love with Sam when I liked Becky. I looked over at the Desk 'You're not Real Sam, you're just some made-up Girl in my Story', I thought... Just at that Moment, I heard a whisper and the smell of the Perfume hit my nose again.

"I love you Danny, my Darling - Good Night".

I flew back, upright in bed and looked around, but there was no-one there. I reached to turn off the Bedside Table Lamp and put my head down for the Night.

CHAPTER 18

It took me a while to get to sleep; I lay there thinking about my Therapy Session and all the Things we had talked about. I was trying to figure out why I had this connection to Sam, a made-up Character in a Story I was writing. How could I be in Love with Someone I had Created in my Mind. She wasn't even real so how could I have these Feelings for Someone that was not Real. I closed my eyes and took some deep breaths and then I heard a soft quiet voice in my left ear.

"Remember me".

I did not open my eyes as I was deep in relaxation, and to open my eyes would spoil the Moment. I started to breathe slower and deeper and deeper. I felt myself going deeper and deeper into a Meditative State. I saw her, the Ghost-Girl. She was very close this time, closer than before. She appeared before a bright, white-light in front of me. I could see her, but yet, her face was still not fully visible. There was golden, white-light around her. I could not speak any words as I was in awe as I felt a Magical Energy come from her.

I am not sure how I knew, but yet, I recognized the Energy. It was so familiar to me like I had been with this presence before. She held her hand out and I reached out to hold it. As our hands connected and met, I felt that I was Home. I was whole and complete. We started to head into the white-light together, hand in hand. As we walked further into the Light, the feeling of Love got stronger. I felt my heart melt and merge with this Light as it ;consumed my whole body. In the distance, I could see a Room that we were heading towards. It looked like a Bar, and I could see People standing around drinking. The Light started to fade and we appeared on the other side in a Bar. The Bar looked very familiar. As I looked around, there were not many People, just the odd few at the Bar, ordering their Drinks. Then I saw her. She stood on her own, this Beautiful Young Woman at the Bar with a glass of Wine, looking around like she was waiting for Someone. I could not take my eyes off her. She looked identical to Sam from my Book. For a Moment, I thought it was. I started to walk over to her but the Ghost-Girl pulled me back.

"Danny my Love, she cannot see you".

She looked Sad and stood there on her own. Then I saw a young Guy walk up to her and start talking to her. They started laughing and drinking together. After a little while, she got her

Phone out and they exchanged Numbers. She kissed him on the cheek and walked past me and Ghost-Girl. I turned to follow her but then remembered that she could not see me. The Guy at the Bar was finishing his Drink, taking one last swig, and placing his glass on the table, he turned around and faced me. I fell back, almost falling in shock. Ghost-Girl grabbed me.

The Guy at the Bar, talking to the Girl that looked like Sam, was me; I was the one with Sam at the Bar. How could this be? Was I dead and looking at my Life? Ghost-Girl looked at me.

"You are not dead Sweetie".

She pulled me into her and kissed me. I felt my body just turn into a Vibration with these Waves of Energy passing through it. I had never felt anything like it, but I did not want this feeling to end, it felt so natural and warm. I opened my eyes and was back in my Room, wondering what had happened. I could not move as I was still feeling the Waves of Energy passing through my Body. She was still with me, but yet, I had no idea who she was and what was she trying to tell me and why did I see Sam at the Bar and myself? Was Sam Real, did I make her up or was she my Future?

***

I woke up the next Morning, only remembering little parts of the Dream I had. I remember Ghost-Girl and seeing me and Sam in the Bar chatting but not much else. I felt very calm, I got ready and went down for Breakfast Alisha had already left for

Work but had put my Breakfast out. As soon as I had eaten, I went back up to my Room, sat at the Desk and started writing again, still not knowing what I was going to write or how this Book would even finish.

***

Matt had returned to the Higher Dimensions after leaving Sam in the Shop. He felt this grief and loss. He knew that Souls could not feel pain but they could take on the pain from their Divine Soul-Partners and he felt her pain, her grief and her loss for him. He could watch over her from this Place but couldn't be with her or intervene as he was not allowed. She had free-will. From time to time, he could let her know he was with her, looking down on her, but it hurt him to see her in pain. He knew that one day, they would be re-united again when her Earthly Life was over.

Was Sam going to make this full Life or would the pain and grief get too much for her and she would have an early return back to the Higher Dimensions? Matt knew though that if she was to do that, she would not be returned to him but she would to go to the School of Re-Training. This was on a different plain to Matt and it was a Place where Souls go who have taken their Life early, to Re-Train, to go back to Earth, and that would mean that they would not be re-united for a long-time. Matt could not let this happen. He wanted Sam to live a happy Life then they could be together again. He pondered a moment then had an Idea. He had learned a lot in the Higher Dimensions since he had been here, and one thing he had picked up on is a Soul-Transfer. It was very rare and never really happened often but this could be a way back to being with his True-Love on Earth. If a Human had died sooner than expected through an Accident that was not their fault, they had a choice. They could go Home or come back into the Body. If they wanted to go Home, the Body would be spared. If it was functional and not too damaged then both Souls could come to an agreement that the Body could be taken over by a Soul that wanted to come back to Earth.

This could be a way back so Matt could be with Sam. If he found a Soul that didn't want to return to their Body then Matt could trade places with them. The only problem was that this was quite a rare thing to happen as if Someone had died at a younger Earthly Age. They wanted to return to their Body to complete Life and also it had to get to a panel of Elders who would make the decision.

Matt closed his eyes and called on his Guardian Angel. She appeared in front of him. She always appeared as a ball of white-light but then changed forms when she communicated with Matt. She transformed into a Beautiful Tall Woman with golden, flowing-hair and a white-robe.

Angels could change into any form and could even look very Human, as sometimes, they needed to travel to Earth for brief

221

moments to Humanly Interact with People, like when you will get a Person, that will appear out of nowhere and give advice then just disappear again or they could work through people doing good deeds.

They could even have full Earthly Lives themselves. Even when a Soul passes over to the other-side, their Guardian Angel will still look after them and be there for them. The Angels were the first point of contact if the Soul needed Assistance. The Angel looked at Matt with a smile on her face; she knew what Matt was going to ask as Angels know everything. She led Matt on a Path that cut through some Trees. At the end of the Path was a bench looking out to the Ocean; they both took a seat and looked out to the Infinite Ocean.

"So, you would like to go back to Earth Matt, to be with Sam as you fear she could end her Life early and you would not be re-united with her", said the Angel.

"I need to go back and be with her. I can't bear to see her in this much pain", said Matt.

"You know that it will have to go to the Elders, and it will be them that make the decision. Also, you won't be Matt. You will have a different Body and Life, also there is the chance that Sam will not take you back".

Matt looked at her, "What do you mean? She Loves me and I Love her".

"As you know, things are different on Earth - They are here, she will recognize you but be confused as to who you are. As you know, you have free-will down on Earth so she might not fall in Love with you down there and who is to say that you will fall in Love with her ".

"What - How can that be? ".

"If this Soul-Transfer was approved by the Elders, first they would need to find a Soul that has just left the Body. It would of course have to be a suitable Body, they would have to agree to stay and for you to enter their Earthly Body, once this has happened you will forget who you are, deep down. You will remember, but unless you tune-in and a lot of Humans don't do that as their Earthly Life is full of distractions - you will forget who you are and who Sam is ".

"Are you trying to put me off the Idea? ".

"No, I am not my Dear, but I have to tell you as it is just so you are sure you want to do it. I can put it forward for you to the Elders "

"How will I know if they say I can? ".

"You will be called to stand and explain your case to them, and it will then be their decision to let you go or not ".

***

Sam was just settling down for the Night, thinking about what had happened that day in the Shop. Another Night alone she Thought. She wished she could just go out and have a normal Life and meet Someone, but she couldn't as she still missed Matt so much. it had only been a year and so it might be too soon to move on Sam Thought, but yet, her and Matt were different from a lot of Couples. It felt like they were Soul-Mates, Twin-Flames, Divine Counter-Parts and she could not live a Life without him.

***

Matt was Meditating thinking about what his Guardian Angel had told him then he heard a soft voice in his ear. He jumped up then he heard it again. He knew he was being called by the Elders. He closed his eyes and appeared in a big Room that looked like a Court-Room, there were three huge Light-Beings behind a big table. The three Beings didn't have any Physical Form. They were just made up of Light. Matt felt a little nervous and excited as he had been called so they must have wanted to discuss his case rather than dismiss it. Matt stood in front of them along with his Angel. They looked at Matt and smiled. Even though they had no faces, Matt could feel their smile. "So, it has come to us that you wish to return to Earth. Your Angel has brought forward our case but we would like to hear it from you".

Matt explained about Sam and that he felt she would take her Life and that they might not be able to re-unite if she ended it early.

"You do understand that it is her free-will and if she wants to take her Life early she has the right to", said one of the Light-Beings.

"She would only take her Life though as I am not in it. If I came back, we could live out Earthly-Life together like we were meant to do".

"As your Angel explained that she might not fall in Love with you or recognize you. Also, you might not remember her".

"He will have some Memories of those and he will remember for a short-time after he enters Earth", said one of the other Light-Beings.

"Wait here".

The three Light-Beings disappeared and Matt looked at the Angel. Nervously, she looked back at him and smiled, placing her arm on his shoulder.

"This is a good Sign, they are discussing it".

"What if they say no", Matt said nervously.

"Well, if it was a no they would have told you and not had to discuss the matter".

Moments later, the three Elder Light-Beings appeared in the Court-Room looking at Matt and the Angel. "Ok, well we have put together a Plan for you, however, if this doesn't work, you can't come back, you will have to continue your Earthly Life until the end". "Ok, what's the Plan?" Matt said, his Energy expanding with happiness, giving off Rainbow-Light in excitement.

"Sam's friend Claire will call Sam and ask her to go to a Bar. It will be Sam's choice if she decides that she wants to go out. Claire and Sam will have a few Drinks, Jack will come into the Bar and start talking to the Girls. Claire will leave with Jack's Friend and Sam will stay in the Bar with Jack. When they leave later that Night, there will be an Accident, Sam will be fine but will get taken to Hospital. Jack, however, will go into a coma. This is the doorway for you then to enter Jack's Body. From here on, you will have free-will". '

'Does Jack know about this and does he agree?". '

'Yes, he has connected with his Guardian-Angel and Higher-Self and they agree to it". '

"Why doesn't Jack want to stay on Earth? He could have so much fun down there".

"Some Souls find it very challenging there and they want to leave early so we can put things in place to make that happen. We don't usually do it, but if it's an old Soul and they may just want to go back to Earth for a short-time then leave".

226

Matt was feeling very excited now knowing he could be back with Sam, his Beloved on Earth. He started to think of all the nice things they could do together. He closed his eyes and went to the Celestial Gardens. The Celestial Gardens were where Souls could look down on their Loved Ones. In the centre was the Viewing Fountain, a big Lake surrounded by Trees and Flowers, Matt walked over to the Lake and placed his hand in the Water, thinking of Sam. He looked deep into the Water; it started to ripple outwards creating a Moving Picture where he could look down on Sam. He saw her sitting, watching TV, wrapped in a blanket, eyes watering. It broke his heart to see her like this, "I will be with you shortly Sweet-Heart", he said softly. Matt saw Sam's Phone at the side of her, light up and start to ring.

"Come on - Pick up Sam - it's Claire", he shouted.

***

Sam was just about to go to bed when her Phone rang. It was her Friend, Claire. She didn't want to answer. She was in no mood to speak to Anyone, but Claire was her Friend and she had not spoken to her in a while.

''Hello Claire", Sam said in a low moody voice.

"Hey Sam, how are you Babe? Clive told me what happened today and I was just ringing you to check in on you to see if you are Ok".

227

"I miss him Claire, I can't get over him. I try but Everything I do just reminds me of him", Sam said, starting to tear up again.

"Well, this is why we now have to Create new Memories Babe, I know it must be hard but you are such a Lovely Person, and you're fit too. If I was a Guy... Like, I'd do you", Claire laughed, trying to make a joke.

Sam smiled and laughed. Her and Claire had been Friends a long-time and she has not made much of an effort with her lately. "Seriously though Babe, you are Gorgeous and have so much going for you and it's time you got back out and had some fun. What do you say we go out on Friday, we don't have to go into Town, we can go to the new Bar that's opened up".

"Oh, I don't know".

"Please do, please do", Matt said excitedly into the Water as he looked down at her. Matt closed his eyes and whispered, "Sam please go for me".

Sam felt a soft voice in her ear like a gentle blow. She closed her eyes and listened to the Silence.

"I will come out Claire. I don't know why but I feel it is right for some reason and I need to".

"Oh, fantastic, so can't wait. It will be nice to see you and have a Girly Night. We might even get lucky".

"Oh, I don't know about that. I'm not thinking about getting with any Guy at the moment", Sam said, taking a big sigh.

"Well, let's just have no expectations and just enjoy ourselves".

Sam felt excited she had not been out in ages and maybe it was what she did need instead of sitting in the House, thinking about Matt. Maybe it was Time for her to move on but her Love for Matt would live on. People would tell her that she and Matt are Soul-Mates. When they were together, they shone out this Love and made Everyone feel happy around them. Sam put down the Phone and went off to bed. She still wasn't keen on going out, but something was telling her she had to but couldn't understand what it was.

***

Matt jumped up and started dancing around the Celestial Gardens as this was the first step to getting his Love back. This first part of the Plan had worked.

***

It was 5pm... Where had the day gone? I looked down at what I had written and read it back. I was shocked as this is not what I thought this Story was going to be like. I was being guided on what to write. I Loved Matt and Sam. They was just the Perfect Couple and for him to come back to Earth to be with his Love was Magical and showed the 'Power of Love'. He did not know that he would be with Sam again, but he was willing to take that chance. Why can't nice things like that happen in Real-Life? All we hear is bad news.

I kind of felt a little envious of Matt as he was going to be with Sam again and yet I loved Sam. I wanted to be with her, I had to keep telling myself though that she is not Real. She is just a Character, but then why did I feel this way? And why did Ghost-Girl show me Sam? And who even was this Ghost -Girl, that kept appearing? I could feel the Magic in my Story, and I started to read the whole Story I had written so far. It filled me with happiness and joy, but also there was that deep grief and sadness in me that I could not seem to shift. I was falling more in Love with Sam, and I could not stop thinking of her. I did not tell Alisha about my Love for Sam and about what happened in my Dream as I felt that this was too much, and she might lock me up for being Crazy, but I had to tell Someone. I guess I will tell Lucy when I see her next.

***

Alisha had called me down to Dinner, but my Mind was too much focused on Sam. All I wanted to do was write and see more of my Story unfold and see where it was going to go as a few Nights ago, I had no idea how to write and now this Story was writing itself.

"Danny are you Ok? You seem a little distracted Tonight. I'm a little worried about you as you have been in your Room all day.

It's not like you at all. You know you can talk to me about Anything".

I started to tell Alisha about my Book, but I didn't say Anything about my feelings for Sam. After Dinner, I let her read what I had written. She loved it and gave it to Tom to read. They both smiled at me.

"Danny, my Sweet, when your Book is done, I want to show it to my friend James. He is a Publisher, and I would Love to get his views on it as I think you could have a Best-Seller here".

"Wow, you think. It's strange Sis as I don't even know what I'm going to write, but then I start, and then I just watch this Story unfold".

"That is a True-Writer, Danny. You just let go and let it flow".

I wanted to tell Alisha about Sam and my feelings for her I needed to get it off my chest, but I was scared that she would think I'm Crazy. What have I got to lose, so what if she thinks I'm Crazy? I told her about Sam and the Ghost-Girl showing me and Sam together in the Bar. Alisha nearly dropped her glass of Water on the floor, her face changed. All the colour had now drained from it and she had turned a pale-colour.

"Danny - The Car Accident - What do you remember of it?".

"Not much at all. The thing is I don't know how it happened as I don't remember driving, but if I wasn't driving then who was? That's the part I'm struggling with. I don't remember"

I closed my eyes and tried to remember, but I saw the Car and the Ocean. There was a Person next to me, but I could not tell who they were and where were they now.

"When is your next Appointment with Lucy?", said Alisha.

"It is next Week, but she did say that I could see her before if I needed to".

"And how do you feel about that? Are you Ok with waiting next Week or do you feel you may need to see her before".

"I don't know. I feel like I need to talk to her before as I'm scared. I don't know what's happening to me or why I feel like this".

I started to cry as I felt this loss and grief inside of me, and I just wanted Sam, I felt so confused. Alisha hugged me and I went off to bed.

***

The next Morning, I called Lucy and told her I needed to see her, I explained to her what was going on and how I was feeling and she booked me in for a couple of days time.

CHAPTER 19

I walked into Lucy's Lounge and took a seat on her Couch; The Room was very calming and had a Relaxing Scent as she lit some Incense Sticks that filled the Air with this very calming Aroma. Once I was comfy and settled, Lucy disappeared into the Kitchen, and I heard the kettle boiling. Two minutes later, she came out with two mugs of hot, steaming Tea.

Today, I had woken up, feeling a mixture of Emotions. I felt so lonely and lost, and I thought that I was doing so well, but Today was different from the other day, it felt like a dark cloud was over me, blinding me from seeing. My heart longed for Sam, and I could not stop thinking about her. It was like she was a Real Person. When I started writing about her, I didn't feel alone.

I am not a Person who tells People how I feel. I sort of bottle it up and get on with Things, but the Truth is, I was hurting so bad like a part of my heart had been taken from me. Something had gone out of my Life, but yet, when I tried to think, my Mind was just foggy.

I felt guilty and confused as I still really liked Becky, but Sam was different. I knew her on such a different level from Becky. Everything seemed to change after seeing Sam at the Bar in my Dream. She was not just a Fictional Character in my Book, she must be Real, for us to be together in my Dream, but then who is she?

Lucy took a sip of her hot Tea then placed the cup down on the Table next to her Chair, she then walked over to her Laptop and put some Music on. It was very soft, relaxing Music, the Sound of a Piano with Waves in the background. She picked up her Pad and Pen and looked at me then smiled, making herself comfy in the Seat across from me.

"Ok, Danny. So, I want you to tell me what has been going on with you since I last saw you".

I started to tell Lucy all about the Dream and Everything that had gone on. She kept looking up at me then scribbling notes down. I told her about Ghost- Girl and the Bar and Sam. I felt a little embarrassed and uncomfortable telling her about Sam as this was probably something she had never heard before: Someone falling in Love with a Character out of a Book. As I continued to talk, I did start to feel at ease, and it was all Confidential. Lucy stopped writing and then looked up at me, taking a moment to analyses Everything I had just told her.

"Danny, can you tell me more about Sam - How you thought her up for your Book".

"Well, it started when I went into this Cafe with my Sister Alisha, and I was given this Pen, and then I started to have strange Dreams, and I kept seeing this Girl, but she did not show me her face. I recognized her but was not sure how. She told me I needed to write, but I have never written before. I did not even know what I was going to write about, but then, when I started, it was just like it came out of Nowhere".

"So, tell me about Sam", Lucy said in a soft, quiet voice, looking more interested now. "I didn't know what I was going to write, but I had an Image of this Beautiful Girl that came into my head one Night. I am not sure where she came from, but when I was writing about her, I started to feel like I knew her. The more I wrote about her, the more I started to fall for her and now I think I am in Love with her".

Lucy was writing down what I was saying to her, she kept putting her head up to look at me, trying to work out what was going on, then she would write down more. She stopped writing, put down her Note-Pad and took another sip of her Tea.

"Danny, so from all the things you have told me, it sounds like Sam could be someone who you have forgotten, Someone close to you. When we write or do Anything Creative, it can open up a little Box in our Mind. In this little Box are all the Things we have forgotten about, but it is still there in our Mind. When I was a Child, I had this little Box. I called it the Memory Box. I put all the Special Things in there, and when I was older, I could open the Box and look back in it and see all my Special Memories.

There was a Photo of me and my Gran who passed away some years ago, but it had all the nice Memories in there. There was even a little Teddy Bear that my Mum and Dad had got me for my first Birthday. Our Minds are the same. We keep a little Memory Box. We can open it, as we do sometimes. There are Compartments in it that are locked. The Memory Box is full of little Compartments, some we can open up very easily, but some, we need a Key, and we can misplace the Key if we have had some Trauma, so we know it is there but just can't open it. We cannot find the Key, so we have to make a new one.

Lucy's voice softened, and I felt relaxed just listening to the Sound of her voice.

"I want to you take three deep breaths in and out, In... Out... In... Out... In and Out. Now close your eyes. I am going to count down from 10-0 and when I go to 0, you will be so relaxed. The only sound you will hear is my voice and the Music. 10 you feel relaxed 9... 8... 7... 6... 5... – You're feeling so relaxed, you feel like you are floating on a Cloud 4... 3... 2... 1... and 0. You can only now hear me and the Music, Danny. I want you to Imagine that you are at a Train Station. You are on the Platform, look around, see, and feel your Environment. The Train pulls into the Station and you board it. This is no ordinary Train. This Train is going to take you back to a Time just before your Accident. There is a Seat by the window, so sit down and relax".

"The Train pulls out of the Station and you look out of the window, seeing the Trees and Fields pass you by. You feel more and more relaxed. In front of you, there is a Screen and on this Screen is the next Destination. It reads a Date and Time. This is the Day of the Event. I am going to give you a few Moments now, just to take in the Scenery outside..."

"You feel the Train start to slow down now as it approaches the Station... Right Danny, it's time for you to get off the Train. When you step out off the Train, you will be in a Place that is familiar to you. I want you now to step off the Train and tell me where you are and what you see".

I started to see an Image appear in front of me, unfolding and becoming very vivid now and clear. I was in my Bedroom at my old House. In the City, there was someone in bed but I could not make them out. Their face was just a blur. The next Image that came to me was in the Car Showroom, picking up a new Car. I was with someone. I tried to focus hard on them, but they were still just a blur. I tried again to really focus on them but all I saw was just the shape of a Woman's Body with no face or features.

237

The next Image I got, I was sitting in the Passenger Seat, we were heading out in the new Car, we turned down this Road, it was the Coastal Road. There was a Car coming toward us, we couldn't stop and...

"What happened then, Danny? You're doing great".

I felt my eyes widen as tears filled, then I saw the Car go over the Cliff and afterwards, heard a scream then all went blank. "Danny, you say that you weren't driving the new Car, so who was it that was in the Car with you?".

I looked but all I could see was this Female Figure but she was just a blur, and I had no Idea who she was. "I don't remember, I can see her but I can't see her at the same time. Her face is just so blurry". I started to cry at this point as I was getting frustrated as to why I could not see her or know who she was.

"Danny, tell me this Person you're with, in the Car - How does she make you feel? Is she close to you?". "Yes, she is, but I can't see her. I am trying to but I just can't. I know I am close to her like maybe we are together but that would be impossible as I don't have a Girlfriend so it can't be that". "OK Danny, you have done really well there, I am going to bring you back into the Room. I want you to get back on the Train and take that Seat by the window. I'm going to count down from 10 again and when I get to 0, you will be fully back in the room 10... 9... 8... 7... 6... 5... 4... 3... 2... 1... 0"

I opened my eyes and stretched my legs out. I was disappointed that I could not see who was in the Car with me, as nothing made sense, like why I was in a new Car? And going to my Sisters and why I wasn't driving? It just left me feeling more and more confused. What I did feel though was the urge to write, and it was very strong this time. Lucy looked at me again and smiled. "Danny, it's Ok you didn't see the Person who was driving. It might be too early for you to remember, but I feel that this Book is playing a part in your Healing and it might even help you remember".

"I couldn't write Today".

"I know you want to, but you can do it Tomorrow - Just take the day to rest, we will do the same next Week as the more we do this Exercise, the more it will help you".

I smiled at Lucy and thanked her, my head felt a little strange like something was happening inside my Brain. Maybe Lucy was right and I had started to make a new Key now for my Memory Box.

***

When I got Home, there was so much going on in my head. I felt this frustration that I could not see who was driving the Car. Why was I not driving as I loved driving and used to drive Everywhere, and who was this other Person, as I pondered over it. I got the Name. Sam who was driving but that would have been impossible as Sam wasn't Real. I had such an urge to write again. It felt like Sam had taken over my head, trying to tell me something, so maybe that was why her Name had come into my head.

My Phone started to ring, I wasn't expecting anyone to Call, no-one called me only Alisha. I think she was the only one that had my Number, oh and Becky did. I took the Phone out of my pocket and looked at the screen for a moment, trying to register who it was, but it flashed up 'Unknown Number'. "Hello," I said in a quiet voice. There was no-one on the other end, just a fuzzy static sound, but as I listened closer, I could hear a whisper, "Hello, who is it? Is Anybody there? I called out, the whisper got louder and a voice came on the line. I could only describe it as Angelic, it was so soft and gentle.

"Danny, Sweetie. I Love You, I always will. Remember me and Love will find you again".

The call ended, I dropped my Phone and nearly fell back. If Sam had a voice, if she was a Real Person, that is how I would Imagine her to sound like. My Phone rang again and a Number came up "Hello". I said in a nervous voice... "Who Is this?"

"Hey, my favorite Man, it's Becky". It took me a Moment to figure out who Becky was then it clicked.

"Is everything Ok, Babe?"

I told her about the Call I had just received

"Did you recognize the voice, Danny?" Becky said in a surprised voice.

"Danny, I have some good and bad news for you, and I would like to see you soon as well. I need to talk to you about Something".

"Have you got a new Phone, Becky. I did not recognize the Number".

"This is my Personal Number, Danny. I wanted you to have it. This is part of my news. You can't contact me on my Works Phone Anymore".

I felt sick, and my stomach clenched, what was she saying? Was she stopping seeing me?

"Becky are you still going to be seeing me?".

"Well yes and no really. Danny, do you want the bad News first or the good News?".

I felt so sick as this could be the end of me and Becky.

"Let's got the bad news over with then", I said sighing.

"I can't be your Nurse anymore as you are physically Recovering well, which is really good News. I am so happy that you are Recovering".

"So, you won't be seeing me again". I felt so sad as I loved seeing Becky, She always cheered me up. I felt like I was going to throw up. Becky was the only friend I had and she was leaving me.

"Just hold on Babe before you start to cry", Becky laughed.

"I'm not going to cry". She did not see the tear but she could hear me trying to hold back.

"You have not heard the good News yet... So, I can't be your Nurse, and this is why I have given you my Personal Phone Number so I can see you and we can ummm... Hang Out - If you want to that is?".

When she had said that to me, I felt like a Kid waking up on Christmas Morning. I wanted to Dance and Sing, hearing her say that and felt stupid that I had even thought she was going to leave me. She did like me so why would she have done that?

"Oh, Wow Becky, I would Love that".

"Maybe we can go for some Food down the Harbour and you can show me around?". My voice had soon picked up now that she wanted to hang out with me. "Are you asking me on a Date?", Becky chuckled down the Phone.

I didn't know what to say to that. Had I just asked her on a Date but then what about Sam? Maybe I needed to Date Becky to get Sam out of my head and Sam was just some made-up Person. Becky was real and I did really like her.

"It could be a Date I mean, if you wanted it to be, you are not my Nurse now Becky".

"Yes, let's do this then, Babe. I wanted to see you and talk to you about something. I'm not free though for another 2 weeks, so I hope you're still around", Becky laughed again.

"Oh, I will be around, definitely. Once I am fully recovered, I will be staying here. I like Palm Bay and it will be nice to get to know it better and to get to know you".

"Ok Babe, that is so cool. Well... I had better go, and I will see you in a couple of weeks. Oh... And save this number and delete the other one" "I will Becky. I'll save it now and I will Message you".

"Not if I Message you first. See you soon, Babe".

Becky hung up the Phone, and I sat on the Sofa, thinking about what just happened. I had never asked anyone on a Date. I had always been a little shy, but I had asked Becky on a Date and I was proud of myself for doing it. Life is too short to hold back. I have always been a little shy but, Becky somehow gave me the confidence.

CHAPTER 20

That night, I sat at my Desk again and looked at what I had written. Lucy had told me not to write Today but I felt the strong urge. I put the Music on that Willow had given me and I picked the Pen up, closed my eyes, took a deep breath and started to write.

***

All week, Sam was thinking about going out and trying to come up with an excuse not to as she was not in the mood, but Claire would not accept any excuse. Friday came and Sam felt a little nervous and apprehensive getting ready. She had not been out in such a long-time. The only place she went was to Work and sometimes to the Park where she would sit for hours on the Beach, watching the Ducks swimming in the Lake. She opened her wardrobe and started looking for dresses, she found a nice white one that flowed just passed her knees. That was Matt's favorite dress. She would always wear it when they went out. He used to say that she looked like an Angel in that dress.

She looked in the mirror and sighed, thinking if it was a good Idea to go out whilst putting on her make-up, trying to motivate herself. Once she was ready, she felt a little better, taking another look in the mirror and scrunching her hair up then pinning it up. She went over to her draw and pulled out her Locket that Matt had given her with a small Photo of them both in. Claire had told her to keep it but not wear it as she could not let go if she still had it around her neck, but she didn't want to let go, not yet anyway. There was a knock at the door and a second later, the door flew open. It was Claire. As Sam walked down the Stairs, she could see Claire, already standing in the doorway inside.

"Oh, Wow Sam. You look Gorgeous. If I were a Lesbian, I definitely would", Claire laughed.

Sam chuckled and smiled. No-one else could get away with saying that to her, but it was Claire. There was no way she could ever be a Lesbian as she liked the Men too much.

The Taxi pulled up and the Girls got in, on their way to the Bar. 10 minutes later, they pulled up outside the Bar, paid the Taxi Driver and went inside. Sam was still feeling apprehensive about the Night. Claire had the tendency to get drunk and end up disappearing with some Guy when she was out but that was not what Sam was apprehensive of.

There was just something that did not feel right. She just had this strange feeling and wanted to go back Home. After some reassurance from Claire, Sam started to settle more. The Bar was pretty much empty, just a few people in. Both the girls made their way over to the Bar.

"What can I get you two Gorgeous Girls?", said the Bartender.

"Can we have two Mojito please?", Claire chirped up.

After a few Drinks, Sam started to feel a bit more settled and they sat in a little quiet Booth, chatting about Life. Claire noticed two Guys, looking over at them, checking them out but didn't acknowledge them as this was not a Night for pulling Guys, but it was about her and Sam having a Girl's Night.

***

"Hey Jack, check out the two Girls over there, they are well-fit. Shall we go over to them?".

"No, we can't. I mean, what if they don't want to be bugged by us. They looked to be in deep conversation and we don't want to interrupt them".

"Jack - How are you ever going to meet anyone if you are scared of talking to Girls? Look Mate, I know the last 12 months haven't been easy for you since you lost Jade, but life has to go on Mate". Ben put his arm around Jack.

"Come on, what have we got to lose Mate?".

Ben and Jack started to walk over to Claire and Sam. Jack was feeling his heart-beat fast as Sam looked over and gave him half a smile then quickly turned back to Claire and started talking again to put the Guys off.

"Oh no, Claire. These two Guys are coming over, and I'm not in the mood to start talking to Guys Tonight. Let's finish our Drinks then go".

Claire took a big Drink and then shouted over to Jack and Ben, "Sorry Guys, not Today. We are not interested".

Jack smiled at Sam and apologized and turned around to go back to the Bar, feeling a little uneasy but with a sense of relief too.

"Hold on Mate. Where do you think you're going Ben?", said Sam, pulling him back.

"They said, not Today, so let's not bother them".

Claire heard them and giggled. "You seem like a nice Guy - What is your Name?"

"I'm Jack, and this is my friend Ben", Jack said nervously, his voice shaking.

"I'm sorry Girls. Jack gets very nervous around fit Girls. He suffers from Social Anxiety", Ben said.

Jack looked at Ben, not impressed by what he had just said. Claire smiled at Sam and then looked at the two Guys who stood at the Table, looking like two little Puppy Dogs, waiting to be fed.

"I'm Claire and this is my friend Sam. Are you Guys just going to stand there all Night or sit down?".

Ben sat with Claire who he clearly fancied; He could not fake it any more, it was obvious: His eyes kept wandering from her face to her chest. She pulled his face back up.

"Oi you, my face is here, not down there", she said laughing as she grabbed his Drink and took a big gulp".

"Excuse me... What the... That's mine!", Ben said surprised.

"Well, you clearly are not buying me one, so I thought I would have yours". Sam looked at Jack, who looked embarrassed and nervous.

"Hey... Would you like to sit here next to me?", Sam said, smiling at Jack.

"Would you like me to get you a Drink?".

"See Ben, that's how it's done. You can learn a lot from him".

Claire was feeling a little drunk now, and she was starting to get loud.

"I'm Ok for a Drink, Thank You Jack, but Thank You for the kind offer".

The Couples got chatting and laughed as time went on. Claire was feeling drunk now and wanted to Dance but this was a Bar and not a Place for Dancing.

"Let's go to the Club, I want to Dance", Claire shouted.

"I'm not really in the mood for Clubbing, I just want to stay here", said Sam.

Jack felt relieved at Sam saying that she did not want to go to the Club as he hated Clubs and would rather be here with Sam. He wanted to get to know her, she seemed nice and if they went to the Club, the Girls might start dancing and leave them.

"Yes, let's stay here. I don't like crowded Places and loud Music where you can't hear yourself think", said Jack.

"Well, Ok then, you two bores. Me and Claire will go and leave you two here to be boring", Ben said.

Ben and Claire got up. Claire grabbed her Jacket.

"You will be Ok Sam, won't you? I will text you in a bit, Ok?".

They left the Bar, and it was now, just Sam and Jack. They looked at each other and smiled. Jake wasn't very good at talking to Girls. He suffered badly from Social Anxiety, it came from him getting bullied as a Child. Sam started to make Conversation to help him out and make it easier for him and she could not leave the poor Guy hanging on. She could see he was shy and nervous. After a short while, the two were relaxed *and enjoying each other's Company. They found out that they had something in common and that they had both lost their Partners. It was not the nicest of things to have in common, but it did make Conversation.*

"Jack, Thank You for Tonight. When you first came over, I thought you were just two Guys that were looking to pull and just wanted to... Well, you know". Jack moved closer to Sam "I'm sorry for my Friend Ben, he is a bit loud and forward, but he is a nice Guy underneath that gob of his".

"Just like my Friend Claire, she is lovely but can be a bit too much, but I Love her. She has been there for me'.

Jack took his Phone out of his pocket and looked down at it for a moment, "Please can I have your Number, Sam...? It's Ok if you don't want to give it to me, I will understand".

Sam smiled and chuckled "Oh Jack, you're so sweet, of course you can". Sam took her Phone out and they exchanged Numbers. It was getting late and the Bar was ready for closing.

"I suppose we had better get going, it will soon be closing time, and I am a bit tired now. We will have to meet up again though, if you like Jack? We could go for some Food next Time ".

Jack's eyes lit up. They got up and Sam grabbed Jack's hand and they walked out together. The Taxis were parked on the other side of the Street. They both stood at the side of the Road, holding hands, waiting to cross the Road. It seemed a little busy for this time of Night, but finally, the Traffic Lights had turned red and they could cross. They were half-way across the Road when they both heard this big screech. Sam turned her head and saw two big Head-Lights racing towards her and Jack. A moment later, she felt herself flying through the Air and then hit the Road. Everything went blank.

CHAPTER 21

It had been a few Days now since I had written anything. It wasn't that I did not want to, it was the opposite. I wanted to continue writing but felt myself getting emotional over Sam and what had happened to her. Part of me felt stupid for even having feelings for her, but I could not help the way I felt. I never knew what I was going to write next until I sat down with the Pen at my Desk, then it just seemed to flow like I was been guided by some Higher-Force. I figured as well that if I didn't write for a few Days and focused on my Date with Becky then Sam might just fade from my heart. Had I just fallen in Love with the Fantasy? As there was not much going on in my Life.

I was excited about my Date with Becky, and I was so happy with myself that I asked her and she said yes. I tried hard to stop thinking of Sam but even not writing about her for a few Days still did not take my mind off her. It felt like I was torn between them both even though Sam was just a made-up Fictional Character in my Story but still, I knew I had created her, so was it normal to feel this way? I loved Sam and I wished that she was Real. When I wrote about her, I could feel myself smiling inside, and I even cried a tear when she was sad, and I wanted to comfort her.

I didn't know how the Book would end or even if I would finish it as this could have just been something to pass the time with, and if Becky and I were to start seeing each other, would I even have time to write but maybe that was just me over-thinking. I had just finished eating Breakfast and was drinking my Coffee when my Phone rang. I picked it up off the side, excited, thinking it was Becky, but an Unknown Number had come up on the screen and I had saved Becky's Number to my Phone, so I knew it wasn't her. I looked at the Screen as it rang, debating whether to answer it or not. This was the second time it had rung with an Unknown Number. I slid my finger over the red button on the Screen and ended the call. A Moment later, it rang again. I looked down at the Screen and slowly swiped up the green button and put the Phone to my ear. The line was very crackly, and I couldn't hear anything. There was no- one there, just the fuzzy noise. I hung up, then it rang again and the same... Just fuzziness. After a few seconds, I was just about to hang up again when a quite, soft voice came on the line.

"Danny, my Love it is me S...". I could only make out the S but it sounded like Sam, but I wasn't sure.

"Hello", I said. My voice was now sounding shaky. "Who is this?".

"It's me, my Love. It's almost time now to let you see, but you must write more or they won't let us see each other. I have to go now. I Love You, Danny".

"Please tell me who you are", I said one more time but the fuzzy Sound had become too loud to hear anything more, then the line cut-off. I checked the Call-Log even though I knew that I could not get the Number, but I wanted to try anyway, but the call wasn't there. The last call showing was Becky, it was like the call had never even happened. I am sure the voice said it was Sam. I definitely heard an S in there. Was Sam a Real Person, and somehow it was her that was making me write? Maybe, she was a Girl that had passed and wanted me to get to know her to help her to move on, but then, why did I Love her and have such a strong connection to her? I sat on the Couch, taking another sip of my Coffee, trying to figure out what had happened. If Sam was Real and had a voice then the Person on the Phone would have been her, her voice just seemed to fit Sam's voice. I thought, maybe I should go see Willow, down at the Shop, but then I remember, she had gone away for a few days.

I felt very alone, yes... I had Alisha, Tom and Becky but I didn't really know anyone here and time was just passing by. I liked it here at Palm Bay, but Alisha and Tom had started meeting up with Friends, and I realized that I didn't have any Friends, and it made me feel a little sad and lonely. I had never really thought about it until now. No Job, and no Friends in a Place I did not know. I tried to fight the tears off but could feel them starting to gather in my eyes as my vision had become blurred. I wiped my eyes and sniffed up, holding back more tears. Was I being too hard on myself? After all I had been through, a very Traumatic Experience.

It didn't help the fact though, that I was still missing Something or Someone in my Life, I just didn't know Who or What. There was an empty hole in my heart that something had been pulled out and had just left an empty Void there.

I knew that I had to write this Book as it had something to do with it. I had always been into Science, but now I started to think that there are things out there in the Universe that cannot be explained. People can be very closed-minded and ignorant, they want explanations and to be told, programmed if you like, and when things happen that can't be explained, they just dismiss it or try to come up with some explanation.

I used to think that when you die that is the end, Game-Over but then how do we know that? If we don't exist, then how do we know that we don't exist?

There must be Something else that knows we don't exist, so therefore, Something must go on when we die. With all the

Events that had happened to me, I was starting to question Science, even the Stars in the Sky. How do we even know that there are Balls of Gas burning so far away? Science tells us they are but who tells them? They come up with these Theories and we just accept them, but how do we know we Humans have never travelled to a Star, to know? All this had me thinking deeply, about my Book, Ghost-Girl and Sam. They were all linked in some way even the Phone Call.

***

I went back up to my Room and sat at the Desk looking at what I had written so far, trying to work out the connection between me and Sam and why I loved her so much.

I switched the Lamp on as it had started to turn dull outside. There was no Sun today just Clouds that had become thick and heavy, like it was going to rain. I picked up the Pen and got a blank sheet of Paper. I closed my eyes and took a deep breath in. 'Ok Danny, what are you going to write today?' I saw a golden-spark appear in front of me then it turned into a mixture of different colours, red, green, yellow, blue, violet and many more. The colours radiated out towards me. I felt so much Love and Peace from the colours. I realized that Ghost-Girl was coming back now to help me write. I opened my eyes, pulled a sheet of Paper out from the pile and started to write.

***

Sam slowly opened her eyes and looked around the Room, she saw other beds next to her and heard voices. She tried to move but couldn't like there was a big weight on her chest. Her legs felt like they were been stabbed with hot needles, her whole body hurt like she had been kicked all over. She managed to pull her head up and looked at her arm as it had gone dead and she could no longer feel it, tubes were coming out of her arm with clear liquid from a machine pumping into her Body. She cried out and was confused as in what was going on. The last thing she had remembered was her and Jack leaving the Bar together. She started to scan the Room, but Everything was a little blurry then she heard a voice that she recognized and felt some warmarms go around her and hug her tight. It was Claire.

"What happened?", Sam asked in a tired voice as she yawed and tried to stretch the best she could without too much pain. "Me and Ben left the Bar, we went to the Club and left you and Jack. I got a Phone Call from the Police saying that you had been in an Accident, knocked over by a Car when you were leaving the Bar. I came as quickly as I could".

"Who did this and where is Jack? Is he Ok?".

Claire looked at Sam and a tear fell from her eye.

"The Police have arrested the Guy who was driving and found him to be drunk", Claire sniffed up. ''And Jack... Well Jack". Claire took a deep breath in. "Jack went into a coma. The

Doctors are monitoring him close. They say the next 24 hours are vital".

Sam started to sob into Claire's arms, she had lost Matt and she had finally met Jack, the first Guy she was getting close to and thought maybe it was time to move on from Matt and now she had lost him. How could this be? How could life be so cruel to her? She started to think that she hadn't woken up and would just die. At least then, she could have been with Matt again, in his arms in Heaven.

***

Jack opened his eyes, he lay there in a bed, but it was not his own. He felt very strange, his body felt so light. He did not know where he was, but yet, there was peacefulness about it and he wasn't scared. Should he be though?

The sun was shining through the window, he looked out and saw Beautiful Countryside, the Sky was a deep-blue with white, fluffy Clouds. He opened the window and a sweet-scent hit him, the smell of Flowers from the Meadows. He could see a little Waterfall and a Stream. Jack didn't know how he got here or where he was, but yet, that did not seem to bother him. He made his way down the Stairs into what looked like an old Cottage-Style Lounge area. He took a seat, looking around, trying to work out where he was but feeling very calm and peaceful at the same time.

The last thing he remembered was walking out of the Bar with this Beautiful blond-haired Girl, Sam. He wondered if this was Sam's House and if they had gone back there. He got up out of the Chair and went back Upstairs to look for Sam, but she was not there. Jack was confused as he had woken up in a strange House, in a Place he had no idea where he was. He should have been panicking, but he was just so calm. He went back into the Lounge and took a seat, trying to figure something out.

"Hello, my Darling Jack", A voice called.

A large Woman walked in, into the room. Jack could not believe his eyes, it was his Mum. He jumped up and ran over to her and threw his arms around her. They hugged each other tightly.

"Mum, I have missed you so much, but what are you doing here and what is this Place?".

"Come on, follow me, and we will talk".

Jack and his Mum left the Cottage and started to walk down the Path and over the little Bridge that crossed the Stream. As they were walking, Jack heard the sound of a Steam-Train and turned to find a large Steam-Train go passed. The Driver waved at them and all the People smiled and waved as the Train raced passed them.

"Wow, this Place is Magical, Mum, but why don't I feel scared here? I woke up in a strange bed, a Cottage, and this Place... I

have no idea where I am but don't feel scared at all, I feel peaceful".

Jack's Mum stopped and looked up at the Sky for a second then looked back at Jack.

"She is coming anytime soon".

A moment later, a Figure appeared out of the Trees. She was tall, slim with long, white hair, her face was young and pure not one wriggle, her eyes were big and blue and she had rosy-cheeks. Jack had never seen anyone so Beautiful. With her was a young Man.

They both approached Jack and his Mum, smiling, they seemed to light up the Path in front of them and Everything around them just burst into Life, Flowers grew under their feet as they both placed one foot in front of the other, walking to Jack and his Mum. Birds flew around them, singing, and one landed on the Woman's shoulder. She turned and kissed it, the little Creature chirped at her then flew off into the Sky. The two Souls stopped and hovered above the Stream, in front of Jack and his Mum.

"Jack - Every Soul gets a choice here, they can choose to return to Earth or go Home", said Jack's Mum.

"But, if I stay, I will die on Earth and Sam... Well, she can't lose anyone else. She told me all about her and Matt".

Jack's Mum stopped him in mid-sentence.

The young Man with the Woman in white, stepped forwards. He held out his hand, he was so handsome and had such a calm, loving Energy about him. Jack went to shake his hand.

"I am Matt, Sam's Boyfriend, and I would like to make a deal with you. I have watched Sam every day and I've seen her struggling. She never fully got over me, she seemed to like you, Jack. You're the first Guy she has liked".

Matt paused for a moment, "Here, you get a choice my Brother, and how would you feel if you were to go to Heaven and I was to come back into your Body as Jack?".

Jack looked confused by this, trying to work out what was going on, as Everything was happening so quickly.

The last thing he remembered was leaving the Bar with Sam, and now he had been asked if he wanted to go to Heaven so Matt could have his Body. "So, let me get this straight. I can go to Heaven and you come back into my Body in the Hospital, but what if my Body is broken?".

"No, it isn't", Matt said smiling.

Jack took a moment to think about it. "She did talk about you at the Bar, she loved you so much she called you her Soul-Mate. I liked her a lot but I just met her and could never have that Love for her as a Soul-Mate - That is a Love like no other. Matt, you and Sam belong together, so Ok... Let's do this. What do I have to do?".

Matt smiled and hugged Jack. There was a golden-glow of Energy around them as they both hugged each other. Matt stepped back.

"OK, my Friend. This is Crystal. She is the Angel that will take you through the Gate into Heaven. Are you sure you're Ok with doing this Jack?", Matt said in a gentle, soft tone.

"Go on my Friend, go be with your Love, your Soul-Mate. She is waiting for you", Jack said smiling.

They both shook hands again and Jack turned to face the Angel, she smiled at him and held out her hand, and walked towards her. He turned to look back at Matt and his Mum. "I'm so proud of you my Boy, and I will be seeing you soon". Jack's Mum smiled and took a step back with Matt now standing next to her.

Crystal looked up and sang the most Beautiful Tune Jack had ever heard, an Archway appeared with a bright-white Light. Jack tried to see through, but the Light was too strong and bright, at the same time and was so Peaceful. The Angel and Jack started to walk to the Archway. As they got closer, the Light reached out, surrounding them both and pulling them in. Jack turned around one more time with a smile on his face and waved at his Mum and Matt, then both the Angel and Jack walked through the Archway then disappeared into the Light. The Archway started to fade away and turned into white, little seeds that hit the ground and within an instance, Flowers started to pop up.

"Are you ready for this my Child?".

Matt looked with a big smile on his face, he was going to be re-united with his True-Love, his Soul-Mate. He did feel a little nervous as what if Sam didn't recognize him or want him, but that was a risk that he was willing to take. They started to walk through the Trees. Matt could hear the sound of Water. They came out onto a Beach where a little Rowing Boat was tied up on the Wooden Pier. They climbed into the Boat, and Jack's Mum started to row further and further out to Sea. The Shore-Line started to become misty and fade away as the Boat got further out. A white-mist started to appear around the Boat. It got thicker and thicker until Matt could not even see Jack's Mum.

"Goodbye, Matt. I will see you soon. Go now and be with her, let your Love shine into Heaven".

Jack's Mum had now disappeared into the thick fog. He could not even see his hand in front of him. He closed his eyes and felt himself fly at such a high-speed, faster than the 'Speed of Light.''

Matt opened his eyes and looked at his new Body, it felt heavy. Matt was not used to having a physical Body now, as it had been a while so he would have to get used to Earth again. Matt took another good look at his new Body 'Not bad this Body'... He thought. No wonder Sam liked him. It felt stiff and achy, but with some little movements, it would be Ok. It didn't feel that broken.

Matt scanned the Room and saw the most Beautiful face looking in on him from the window to his Room. His heart skipped a beat as she looked at him. A tear rolled down his cheek, but then a thought came into his head. What if Sam did not like him as he wanted her to, he was in the Body of Jack and it has been so long. Matt didn't like thoughts. There were no bad thoughts in Heaven, it was just Love so he wasn't used to this. He told himself it was going to be Ok and the Thoughts soon disappeared. Sam came bouncing into the Room and put her arms around him and their eyes met. She pulled him close to her and kissed him.

"Oh, Matt. I thought I had lost you", she realized what she had said and started to blush. ''I am so sorry, I meant Jack".

Jack just laughed. He wanted to tell her he was Matt, but now wasn't the time. "I don't know why I called you Matt".

Sam was a little confused by this as there was something different about Jack, something in his eyes she recognized.

"Sam, would you like to go on a Date with me when I am out of here?".

Sam smiled and kissed Jack again, she looked into his eyes one more time and looked confused. There was just something different about Jack, it was like she had known him all her Life and throughout time, but yet, she had met him once at a Bar.

***

11pm, and I was still writing. It took me a little while to come back as I seemed to have got so lost and deep into my Story. I looked back, and what I had written was so Magical, the way Matt and Jack had made the deal so Matt could come back to Earth to be with his True-Love. I wanted it to be Real and I did wonder if that did happen and some Souls have come back into different Bodies, to be back on Earth to be with their True-Love. The Book was coming on, and I thought that it could be a Best-Seller. I wanted to get it finished so I could let Becky read it. She would Love it as she loved things like that. I Looked out of the window to see if Ghost-Girl was there, but she wasn't there.

CHAPTER 22

The next Morning, I woke up early, the Sun was shining through the window. I could hear the Birds singing in the Trees, outside the window. The first thought that had come into my Mind was Sam and how her and Matt were to be together again. It was Magical how two Souls had parted and then re-united. I hoped that she recognized him - How could she not? What was going to be the ending to this Story? I wasn't sure how this Story would end, but right from the start, I didn't know what I would write next as it just seemed to flow out, so the Story could end in any way.

Parts of the Story seemed very Real-Like, as if it had happened to me. I wished the Story was Real and things like that happened to People, but the World wasn't like that or was it, but we as Humans are just so cut-off and disconnected that we do not see the Magic in Life. I did not know what I thought anymore, all the things that had gone on in my Life, could I even trust in Science? I had fallen in Love with Sam, my own Character from a Story that I had made up. What would Science make of that? It would probably label me as crazy.

I got ready and went down for Breakfast. Alisha had already gone to Work, and I had started to feel lonely as Alisha and Tom always seemed to be out now, having their own Life, and I was just left on my own, but I would not expect them to give up their Lives for me and besides they had given me a Home. I made my Morning Coffee and sat in the Back Garden with it. The Air was fresh and slightly cool as the Sun had not come around yet. I looked out towards the bottom of the Garden where the Gate was and the Steps down to the little Beach. I heard the Sound of the Waves, I had started to wonder what my Future would be and what would happen. I had no Job here and would Alisha and Tom want me to stay here for the rest of their Lives? Would I be even able to afford a Place here in Palm Bay or would I have to move back to the City, but what was there for me? All of a sudden, I felt this wave of sadness that I did not belong Anywhere. I didn't have a Home, I had no Memories of the Accident or even who was driving the Car. That part of my Life had been wiped clean out. All that was left was just a hole in my heart, a void where something should have been. I missed Someone. I had lost Someone close to me, but yet, I didn't know who. I finished my Coffee and went to my Room to start writing again. I sat at the Desk and picked up the Pen, but nothing happened.

What is going on?... I thought to myself. I just couldn't write, nothing was coming out. I read the last bit I had written where Matt had come into Jack's Body and had just come out of his coma, but what would happen next? I tried to think of what to write, but nothing came out. My Mind was blocked. If I didn't get this Book finished then what would I have? I would have to look for a Job and I didn't want to do that. I didn't feel ready to. I thought that maybe it was because it was Morning and I usually did my writing in the Afternoon or at Night. I put the Pen back down and went back downstairs into the Lounge, wondering what to do.

I must have sat in the Lounge for what seemed like Hours, but I looked at my Phone and only Minutes had passed. The Sun was beaming in through the front-bay window and heating the Room. I thought about trying to go for a walk again into Town but remembered what happened the last time when I passed out, but I couldn't stay here all Day. Maybe if I just took it easy, I could manage, and I had all Day to walk. I got ready and set off into Town and maybe going for some Lunch once I got there.

***

I was walking down the Main Road, and something caught my eye. I looked over into the Trees and saw a Figure looking over at me. It was Ghost-Girl. Strangely, I felt happy to see her as it

269

had been a while since I had seen her last. This was the Day-Time though and she never came out in the Day. I still couldn't see her face, just the outline of her Body with a golden-white Light around it. She just stood there, looking at me; I took a few small steps forwards to get closer to her and squinted my eyes to try and get a better look at her and to see if I could make out her face. I took a few more steps forward, and she turned and started to walk away. I stopped, and then she turned to face me again. I felt the pull to follow her, so I started to walk toward her and she continued walking into the Trees, down an over-grown Path.

I continued until I could see openings that led out onto the Beach. I looked around, but she had gone.

I scanned the whole Beach, but she had vanished. Why had she wanted for me to follow her, for her just to disappear?

I had never seen this part of the Beach before, it was like a little Cove that had been carved out of the Trees. There was an old, wooden Rowing Boat on the Sand that looked to have been washed up many years ago. On one side of the Beach, in the distance, were the Cliffs that our House stood on top of and the Rocks that separated the Cove from the little private Beach, to the other side of me I could see the Main Beach of Palm Bay. The Sand was untouched and was just soft and smooth. I could tell that not many People came to this part of the Beach, but there was no reason to as it was out of Town, and there was nothing here, just a bit of Sand, surrounded by Trees. I found a nice, big Rock to sit on, nestled in the Sand. I sat there for a moment, trying to figure out where Ghost-Girl had gone. I did think it was a bit strange how I wasn't scared of her and that I was crazy to even follow her into the Trees and then onto the Beach, but I can't explain it, but something told me to follow her here, and I was so drawn to her. The Tide had started to make its way in and was bringing in a cool Sea-Breeze with it. I looked up at the Sky and the Sun had now gone behind the Clouds, lighting them up a golden-colour. I got up off the Rock, ready to start walking along the Beach into Town. As I pulled myself up, I heard a whisper in the Wind.

"Danny, my Love".

I looked around to see where it was coming from, but there was no-one there, then I heard it again... I quickly turned to see Ghost-Girl stood on the Rocks.

I shouted to her, "Hey, who are you...? Please tell me who you are and why I keep seeing you. What do you want from me?". She just stood there, still on the Rocks, not moving a muscle. I started walking toward her, going in the opposite direction, to the Town where I had intended on going, but I needed to find out who Ghost-Girl was now, for once and for all.

I was climbing over the slippery Rocks to her, my feet slipping all over. The Waves were hitting the Rocks, splashing me in the face. I had just regained my balance when a huge Wave came

271

out of Nowhere and knocked me off my feet. It was like slow-motion, as I fell. I could see Ghost-Girl standing a few Metres away from me. I looked at her and got a glimpse of her face. I had never been this close to her. Then, I lost all vision as my head hit the Rocks with a thud.

***

"Danny, my Love",

I heard a voice call. I opened my eyes, and there she was, standing over me. It was Sam. She was so Beautiful – Long, blonde-hair, big-eyes, perfect white-smile. She looked down and reached down to grab my hand. I reached up for her hand, and she pulled me up. She pulled me into her, and we embraced. I looked into her eyes, and I was Home. I knew Sam was real and that I hadn't made her up. Ghost-girl was Sam. "Sam - Is that you? Are you Ghost-Girl? She pulled me in and kissed me, her lips were so soft. The kiss felt so familiar to me, she pulled back and smiled at me, still holding each other.

"Danny, my Love. I am not Sam. I look like Sam, but I am not her".

"Who are you, and why do you look like Sam?".

"Let me show you, it's time Danny, my Love".

Ghost-Girl/Sam led me back through the Trees, but this was not the Beach, it was another Place. The Sky was a deep-blue colour, and the Clouds were a pale-pink colour. The Flowers were tall, and some I had never seen before. As we walked through the Trees, a Rabbit hopped up to me. I bent down to pet it, and it sniffed me then jumped into my hands. I was shocked as Rabbits are scared of Humans, but this one wanted me to hold it. "Danny, Nothing is scared of you and there is Nothing to be scared of", said Sam.

We walked further and further until we got to an Opening, there was a big Lake with a Waterfall at one end with Trees all around. The Air felt very different, it felt so fresh and clean like the more I breathed, the more alive I felt. Sam led me to a Log next to the Lake and turned to me.

"I am not Sam, my Love. My name is Sian, Danny. After the Crash, you lost your Memory of me. I needed you to write the Book to help you remember me. I guided you to write, it was me you were writing about, not Sam. Danny, I am Sam the Character in your Book".

I pulled away, as I was now in confusion. I had no idea where I was and there was my Character, Sam, telling me her Name was Sian, my Girlfriend. I started to panic, wondering what was going on. Was I Dreaming again and was I going to wake up in my bed? I looked at Ghost-Girl again, and her eyes were staring into mine.

I felt my heart melt away, and the last thing I remembered was hitting my head on the Rocks. Was I dead and Ghost-Girl was an Angel looking like Sam to take me to Heaven. A tear fell from my eye as I thought of Alisha, Tom and Becky. I had not even had a chance to say Goodbye to them. Ghost-Girl put her arms around me again and pulled me close to her. I smelt the sweet-scent of Summer Flowers.

"Danny, you have felt Something missing, felt like you were missing Something, a hole in your heart. It is me that you were missing, my Love. I have tried so hard to help you remember me so you can move on. I want to show you Something".

Sian put her hand in the Water and swished it around, making ripples. An Image started to form, it was a Photo of Sian and me together not long after we had met. Sian got up off the Log and walked into the Lake, she grabbed my hand, pulling me into the Lake with her. It wasn't like a normal Lake, the Water felt very warm and clean, and I could feel this Healing Energy around me. She put her arms around me and we both started to submerge into the Water. As we went further and further down, I realized that I could still breathe under the Water, I could feel my whole-body Healing. She looked into my eyes as we both sunk further and further down into the depths of the Water, holding each other.

"Danny, close your eyes - Let me show you".

I found myself in bed, waking up next to Sian. We kissed and then got up, ready to pick up the new Car and then go to my Sister's House, to visit Alisha and Tom. They lived in a small Town by the Coast called Palm Bay.

The next Image I got was in the Car Showroom, picking up the new Car and then Sian driving it away. After that, I saw us both together, looking at the Viewing-Point, then the next Image was the Car skidding off the Cliff and the look on Sian's face. All my Memories came flooding back to me and my heart started to feel full again. She was the one I was missing, she was the one I had lost, and now I was back with her, back with my Love. Tears rolled down my cheeks, and I felt so happy and was back with her. Nothing mattered now, only her. I was back with my True-Love.

"Why did you have to leave me, Sweet-Heart? Why did you have to go? It's all come back now and why do you look like Sam in my Book? I had so many Questions. Sian looked at me and we both started to rise back out of the Lake. I appeared in what looked like a white-marble Temple with big, huge Pillars at both sides. Surrounding the Temple were Waterfalls and Gardens. At the far end of the Temple, there was a big Archway with Stained-Glass that had Angels and Clouds. It looked like an Image of Heaven. We walked over to the glass.

"Danny, before we come to Earth, we have a meeting with our Angels and talk about what our Life will be like on Earth, what will happen and who we will meet. This is all part of the Plan. You planned to meet your Soul-Mate and spend your Earthly Life together with her".

"Are you not my Soul-Mate, the one I would spend my Life with?".

"Yes, my Love. I am your Soul-Mate, but I was only there to Guide you to your True-Love, the one you would spend this Life-Time with. Let me explain.

You and I made an Agreement before we came to Earth that we would get together but it would only be for a short-time. We would get the new Car and I would drive it, but the brakes would fail and the Car would go over the edge. I would die, but you would survive. You go into a coma, and then, when you come out, you have no Memory of me, but there is a young Lady who you grow fond of, she looks after you and you get close to her. She is the one. I have been giving you Guidance to write, you fell in Love with Sam but you didn't know why, but it was me all along. I am Sam in your Story".

"Who is my Love then, if you're not?", I said, my voice all quivery now.

Sian pointed to the big Stained-Glass Arch Windows and an Image appeared on them. It was Becky, singing in a Kitchen, preparing some food. It was the same Place that I had been to when I was in the coma; I had seen Becky before. I had met her.

"What happens now? I don't want to lose you, Sian".

"You continue with your Book, my Love, and you and Becky live a 'Happy Life' together. Remember everything in Life happens for a reason and you are always on the 'Right Path', my Love. I am going to help you finish your Book and will always be by your side".

"Now, I have seen you, and remember how I can even continue with my Book and even in Life".

Sian looked at me and she wiped a tear from my cheek. I didn't want to leave her. I had lost her, and now we were back together - How could we part again?

"Becky is your True-Love in this Life-Time. She is waiting for you. You saw her when you went to the other side in the coma. That is who the girl was in the Beach House. She will support you and help you get the Book Published. You shall walk side by side together, and you will go on to write many more Books, and I will help you, Danny".

"At least I am not Crazy, 'Falling in Love' with my own Character". I sniffed up and smiled, wiping a tear from my eyes.

"It was the only way you could remember me so you could move on, but then things changed. I knew you were struggling, so I had to step in and bring you here to show you. Now that you know, you can write about Sam with even more love in your heart and know that Sam/I will always be with you".

"What is Heaven like Sian? Can you show me before I go or am I in Heaven now?"

"Heaven is Beautiful, we can watch everyone on Earth and help them out when they need us, most People don't know we are helping them as we give them Messages in any way we can, like I helped you remember me by writing a Book".

"You can have Anything you want here, be Any Age or be Anyone you want -There are no limits, but this is not Heaven you are in, Danny - This is the In-Between Place – We can meet Souls here from Heaven, but it is not your time yet, so you cannot see Heaven or go there yet, but what you can do is Create your own Heaven on Earth".

"I have been through so much Sian, and how can I go back, now knowing all of this - How can I even write my Book, knowing that I am writing about you".

"From suffering, comes great Love. We have to go through the pain and Trauma to get us here now, to help us to grow. By losing me, you met your True-Love. You both shall grow together and be very happy".

"How can I continue to write though?".

I knew I couldn't bear to go back to the Book and start writing about Sam. It would make me too sad.

"You will, my Love. For we shall write it together, you have to - it is part of your Mission here, to Inspire others, to show them the Magic, to give them Hope and Faith".

"Can I have one more kiss before we part?".

Another tear fell from my eyes as I knew I couldn't stay here, there would be People who missed me, and me and Becky were to be together. Sian pulled me into her and our lips met and we kissed, one last time. I did not want the kiss to end.

***

"Fred, get over here – Now, call an Ambulance!".

"What is it - What have you found?", a Man shouted as he came running over, on his Phone.

"He is alive... You Ok, Son. It's Ok, the Ambulance is on its way".

I opened my eyes to find myself, lying there on the Beach, soaking wet and cold with two Men around me and a Team of Paramedics.

"What happened - How did I get here?", I said. I was so confused as I had just been kissing Sian, and now, I was so wet and cold on the Beach with People around me. I looked through a gap in-between Paramedics and saw Sian there, watching me. She blew me a kiss, a ray of light shone down from the Sky and she started to ascend into the Clouds. From the Clouds, came down hundreds of white Butterflies. The two Men and the Paramedics looked at the site in amazement. The Butterflies came fluttering over my body with the scent of Summer Flowers, then they flew off into the Sky. The Clouds parted and a 'Golden Ray of Light' shone down on me.

"Would you look at that Fred", the Man said to his Friend.

He looked at me and smiled.

"It's not your Time, is it my Boy?".

The Man's Accent had changed into an Irish one, and even the look on his face had changed, it was the Man I had met in the coma... Patrick, my Guide who brought me back to Earth. He smiled at me one more time then changed back into Fred. The Paramedics lifted me onto the Stretcher and put me in the Ambulance to check me over. I didn't want to go to the Hospital, but the Paramedic insisted as I had had a Head Injury and needed a Scan, just to make sure there was no serious damage.

***

I lay on the bed, resting, waiting for my scan results, thinking about what had just happened. All my Memories had returned, and now I had to face and deal with the death of my Sian, my Girlfriend. I took my Phone out of my pocket. Surprisingly, it was undamaged, and a Message appeared.

"Danny, my Love. Don't be sad now that I am gone. We have spent many Life-Times together, and we shall spend many more together but spend the rest of this one, with your Soul-Mate - your True-Love, and we shall be re-united again. I Love You for all of Eternity Darling, Sian xxxxx".

As I read the Message, the words began to fade until the Text had fully disappeared. I heard some familiar voices in the corridor and Becky, Alisha and Tom came into the Room. Becky bounded her way over to me, threw her arms around me and gave me the biggest kiss ever, on the lips. She stepped back and giggled, remembering where she was and who she was, in front of Alisha who just smiled and didn't want to make Becky feel more embarrassed than she was.

"I remember", I said quietly. "I remember", I said again but a bit more-louder, this time, "I remember it all, the Accident... Sian". I broke down in tears. "Why did you not tell me, Sis?".

Alisha looked like she was going to burst out crying.

"Danny, we all wanted to tell you, but you had been through so much, and you needed to get strong again. It was killing me inside, seeing you go through this pain and not knowing why".

I explained to them what had happened, the Ghost-Girl on the Beach and Sam. Even the things I saw in the coma including seeing Becky. Becky rubbed a tear from her eyes. I looked at the three of them, standing there around the bed. I was upset that they had not told me about any of it, but would I even believe them? They did what was best for me so how could I not be mad at them for not telling me - It was for my protection? "You all probably think I'm Crazy for saying this".

"No, I don't think you are Babe. I had a Dream last Week, I was visited by this Beautiful Girl, she looked like an Angel, she said her Name was Sian and we knew each other from our previous Life. We were Friends and that she had to connect me to my True-Love in this Life-Time. She did not want to do it this way, but the Elders told her that this had to be done like this, she would have to leave the Earth in a way that you and I could connect, and this was all planned out. So, it looks like your Girlfriend Sian had all this planned out, to bring us together, Babe".

Becky kissed me again, and this time I kissed her back. It felt like I was kissing an Angel. Alisha was sobbing in Tom's arms, and even Tom had tears in his eyes. We all tried to compose ourselves as I saw the Doctor coming over.

The Doctor came in with my Scan Results, pulled up a seat and looked through the Papers. The Scan was all clear, but I needed to take it easy for a few Days. I now knew I had to finish this Book and Sian was going to help me finish it, finish the Story of Sam and Matt. I had felt so much Love, happiness and joy now, it was like the dark Cloud had been lifted and the hole in my heart was now filled back in.

I looked at Becky and the Love I felt for her, and I knew part of Sian was in her - They were connected.

CHAPTER 23

I lay there on my bed, thinking about the Day's Event. I started to feel angry at Alisha for not telling me about Sian, my stomach started to hurt, and I wanted to smash my Room up to get the anger out. I had never felt so angry in my entire life. I shouted out, swearing and cursing, tears streaming down my face. How could she hold something like that back from me?

I sobbed into my pillow, and Alisha came bursting in through the door, she grabbed hold of me and pulled me into her arms.

"Why Sis, why? Why didn't you tell me?", I cried.

"Danny, I am so sorry. How could I? You had been through so much", Alisha cried.

We just both sat on the bed, hugging. I knew it must have been so hard for her to keep it from me, and I knew in my heart that she was only looking out for me, and would I even believe her if she had told me? We have to figure Life out ourselves, it's the only way we can move forward, and for her to keep such a thing back from me, was her way of protecting me.

So, Sian my Girlfriend who had died in the Car Accident was Sam who I had been writing about, and that was why I had fallen in Love with her.

I wanted to stop writing and just give up. What was the point in any of it, what was the point in Life itself? I felt like I had nothing in Life to live for anymore. Sam was Real, but only she was Sian who comes through as Sam in my Story. I heard a tiny whisper in my ear.

"Please don't give up my Darling, Danny. I promise you. I'm here with you and you will finish this Book, and it will change your Life. I Love You".

I felt a glimmer of Hope and wiped my eyes dry. Alisha pulled back and kissed my forehead.

"Danny, you are strong - You can get through this - We are all here for you", Alisha said softly, before going down to make Dinner.

***

I went down for Dinner where Alisha and Tom were sitting at the Table waiting for me to join them. She had cooked Steak and Chips with Mushrooms and Onion Rings. It was my favorite Meal. I sat there in silence for a Moment, not knowing what to say to them both. I looked up at them both and the anger just disappeared. I could not be mad at them, they were two Angels that had been sent to me. I took the first bite of my Steak, she had cooked it just how I liked it – Medium-Rare, so it was just perfect. "Thank You", I said, swallowing the piece of meat.

"Danny, I am so sorry we didn't tell you, how could we? It was too soon, and it was killing us both inside to keep such a thing from you. I want you to understand, we did it to protect you. I knew in time that you would find out and we wanted you to be strong enough to be able to deal with it", Tom said.

I looked up at him, and I felt his sadness. I got up off the Chair, walked over to him and hugged him.

"It's Ok Tom, Mate. I know you were both only doing it to protect me and it must have been so hard for you knowing it and not being able to tell me. I Love You both so much and I am so grateful to you and Alisha for Everything".

"Danny, Mate, we are here for you and we always will be. I could not even begin to Imagine what you are going through".

"Danny, we are here now and we will support you and help you through it", Alisha said.

"What about the Funeral. Did I miss that? I didn't even get to say Goodbye to her".

I broke down in tears and sobbed into Alisha's arms. I had not only lost my Girlfriend, but I didn't even get a chance to say my last Goodbye to her. "You were in a coma and me and Tom wasn't sure if you would pull through. It was a Beautiful Service though, her Mum and Dad talked about you both and how in Love you both were with each other, and her Mum prayed for you, asked the Angels not to take you as well and for her Daughter to watch over you. Danny, you missed the Funeral but we are going to hold a little Service for you to say your Goodbyes to her".

After Dinner, I went back up to my Room and looked at the Story that had been written so far. It was Magical and Emotional. How could I leave it now? I had to finish it now. Sian wanted me to, and this wasn't just a Story now, it was how I remembered Sian. She lives on in me and through the Story. I thought about what Sian had said to me down at the Beach when I had left my Body, how things happen for a reason, and sometimes in Life, we have to face pain, loss and suffering to help us along, to get us to where we are now and to connect us to our True-Love in this Life-Time. Love is Love, and it comes through in Everything and Everyone. It was the same Love that Becky showed to me, just like what Sian had shown to me, just in a different Person. I sat at my Desk and picked up the Pen, took a deep breath and looked at the writing on the Pen that Read, 'Remember me'. I started to write.

**

It had been a few weeks since Sam and Jack had been in the Hospital. They had not contacted each other, but it was Saturday Night and Sam was doing her usual thing, curled up on the Couch, watching a Movie. The thought of Jack popped into her head and she picked up the Phone, but then placed it back down next to her, hoping that he would call her. Should she call him she thought for a Moment...

A Moment later, her Phone rang, and it was Jack. ''Hello'', she said.

"Hi Sam, it's Jack. I am so sorry I have not been in contact after the Accident, I needed a little bit of time. Something happened to me when I was in the Hospital, and I feel like I need to get used to this Planet again", Jack laughed. "Sam, I like you a lot. I know you have been struggling since you lost Matt, but please, can I take you out on a Date?".

Sam was a little shocked and surprised. She was not expecting that. She smiled at the thought. Maybe it is time to move on. "Oh Ok, yes that would be nice Matt, Thank You.... I mean Jack, I am so sorry". Sam started to blush down the Phone. "I'm sorry Jack, I did not mean to call you, Matt. I did not know where that came from".

Jack just laughs a little.

"It's Ok Sam, there is something I need to talk to you about".

***

The following week, they went on their Date. Sam was waiting for Jack in the Restaurant. She had put on the same Outfit as she had done for her and Matt's first Date together, not knowing she did that. She scanned the Restaurant and then the door, looking for Jack. She started to feel sick, as thoughts kept coming to her, that he wasn't going to turn up or if he did, what did he want to tell her?

Was he just going to say that he just wanted to be Friends with her. After a few more Minutes waiting, Jack walked in and he was wearing the same shirt and jeans Matt had on when they went on their first Date together. Sam jumped up, her heart beating so fast. Jack looked different to how she had seen him in the Bar, but she could not work out how or why. He saw her and started to make his way over to the Table. He looked at his heart pounding, his legs feeling like jelly.

They both looked into each other's eyes and embraced. Sam got a scent of Jack's aftershave, it was the same that Matt used to wear. She buried her nose into his neck, inhaling the sweet-smell. She looked into his eyes and pulled him in closer to her, their lips met and they kissed each other, deeply forgetting where they were, but it didn't matter, as the kiss took them into a different Place. Sam pulled back and then looked into Jack's big, wide eyes.

"Why do I feel like I know you?".

"We went out for a Drink to remember Sam, that's where we met", Jack said, trying not to let on he was Matt in Jack's Body, as he did not want to freak her out, she had been through enough.

They both sat and ate their food, enjoying the Night. When they had finished and paid the Bill, Jack did not want to leave Sam, so he offered to walk her Home. They crossed the Road into the Park. It was a clear, starry Night, the Air was cool, and the Moon was almost full, lighting up the whole Sky. They both did not say much but were just enjoying the Moment together. Jack stopped to face Sam.

"I Love You Sam, my Beautiful Angel".

Sam looked at Jack, and her heart raced as Jack's voice changed into Matt's. Matt used to call her his Beautiful Angel. She stepped back and looked at Jack, confused but in Love. "What is going on?". She stepped forwards and looked deep into Jack's eyes.

"Matt", she cried. "Is that you?".

"Yes, my Beautiful Angel, Sam, it's me, Matt".

"But how? You are gone and in Heaven. I lost you, and Jack... Where is Jack?". Sam's voice was now shaking and tears filled her eyes as she looked at Jack and saw Matt's Soul in his eyes.

Jack explained to her what had happened and how Matt wanted to come back to be with her, so when Jack was in the coma, he and Matt did a Soul-Transfer where Jack stayed in Heaven and Matt came back into his body. Sam didn't know how to react, she did not even think this was possible, but yet something told her that this was Matt. She felt his Love so strong and everything about Jack reminded her of Matt, but her Mind did not want to allow it.

"If you are My Matt, then tell me something that no-one else knows but you".

"The first Night I stayed at your Place, you told me that as a Child you used to line all your Teddy Bears up and pretend that they were all at your Wedding".

Sam stepped back, shocked. How did Jack know this? - The only Person she ever told that to was Matt.

"Ok, if you are Matt - What did you say to me when at the Theme Park on our 3rd Date?".

"I said that I think I'm in Love with you, and I want you to be my Girlfriend".

"Matt, it is you", Sam said, still shaking a little.

He pulled her into him and kissed her, it was that kiss that made it all clear as he kissed the same way as Matt. She looked at him again".

"Matt, is that you - Are you in there?".

'Yes, it's me. I am here, and I am not leaving you again. I'm so sorry for leaving you".

"I want you to stay with me Tonight, Jack. Come to mine and stay with me the Night".

They both walked to Sam's Place, hand in hand. When they got to Sam's, she led him upstairs and started to take off her clothes and pulled Jack into her.

''Make Love to me Jack, just like we used to".

Both their bodies entwined and the two Souls had re-united.

CHAPTER 24

I had got so lost in the Story with Sam and Jack, and it felt like I was Matt and had been re-united with Sam. It was so strange that a few weeks ago, I could not write, and I had not even read a Book and now... All this. I started to feel tired now and it was getting late, I put down the Pen and walked over to the window. The Moon was out, shining bright, lighting up the Sky. "I Love You Sian, Sweet-Heart", I said, as I looked up at the Moon. I felt two hands come behind me and the smell of her sweet Perfume.

"I Love You too, Babe", I heard a voice whisper in my left ear, I felt her lips kiss my neck, and then she was gone.

Even though I was tired, I struggled to get to sleep as all I could do was think of Sian. I loved her so much, but I was going to have a Life with Becky. Could I Love Becky like I loved Sian? Life moves on, I guess, and Becky was amazing, she was fun and attractive, but could she Love me as Sian did? Becky made me laugh but was she more of a Friend than a Lover? Sian had shown me Becky, when I was in the coma. She stood in the Kitchen with her shoulder-length, shiny, dark-hair and her tanned-skin.

I was amazed that I had been shown Becky before I had even met her, how amazing Life works. It has all been planned out, and we just have to go with it and trust in things, knowing that we are always on the 'Right Path', no matter how hard Life may seem. I had spent my Life working in an Office, trying to work my way up and be Someone, and what for? I had lost the Love of my Life, and no money could get her back. I was now writing and getting so much Joy from it, so much fulfilment from it. Life is there to Live, it is so precious, and we do not know when our final Day is. I had worked with a Man years ago in one of my first Jobs after leaving School. He worked 60 hours a Week, saving up and saving up for his Future. He would tell me that it's important to save for the Future so we could enjoy Life when we retire. Then, one day at work, he collapsed from a heart attack and died. He had no Family or Kids so all the Money he had saved up, just went to the Government. After what had happened to me, I realized that I needed to live. I nearly died that Day, all the Money I had saved up and working to the Promotion, I had worked hard for and for what? Just to go telling People what I did and how much Money I had.

Everything made so much sense now. Sian was right about Everything happening for a reason. I knew that. I had to have the Accident and lose Sian so that I would meet Becky and write a Book. It was my Purpose. Writing a Fictional Novel could be so inspiring to People and help them in so many different ways, even though it was a made-up Story, but there is Truth in Everything, and it Creates Magic. People need to take time out and get lost in a good Book once in a while.

I stared out of the window for another few Minutes, to look at the Stars. We are like Stars, we die and get re-born. When a Star dies, it then creates other Stars and this is the Circle of Life.

***

Today was going to be a sad Day as I never got the chance to say my last Goodbye to Sian. Alisha and Tom wanted to do a little Service for me so I could say Goodbye. My heart felt like it had a lead weight on it, crushing it down. She had asked Julie and Robert to come around. Sian's Mum and Dad, I had not seen them since before the Accident. I felt nervous about seeing them and guilty for some reason. Why did she have to go and I stay, why couldn't we both have died or survived? Alisha had asked me where I wanted the Memorial Service to be. The last time we held each other and kissed was at the Viewing Point, just outside Palm Bay, so I wanted it there. I had not gone back there since, so this wasn't going to be easy at all. I saw Julie and Robert pull up outside the House. When they saw me, they came running up to me and hugged me, both crying, that in itself made me cry.

"I miss her so much, Danny. Life is just not the same without my Beautiful Girl".

Robert pulled a tissue from his pocket and passed it to Julie. They got back in the Car, and we got in Tom's Car and set off to drive to the Viewing Point. It was a nice, sunny and warm Day. As we approached, I felt sick and wanted just to turn back, but I couldn't as this was my way of saying Goodbye and letting go now.

It felt strange being there, as I had not been there since the Accident. It felt lonely there now, even though I was with Alisha, Tom, Julie and Robert. I didn't have my Sian with me. I looked out to the Ocean, the Breeze blowing into my face, the Sun was shining down, making the Water sparkle. Julie took out her Phone, and I played Faith Hill, 'There You'll Be'. It was Sian's favourite Song. As I listened to the Words, I broke down and fell on my knees. "Why God - Why did you have to take her from me? Why couldn't you have taken me instead or taken us both?".

I cried out, and Alisha came running over and picked me up. Julie walked over to the Car, pulled a big jar out. It was the Urn with Sian's Ashes in. She handed them to me.

"Danny, my Lovely - It's time to let her go now. I want you to take these Ashes and scatter them".

I took the Urn from Julie and opened it up. I held it up to the Sky. "Sian, I remember when we first met, that first kiss we had, it was like a Dream. I never thought that I could be in Love, but you showed me. I remember all the times we had together and the Weekend away with your Friends. You didn't want to leave me, but I told you, you had to go and spend time with them, and when you got back, you were so happy to see me. It felt like we had been apart for Life-Times. I know you are with the Angels now Sweet-Heart, they are looking after you. You loved the Ocean so much, and we would come here and watch the Sun go down together and the Stars come out. We would look up at those twinkling Stars and wonder what was out there and what they were. Now, you are one of those Stars twinkling down on me, Sian. I now scatter your Ashes in the great Ocean, letting the Water and Wind take you to Wherever you want to go – You are free to fly now, my Love, my Sian".

I threw the Ashes over the rail, down into the Ocean, and the Gentle-Breeze carried them into the distance. I felt a warm, loving presence come around me, a white-feather fell from the Sky and landed in front of me, just by my feet. The Clouds had now covered the Sun, leaving a golden, ray of Light, shining through. I knew she was here with me and she always would be watching over me. I felt a little tickle on the back of my hand; I looked down to find a white Butterfly. It stopped and looked at me then flew up to my face and landed on my nose. It stayed still for a few seconds then flew off towards the golden beam of

Light and disappeared into the Light. I looked back at the others to check if they had seen it. Julie smiled with tears in her eyes and waved Goodbye.

"I will miss you my Darling Daughter". She wiped a tear from her eyes. "Look after her, God".

My heart felt warm. I knew she was home, back with the Angels where she had come from, and I didn't feel so sad, as I knew I would see her again, and we would be together in another Life-Time. Julie reached in her pocket and took Something out. She passed it to me, it was a Photo of Sian and me standing together on some Rocks from the Day I met her Mum and Dad for the first time, and we went out for the Day. I will never forget that Day.

I was so nervous, hoping that they would like me and that I was good enough for their Daughter, but they both liked me and treated me like their own Son. "Danny, I want you to have this, and I want you to move on in Life, meet a nice Girl and settle down with her. Robert and I will always be here for you and we will keep in touch, my Love".

Sian's Mum and Dad walked away, back to the Car and drove off. I felt so sad for them. I had lost her and that was hard enough, but they had lost their Daughter, and now they had to continue their Life without her. I looked at the Photo of me and Sian in my hand - A tear fell onto it, I gazed up at the Sun.

"I will always love you Sweet-Heart", I whispered.

***

On the way back to Palm Bay, I sat in the Car, silently staring out of the window, feeling at peace and warm, knowing that my Sian was Home with the Angels, but I felt sad knowing, that in this Life-Time, I would not be able to kiss her and share my Life with her. I needed to live now and get on with my Life. I had said my final Goodbye to her, her Spirit would be with me always, and we would be together again in the next Life-Time. I needed to finish writing my Story and get to know Becky. It was me and her now - She was my Love in this Life, and we would make Happy Memories together. Sian was part of Becky as they had pre-planned Everything before they came to this Earth

CHAPTER 25

I woke up the next Morning feeling better. I still missed Sian so much, but after scattering her Ashes, I had to let go now and move on. Besides, she was still here, helping me write.

Today was the Day of my Date with Becky, so I was excited for that but also a bit nervous too. I found Becky attractive, and I did like her, but we got on so well, it felt more like a Friendship, and I started to think in the back of my Mind. -What if it didn't work out between us - Would it ruin our Friendship? Why am I even thinking about that? I thought as I got ready.

I went down for Breakfast and was greeted by Alisha. Tom had left for Work. She had made me a full fry-up. We had our Breakfast together; it seemed so long ago since we had sat down for Breakfast as she had to go back into the Office, so it was nice to eat with her. She looked happy this Morning, a smile on her face looking over at me.

"Big Day Today Bro, I'm so excited for you".

"What if she doesn't like me like that Alisha?".

"You are joking right, Danny. Were you not there when she kissed you in the Hospital. That Girl has been crazy about you since that first Day you met".

I felt a lot more at ease and better about my Date after Alisha said that. After Breakfast, I headed back up to my Room, as I needed to write and continue the Story. I needed to know what was going to happen with Sam and Matt... Well Jack - Who he was now? I closed my eyes and called out to Sian. I felt her presence with me, and I started to write.

***

Sam woke up in Jack's arms, she looked at Jack who was still sleeping and started thinking about all the times they would have together and how Happy their Life would be. Sam gently kissed Jack, waking him up. He slowly opened his eyes and saw her staring at him, smiling.

Later that Day, they decided to go into Town for Something to do. They had walked past a Shop that they had never seen before called Paradise Travel. It had just appeared out of Nowhere. Sam was confused as to how she had not noticed it before as it was very bright and colourful. Sam had wanted to go on

Holiday for some time as she felt she needed some time away. "Come on Jack, shall we go and have a look?". She grabbed his hand and pulled him inside the Travel Agents. There were no Customers in, only Sam and Jack. There weren't many Holiday Brochures, just one shelf, and they all seemed to be the same. Jack picked up a Brochure and started looking through it to see if Anything had caught his eye.

A few Moments later, a Woman came out from the back and greeted them. She was an older Woman with white-hair but yet looked very young in the face. Jack recognized her but didn't know how. Her face was so familiar as he had seen her before. She smiled at Jack. Sam looked at them both, thinking that they knew each other.

"Please take a seat, welcome to Paradise Travel. My name is Angela", she said, in a soft voice. ''So, do you have Anywhere in mind that you would like to go".

"No, we don't... We thought maybe you could help us out", said Sam.

"Oh, perfect - Let me see what I can do, when would you be looking to go?".

"Soon as really, the sooner we leave, the better. We both need time out of Life", said Jack.

"Let me see what I can do. Angela started typing away at her Computer and kept looking up at Sam and Jack "It's so nice to see two Souls re-united".

"What do you mean?".

Sam looked at Angela, puzzled, not understanding what she meant by that, but then quickly dismissed it when Angela turned the Computer Screen around and showed them a Package she could do them. It was a 14-Night -All Inclusive to the Bahamas and the flights were perfect. Angela turned the Screen back around and made a Phone Call.

"Right, Ok guys. So, I have a deal for you. I can get you £500 off if you want to go at the end of this Week. I know it's short-notice but they are also giving you a free upgrade as well".

Sam turned to Jack and grabbed his hands, they started talking quietly then turned to Angela and agreed to take the Holiday Deal.

"Perfect. I just need to fill out the Details and get your tickets printed off. A few Moments later, she came back out from the Back Office with tickets and some forms. "Please read through these and sign for me". The print was small, too small to read. "I hope I'm not signing my Life away", Sam chuckled.

Angela looked and just smiled.

"So that's all done Guys, enjoy your Holiday and I shall see you soon".

Sam and Jack left the Travel Shop and walked around the corner to the Coffee Shop. They got their Coffee and found a nice spot in the corner.

"Sam, are you Ok? You look confused", Jack said as he sipped his Coffee.

Angela, in the Shop. Don't you think she was a bit strange like when she said see you soon, like how will she see us soon and when she said two Souls re-united".

"She also looked familiar too, but I couldn't think where I had seen her before", said Jack. "Maybe ,we are just over-thinking things".

That Week, Sam had to go into Town to pick up some things for their Holiday. She was Super Excited as the last time, she had been away was with Matt. She went passed the Building with Work Men around it. She could have sworn that that was where Paradise Travel is. No! It was where Paradise Travel was. She made her way over to one of the Work Men and asked what had happened to the Travel Agent; He looked at her with a confused funny look.

"I'm sorry Love, I think you have mistaken this Place for Somewhere else. This Building has been empty for years, and before then, it was a Bookshop, and in a few months, it's going to be New Look, so it's never been a Travel Agent". "Maybe I was thinking of Somewhere Else. I'm sorry to bother you. Have a nice Day now". Sam turned and started to walk off.

*"Excuse me, Love - What was the Shop called Sweet-Heart?",
said the Work Man.*

"Paradise Travel".

*"Not heard of it. I have lived in this Town all my Life, and I have
not heard of that one. Me and my Wife have visited a few round
here but never come across that one".*

"Oh, Ok no problem then, well you enjoy your Day".

"You too, Miss".

*Sam went on her way, confused, as she was sure the Shop was
there - Had she just Dreamed it up? She got the things she
needed and then went into the Coffee Shop, still confused about
the Travel Agent.*

*A few Hours later, she was back at Home, waiting for Jack to
come in so she could tell him about the Shop. When he arrived
from Work. She took one look at him and forgot all about the
Shop, she was just Happy to be making Happy New Memories
with him. That Night, they curled up on the Couch together. Sam
had spent many Nights alone, crying, wishing Matt was with
her, and it all still seemed like a Dream that he was back with
her now, only in Jack's body. She did slip up a few times and
call him Matt, but they just laughed about it as he was Jack,
now in this body, and this Life-Time, and she would have to get
used to that.*

***

It was the Day of the Holiday and the Taxi had just arrived to pick Sam and Jack up. They loaded the Car up and set off to the Airport. It wasn't too far, as Sam only lived about 20 Minutes away. They checked in and got food then sat and waited in the Airport Lounge, waiting for their Flight. Jack was like a little Boy watching the Planes take off and land, out of the window. He loved Planes. It was now time for them to board, and they both made their way down to the Boarding Gate. Time seemed to pass quickly, it had been 4 hours and they were boarding the Plane, but yet, it seemed that Minutes had passed from when they set off from Sam's House. As the Engines revved up, ready for the Plane to take off, Jack closed his eyes for a Moment and saw Angela, the Woman in the Travel Agents and then saw the Angel who was on the other side when he and Matt swapped Souls. They looked the same. Jack opened his eyes and looked at Sam, reached over and kissed her, grabbed her hand and held it.

"I Love You, Sam. I always will. We will always be together. I want to you know that".

"I Love You too, Jack". Sam reached over and kissed him".

The Plane started to move, picking up speed, down the runway. There was a loud bang and the whole Plane shook, but the Pilot reassured everyone, it was Ok and the Plane lifted off the ground.

It was a good 3 hours into the Flight, and food was being served. Sam was just buttering her bread when there was another loud bang, and the Plane shook again. This time, an alarm went off and the Oxygen-Masks fell from over-head. The Air Steward advised Everyone to get into the Brace-Position as the Plane started to descend.

'MAY DAY, MAY DAY' the Captain called over the Radio, but there was no response. A few seconds after, there was a loud Explosion. Sam grabbed Jack, and they held each other tight.

''Please don't leave me'', she cried.

"I'm here, I will never leave you", said Jack, holding Sam even tighter in his arms.

He felt a blast of hot-air and looked up and saw a fire-ball racing toward them. The whole Plane had turned into a fire-ball in mid-air.

***

The Couple opened their eyes and found themselves laying in the warm- grass in a Flowery Meadow. The sound of Birds singing and the Bees buzzing, there was a sense of Peace and calm. Sam looked around and wondered where she was. She remembered an intense heat for a second then Nothing. She looked down at her body, but there was not a mark or scratch on it. She looked at Jack, but Jack was gone, it was Matt that laid next to her. She pulled herself up and looked around at this

Beautiful Place she was in. She felt so Peaceful and Happy, this was not Earth. Earth was not as Beautiful as this, the Birds, the Trees, the deep, Blue-Sky and the soft, Green-Grass. Sam looked over at Matt and then realized she had died in the Plane Crash. Matt opened his eyes and looked at Sam and pulled her on top of him and kissed her.

"Sam, we are going Home now, where we can be together and be Happy".

A beam of white, golden-Light came from the Sky and a Figure appeared out of it. It was Angela, the Woman in the Travel Agent, but she was not wearing her Uniform, she was dressed all in white.

"Angela, what are you doing here?".

"I said I would see you soon", the Angel said, smiling. "It's time to go home". A big Archway appeared with a bright, white-Light beaming from it. The Angel started to walk towards it, then she turned around and looked at Matt and Sam.

"Follow me", she said in a soft voice and a big smile.

Matt and Sam followed the Angel, hand in hand, as they walked into the Light together, their Energy merging, creating a golden, white-Light around them both as they both walked through into Heaven together.

The End

***

"Thank you, Sian for helping me write this Beautiful Story", I whispered.

My Story was complete and even though Sam and Jack had died in the Plane Crash, they could now be together in Heaven as Sam and Matt - two Souls re-united, together for Eternity.

CHAPTER 26

It was getting late in the Afternoon, and my Phone hadn't rung all Day. I checked for Messages to see if Becky had text me but she hadn't. The last Message from her was Yesterday, telling me to meet her at the Italian Restaurant at 7.30pm. I was getting a bit worried now - What if she had backed out – backed off. I got in the shower and got ready, hoping she would turn up. Alisha had come home from Work early as she had been called back into the Office not long after we had had Breakfast. She and Tom were going away for a long Weekend, and she needed to get ready. I came down to greet her all, ready to go in my white shirt and jeans. The last date I went on was with Sian, so it felt a little strange. I didn't want to over-dress but didn't want to look too casual, so I went half and half with a white-shirt and ripped jeans.

"Oh, Wow look at you, Danny. You look so Handsome and you smell Gorgeous", said Alisha in an excited voice.

I don't know who was more excited, her or me? She wanted to see me happy and smiling again. She and Tom had a Life together and they wanted me also to have a Life and to be happy.

***

The Waiter showed her where I was sitting. She came walking over with the most Beautiful, beaming-smile. The vision came to me of her singing that Beautiful Tune in the Kitchen when I was in the coma and I had gone to the Beach.

"I'm so sorry I'm late, Babe. My Taxi was late, and my Phone needed charging up, so I couldn't text you and let you know. I'm sorry".

"It's Ok, you're here now... Wow, Becky, you look amazing", I said, trying to keep my eyes on her face rather than on her low-cut top.

"I scrub up well, don't I?" Becky said, laughing.

She pulled me into her and kissed me then sat down across from me.

I found my eyes wandering down to her chest as her dress was quite low. I think she knew that my eyes kept wandering, but she was just right.

"Oi, you... Mr. - My face is here, not down there".

As she was chatting, I looked at her, and I knew that I would spend the rest of my Life with her. I would always Love Sian, but Becky was the one for me in this Life-Time and I knew that now. I had to remember Sian so I could let her go and be with Becky.

***

After Dinner, we decided to take a walk down onto the Beach from the Harbour as it was still pretty early. The Moon was full, lighting up the Sky, and the Sky was littered with Stars. It was so Peaceful, just me and Becky holding hands and the sound of the Waves crashing on the Shore. I knew I was Home and this is where I wanted to spend my Life, and I wanted to spend it with Becky.

"Isn't life just so Amazing and strange how Everything unfolds like you had that Car Accident, driving to Palm Bay and ended up in the Hospital where I was working. I mean, you could have gone to any Hospital, but the Ambulance took you to mine and we met, and now we are here, together on our first-Date. It is like it's all been planned out before we even came here, and yet, we forget it all", said Becky as she looked up at the Stars.

I looked up at the Sky and a Star appeared before my eyes. It appeared bigger and brighter than the rest of them.

It twinkled so bright that it made my eye squint for a second then it disappeared.

"I believe Everything does happen for a reason and sometimes, things happen in life that we don't like. There are Sad Moments, but they bring us to Happy Moments and sometimes, unpleasant things happen, and we suffer, but it is the suffering that takes us to where we are now, making us who we are", I said, looking into Becky's eyes as we cuddled up together on the Beach.

"Wow, that is so Beautiful Babe", said Becky as she pulled me in close into her and kissed me deeply.

After sitting down at the Beach for a while, talking, the Air had started to turn chilly. We both started to shiver and decided to call it a Night. We headed back up to the Harbour where the Taxi Rank was. I saw her into the Taxi, Home, and then I waited for my Taxi.

When I got Home, the House was silent as Alisha and Tom had already left for their Weekend Away. It felt a little strange being in the House on my own at Night. I wished Becky could have come back with me, but I liked her a lot and had to be a Gentleman and respect her. I knew she didn't want to go Home alone but she was been respectful too. I picked up my Phone and there was a text on it from Becky. "Hiya, my Darling Danny. I have just got Home Thank you for this lovely Evening. I wish you were here, snuggled up to me in bed. Lots of Love Becky xxx".

I smiled and replied back and then went up to my Room. I looked at my Story and the Pen that had the Inscription on it,

'Remember me'. "Yes, I do remember now, Thank You", I whispered. I read the last few lines of the Story where Sam and Matt walked into the Gates of Heaven, hand in hand. I knew this was going to be the start of my new Career, writing and telling my Story. I slipped into bed and drifted peacefully off to sleep with a smile on my face.

CHAPTER 27

6 Months Later.

"Babe, it's time to get up - Wake up".

I felt a nudge and slowly opened my eyes to find Becky smiling at me. It was the day of my Book-Signing. I had sent it away to a Publisher a few months back and it was a Big- Seller, the Reviews were so nice from People. I had only come across one bad Review, and the Person said the Story had lacked a lot of detail and I should have gone into more explanation with things, but I had written it that way so the Reader could use their Imagination to Create their own World.

Oh yes, and I now lived with Becky. After our first Date - That was Amazing. Things moved pretty quickly from there. We started to see each other, go on more Dates, even went away for a Week together up to the Mountains and stayed in a Log Cabin. It was a few Weeks after that, she asked me to move in with her.

That was an offer that I couldn't refuse. I was together with my Best Friend. Living with Becky was Amazing and Fun, she was always so full of Life and Happy. There was just a few times that I knew that she was a little moody, but I always cheered her up, so life was pretty good. Oh, and Alisha and Tom had got engaged, it was about time. Tom had asked me if I was Ok with him, proposing to my older Sister. I did not object. He took her away for the Weekend and got down on one knee, the poor Guy. I bet he was so nervous and embarrassed as he hates having attention drawn to him. So, a lot has happened in the last 6 months.

***

"Come on, Babe - Are you getting up? I made Breakfast".

I got up, put on my Night-Gown and went through, into the Kitchen Area. She was an Angel to me. Becky had quit her Job being a Nurse, and she now worked with Willow, full-time, down at the Crystal Shop at the Beach. She wanted to learn more about Crystals and get more into the Spiritual side of things after all that had gone on. Life just seemed perfect now, I had started writing my second Novel too as lots of People wanted to know about Matt and Sam and what happened to them when they went into Heaven together, so I had started to write another Story, with Matt and Sam in.

After Breakfast, we both got ready and got on the Train into the City where I was going to do my Book-Signing. Alisha had offered to take us but getting the Train was nice as it was a Day Out. The Train was nice and quiet so getting a seat was not difficult at all. It was busier in the Summer-Time when People would come from the City to Palm Bay. I did not miss living in the City at all, it was too busy and fast-paced. I don't think I could handle that now.

I had gone from this Office Corporate Life, trying to be a High-Flyer in the City to writing Books and living in a little Coastal Town, but I loved my Life. I was Happy and that's all that mattered to me.

I loved looking out of the window on the Trains and watching the World go by. It reminded me of the Hypnotherapy Session with Lucy when she put me on the Train. Wow, that seems like a Life-Time ago now. It was about an hour on the Train to the City. The Train ran alongside the Ocean for a few miles, then the line reared off Inland towards the City through the Hills. The Train finally pulled up to the Station and we got off, trying to look where the Exit was, through all the People. I felt myself start to get stressed out as I never liked crowded Places. Everyone was always in a rush. Becky and I finally found the Exit to the Station after fighting through the crowd of People. I heard someone shout my Name, and I turned to see where the voice was coming from. A couple of Teenage Girls came running over to me screaming and all hyper. Becky looked at me as if I knew them.

"Danny, is that you? OMG is it? I am such a big Fan of yours. I like to read your Book - 6 times", one of the girls said excitedly.

"Oh, Thank You. I am glad you enjoyed it", I said in a quiet tone. I did not know what to say as I had never been approached by two Fans.

"Please can you sign our Copies for us, it would just make our day so much. Oh, and can we have a Photo with you to show our Friends".

Becky grinned at me as she could see the embarrassed look on my face. After I had signed their Books and had my Photo taken with them, the two Girls walked off, smiling and laughing, and we continued to make our way to the Bookshop through the City. The City Centre was very busy, and trying to find the Shop was a bit of a challenge. We both knew it was somewhere in the main Shopping Area so I scanned one side and Becky scanned the other side.

Becky spotted it and grabbed my hand. It was a big Building with a glass-front, but on the inside, it was old but had been modernized. It had two floors on the ground floor, there was a Reading Area and Cafe with lots of different sections for different Books. We walked up to the Counter to ask where I was meant to be. The young Woman behind the Counter, took her eyes off the Computer Screen and looked up at me.

"You must be Danny", she looked at my Photo on the back of the Book.

"Follow me... It's so nice to meet you, your Book is Amazing by the way. It is such a Beautiful Story".

"Thank You", I said, blushing a bit. I never could take compliments. She led Becky and me to a Table that had been set up with lots of Books on it. There were some seats set out in front of the Table, next to the Cafe.

"Would you both like a Drink? It's on the House. Get yourself settled and I will go get you a Drink, what you would like?".

"Just two Coffees please, one sugar in both and milk", said Becky.

The Woman went off to get our Coffee, and we started to get set up. Now I was here, I wasn't as nervous, but it was all new to me as I had never done anything like this before. Once we were settled and had our Coffee, we just waited for people to arrive. I looked down at the Front Cover and thought of Sian. I had not seen her in Months – Ghost-Girl had not come, maybe she had moved on or was looking down on me, and when I needed her, she would be there.

***

People started to arrive and take seats. Once all the seats were filled, I introduced myself and started to talk about the Book and the reason I wrote it and the Story behind it. People started to ask questions and talk about their favorite bits. One Woman put her hand up and asked me about Sam, as she was very interested in Sam and wanted to know more about her.

"Sam was my Girlfriend, Sian who died in a Car accident. I went into a coma and lost my Memories of her but she came to me and helped me write my Story. I fell in Love with Sam, but I didn't know why until it all became clear. Sam was Sian, and the only way to remember her was writing a Book".

The Woman's eyes filled with tears, she took out a tissue from her pocket, sat back down and blew her nose and wiped her eyes.

"That's so Beautiful", she said, sniffing up.

After the Questions, People came up to get Signed Copies,

Becky had gone to the Toilet and the Shop was nearly closing, so I started to pack my things away. All the Books had gone, apart from one. I looked around me as the sound of silence hit me. Where had Everyone gone...? I thought. Then, I heard a door creak open. I looked up to find a young Woman there, smiling at me. I jumped back in disbelief. It was Sian, but she looked as solid as a normal Person.

"Hello, my Love", she said as she picked up the Book. "I'm so proud of you, Danny. Please may a take a Copy and can you Sign it for me?"

I took the Book from her hand, her skin was so smooth and warm with a pinkie glow to it, and I Signed it and handed it back to her.

"Danny, my Love. This will be the last time I will come, but I want you to know that I am watching over you always, and we will be re-united again in Heaven, and we will be together again. I Love You for Eternity".

Sian turned around and walked away, back through the door she had come in from, the door closed behind her and then she faded away into a white-smoke. When the smoke had cleared, there was no door - just a Book-Case. I heard the sound of voices again and looked down - The last Copy had gone -She had taken it. Becky came back and put her arms around me.

"I Love You so much, Danny. Thank You for being a part of my Life".

I kissed her and held her in my arms for a long Moment, and then, we left the Book-Shop to get the Train back Home. On the way Home, Becky fell asleep, her head resting on me. I sat and watched out of the window as we left the City, back Home. I thought about how much my Life had changed over the last year, it was quite overwhelming. I learned to live and not to take Life too seriously. I am not saying quit your Job, but do something that fulfils you in Life, makes you Happy, brings you Joy, because you never know when your last Day on Earth will be, and you can't take all the Money you saved up from your Job, with you.

There may be many sad Chapters in your Story but they lead to a Happy Ending if you choose them to.

The End

Matthew Smith

Printed in Great Britain
by Amazon

21034074R10192